GRUMPY GOALIE

WILCOX WOMBATS
BOOK 2

DELANCEY STEWART

For Dawn, who knows how to do magic.

PROLOGUE

JULIUS RAMON (AKA ICE RESURFACING MACHINE DRIVER)

Driving a Zamboni is a rewarding job.

It allows you to smooth out any past negativity, clear away previous scuffles and transgressions, leaving behind only a clear sheet of pristine ice.

Many of us wish such a thing were possible in our own lives—to wipe away all the mistakes, all the heartbreak and hurt we might have caused. But life is not like ice.

The mistakes we make with those we love leave more permanent marks. And depending on who you love, the marks might never fade.

For the lucky ones, the opportunity might one day arise to pour a fresh layer over the mistakes of the past, to cover those marred spots with better choices made in the present.

For me, the past is done.

I made my choices, and I live with them today.

They were not right or wrong. They were the things I chose at the time. And the past is gone.

But my nephew has opportunities I never did. Many of these players do. They're young and the years haven't marked them yet.

They're not all my blood. In fact, none of the Wombats are my actual family. But I look out for them as if they were because I know too well the way hockey can play into those lifelong scars if you're not careful.

And the one I look out for most especially?

The goalie.

Stephano.

CHAPTER 1
STEPHANO
WORSHIPPING PASTA

"He's green." I muttered it, not really intending these words as a public critique of our second-string goalie, who Coach Merit had dropped in for the last period of the game against the Bolts. Never mind that the guy couldn't possibly lose the game for us now after we'd served up four goals to their paltry one.

And for the record, Samuels let that one in, not me.

"He was the best goalie coming out of the draft, Mizzoni. We were lucky to get him." Cade Simpson was at my side on the bench, waiting for his next switch. "And you're the one who's been training him."

I hated Cade's good-natured, level-headed attitude.

I hated the new guy.

I hated the whole situation. I knew I wasn't invincible. A second-string was necessary and our last one had gotten picked up by the Titans to start, but that didn't mean I had to like any of it.

Samuels was good. I could admit it, at least to myself. Quietly. When I was barely even paying attention and no one else was around. But Samuels was something else too. He was young. Likable. Charming.

Things I couldn't be if I tried.

And the writing was on the wall. I was getting older. One day I'd age out, or my body would give in to the constant demand of pushing myself around in front of the net, trying to block every centimeter of free space. Or I'd get an unlucky puck to some part of me that wasn't protected—although that was not something I intended to let happen. Ever. I'd give up the position first.

Coach swapped in the third line for offense, and I watched as Braunstein and Solamentes switched out seamlessly with Rubio and Craft to play the final forty-five seconds. We won, so that was something. But the goal Samuels allowed ruined my shut-out, which steamed me a bit.

When it was all over, Samuels faced me in the dressing room.

"So?" he asked, waiting. In the past, I'd pointed out details I'd noticed, issues with his play that could be improved. But tonight? I had a few other things on my mind.

"You did okay, kid."

He stared at me, and his mouth dropped open just a centimeter or two. "I let in a goal."

"Yeah, don't do that." I pushed him aside and grabbed my shirt out of my locker, pulling it over my head as he watched.

"He wants his usual tough love, Mizzoni," Sly told me from a couple spots down. "You know, where you tell him how much he sucks."

"I can tell you how much you suck, if you want," Tyler "Corny" Cornwall stepped close and gave Samuels a quick up-and-down look.

"Back off," I suggested, pushing my chest into Cornwall's personal space.

He raised his hands and stepped away, chuckling.

"You did fine," I told Samuels, relief washing through me as he finally turned away, headed for the showers.

I wasn't built to be anyone's mentor. I could hardly manage myself. But this kid had glommed onto me the second he'd joined the team, and I knew it was my job to make him the best goalie he could be. It wasn't about me, or how much I needed to keep my position at the top. It was about the Wombats. It was about the game.

My life kind of went like that, I thought. I'd been given what many would call a gift at birth. The hockey, obviously, but the other thing too. And I had no real idea what the fuck a pro-hockey goalie was supposed to do with the irritating tendency to see colors emanating from everyone he met. Auras, they were called. And while sometimes they gave me tidbits of information that proved useful (like when Corny's aura turned from his usual blue to almost black right before he hurled his curly fries into Deck Gillespie's skates), they were mostly annoying.

"Heading to Whiskey's," Rock Stevens told me as he picked up his bag and turned for the door. "See you there?"

"Not tonight," I told him. The guys didn't party during the season, but Whiskey's was our usual hang out after an early game —unless I invited everyone to my place. But tonight? I wasn't up to it.

"What's wrong, your chakras off or something?" Stevens teased. I should never have told that guy anything about auras.

"Yeah. Heading home to sage that shit," I said.

"Okay, old man. See you tomorrow." Chris Houstein said this as he departed with Rock, and I took my time getting my things together. He hadn't meant anything by those words, I knew.

But I did feel old. And I needed a few more years to cement my future. And my family's. I couldn't be old yet. And I couldn't allow myself to be replaced.

I hated that if I squinted and stared out at the ice, I could see the beginning of the end. And the low ache in my groin chimed in to add detail to the image.

I had things to accomplish still, things I'd promised myself. And I wasn't finished.

The house was quiet when I arrived. The way I liked it. Maybe it was a little big for me—what single dude needed six bedrooms? But I'd gotten a little carried away when I'd built it. My mom's voice had been in my ear, telling me I was a family man, that I needed space for all those kids. The ones I was pretty sure I'd never, ever have.

It wasn't that I didn't want them.

It was more that they just didn't seem imminent. I'd been too busy stabilizing my own family. My own life. Starting another seemed unlikely.

But this house?

Yeah, it was mostly for me. I hadn't lost sight of the goal while I was having it built. I took care of my family back home first. And if worse came to worst? Mamma and my entire family could live here with me. Not that Mamma would ever leave Italy for good.

But I really didn't want that. As nice it would be to see my nonna and poppi, to have Mamma and Cristano and Luca all here with me for a while, I wasn't a family man. Not like Dad had been. Not the way Mamma had always told me I would be.

I liked my space and my silence.

I settled back into my Eames lounger and sipped the club soda I pretended was Scotch and took a deep breath, looking around at what I'd accomplished. What I'd built.

The night had just drifted into the kind of darkness that pressed itself up against the windows of the living room, bringing that biting winter cold that made you glad for a warm lamp and a blanket. My phone buzzed next to my empty glass beside me. It was one o'clock in the morning, and the number confirmed that Mamma was up early again.

She always called at this hour. She knew I didn't sleep until late, and she still liked to wish me goodnight. Plus, they would have gotten the news of the game, even if they hadn't watched by now.

"Mimmo!" she cried when I picked up, before I'd even said hello.

"Ciao, Mamma." We spoke Italian on the phone. It was the only time I ever got to practice my native language.

"You won your game," she said, pride radiating in the lilt of her voice. "You are the best goalie in the league." There'd never been any shortage of encouragement from my family.

"That's not quite true, Mamma, but thanks."

"Tell me how you are."

I told her the same things I usually did, about practices and schedules, about the other guys on the team.

"And you are cooking?"

"Now and then."

"It feeds the soul, Stephano." Mamma was Catholic, but her real religion was food, her sanctuary the kitchen. She'd taught all her sons to cook, and insisted we go to that altar whenever anything was bothering us. She wasn't wrong about it having mind-soothing qualities.

"I know, Mamma."

"And how is my future daughter-in-law?"

"That, I wouldn't know."

Mom made a clucking noise, the one she used to demonstrate disappointment. She certainly appreciated the money I sent home, the way I took care of my family, but what she had always wanted was a daughter-in-law and a house full of grandbabies.

"You haven't found her yet." She sucked in a quick breath. "Unless . . . perhaps it is a him?"

"It is not."

"Good. I think maybe that is for the best."

This was a strange turn. Mamma usually suggested I start hanging around the grocery store and farmer's market trying to pick up the kinds of women who liked to cook. She definitely had never suggested that me not dating anyone was a good thing.

Dating wasn't really on my radar anyway. The very idea was not appealing. Women liked me. For a while, at least. But in the long run? I was not the man of most girls' dreams. "I'm too busy for anything like that, Mamma. Nothing's changed."

Mamma was still clucking, her tongue making a little echo down the phone line that told me she was thinking.

"What's wrong?" I was happy to change the subject, but Mamma only made that sound when she was worried.

"Nothing is wrong. But I would like to see you. We are coming for a visit."

I sat up straighter in my chair. I was torn. I loved my family and wanted to see them. But Mamma's past visits had involved her efforts at matchmaking, and right now I didn't need any distraction from the season. I had enough to handle with the new goalie speeding around me like a puppy and an injury I was trying to will away. I didn't need Mamma to play matchmaker, and I didn't need them to know I was injured. "You should. That would be nice. Christmas, maybe?"

"No. Sooner, I think. Next week."

Next week? I put the phone down for a second and took a deep, calming breath. We'd be in the midst of the season, but I couldn't argue about travel schedules because Mamma knew every detail of my schedule, and undoubtedly knew that we had more home games in a row than usual over the next couple weeks.

"That would be nice, Mamma." What else could I say?

"Maybe your brothers will come too, though Cristiano is impossible to get answers from lately."

I sighed. As much I loved seeing my little brothers, at seventeen and twenty-one, they hadn't exactly matured to the point where I saw them as peers. Mamma had me when she was seventeen. And then she didn't have my brothers until I was already twelve years old. In some ways, I felt like I'd raised them as much as she had.

"That would be nice." There was only one right answer.

"I will send you our travel plans. You can . . ."

"I'll book everything for you, Mamma. Just like always."

"Good boy. *Ti voglio bene, figlio mio.*"

"I love you too, Mamma."

CHAPTER 2
HILLARY

IT'S NOT THE TIKTOK POOP SHAKE.
I DON'T THINK.

"This is the life!" I spun in a circle, one arm flung out wide and the other still holding my phone pressed to my head as I celebrated my latest accomplishment.

"That," my sister drawled, "is actually someone else's life."

I stopped spinning, letting my eyes readjust to stillness with a sickening swoop around Teresa Palmer's living room. "It's mine for a month," I reminded my too-practical sister, Helena. "And it is gorgeous, Helly."

"I'm sure it is. You don't become the first lady of rock to live in a shack. I bet her place in LA is even better."

I looked around, taking in the plush carpet, the thick drapes, the sleek furnishings, all of which screamed "music money" loud and clear. "I don't know how that would be possible."

"Well, enjoy," Helly said.

"I plan to."

"And what's the plan when the month is up?" she asked.

I dropped onto the leather couch that was so soft it felt like maybe the leather had been rubbed down with coconut oil or something before being turned into a couch. Synthetic leather, of course. Teresa Palmer was a noted defender of animal rights. I could still hear the song from the radio commercial she voiced, asking if I could spare just a few dollars a day for feral hedgehog rescue.

I sighed. "The universe will let me know when it's ready."

"The spare room at our place will be ready if the universe is not, but I'm not sure the med school loan people will take IOUs from the universe, anyway."

"Won't need the room," I assured my sister, a black hole opening up in my gut at the mention of my school loans. "I can feel something coming."

"Have you pooped today? Could be that poop shake from TikTok you told me about."

"Ew. And that was weeks ago."

"Maybe the universe will bring you a real, grown-up job." Hel was beginning to sound like Dad, and I wasn't fond of her tone.

"I am a house sitter."

"For now."

"There are always houses needing to be sat. I could travel the world this way. I can totally pay back my loans on this," I told her indignantly. My indignation, however, was partially feigned. House sitting jobs weren't that easy to come by, and though I'd earned a place among the elite house-having population as reliable and trustworthy, the jobs weren't exactly lined up. Also, I could not pay back my loans this way. And I'd missed a few payments now.

But the universe, I was confident, would provide.

"I wish the universe would get you to finish your degree," Hel said.

"Stop being my older sister."

"Can't. Assigned at birth."

"I like you better as my friend."

"The only friend you have that tells you the truth."

"Maybe." I pushed a hand to my stomach, which was grumbling loudly. "I'm gonna run and get some food."

"Okay, Hill. Be good."

"Always. Love you."

"You too," Hel told me, and I pictured her putting her phone down on her responsible oak coffee table and kicking up her feet onto her IKEA couch. Helly, like her furnishings and everything in her life, was solid and reliable. So much so that I was pretty sure she'd sopped up all the available genes from that department and left me only with enthusiasm and poor planning to choose from.

I'd done fine with what I'd gotten, though. I couldn't imagine working in medicine like Helena did. I needed freedom, fresh air . . . But like everyone else, I also needed cash. Rather immediately. And one day, much as I hated to admit it, it was possible I might need a bit more financial security than house sitting provided. Hel wouldn't always have an available room for me. She was engaged, and her beau Anson didn't find me nearly as charming as most people seemed to. When they got married . . . well, it didn't make sense to worry about it now.

Not when I had an enormous modern home to explore.

I wandered through the kitchen, picking out a fancy kombucha and a salad left by the personal chef who was evidently going to stock the fridge for me once a week. I scarfed the salad, and then I took myself on a tour.

The house, needless to say, was enormous. Teresa Palmer had built a career producing women in rock, and I was pretty sure she had houses all over the world. She'd asked me if I'd be willing to spend a month in Wilcox, Virginia after her bestie—a high-profile photographer of fancy weddings—recommended me since I'd managed her NYC penthouse apartment and two very demanding chinchillas for two months over the summer.

I could live like this, I thought, stepping into yet another bedroom furnished like it was prepped for a photo shoot happening any minute for some swanky home magazine.

Only, to live like this, I'd have to actually choose a place to live. And maybe figure out a way to earn real, actual money.

I let out a long sigh as I concluded my tour by passing through the movie theater and recording studios set up in the basement. I spent a long time lingering in the latter, deciding that it would probably be okay for me to test out the studio a bit at some point, and then I returned myself to the kitchen with its waterfall quartz countertops and gleaming appliances.

"It's definitely too much," I told myself. I didn't need fancy.

But that was the problem.

I had no idea what I did need.

I did know that three quarters of a medical degree did you very little good in the real world. But, I reminded myself, having a very expensive degree you had no intention of using did you no good either.

I squeezed my eyes shut against the memory of Dad's face when I told my parents I wasn't going to be a doctor.

"All that time, all that effort Hillary. The money. Your loans," he'd said, looking as pained as if he'd been the one to put in the hours, pull the all-nighters, talk Kamala Yadav away from the third pint of Ben and Jerry's when her Step One USMLE hadn't gone well.

"It's not the right fit," I'd told him, my voice weakening as his anger grew. "I'll pay you back."

"How?"

It was a fair question. I'd taken Dad's money for some of my tuition—he'd been happy to give it to secure the pride of having a doctor in the family to add to his status after Helly had become a nurse practitioner. But now that I was not going to be a doctor, he had little to show for the investment. And my promise to pay him back was half-hearted at best. We both knew I couldn't.

"I just need a little time," I told him.

"To do what exactly?" Dad's silver brows had pulled down low over the deep brown eyes he'd passed on to me. Only I hoped my own eyes were never as disappointed as his had looked at that moment.

"I don't know," I'd told him, the pain of his regret slicing through me. I didn't like letting him down. But I couldn't be a doctor, either. And it was my life, not his, even though he seemed mightily concerned about my credit and financial future as my loans came due.

I stared out Teresa's floor-to-ceiling windows at the pool in the backyard, covered now for winter, and let out a yell to banish the negativity flowing through my mind.

If she had a pool, did that mean she had a hot tub? I hadn't noticed one when I'd arrived, but I could practically picture it out there in that perfect yard, nestled off to one side of the pool, just waiting for me to come out and slip into it beneath the stars.

I carried my bag to the middle bedroom—didn't ever feel right to sleep in the master—and pulled out my bikini, which I traveled with no matter what the season. A quick trip through the bathroom for a towel and a stop by the fridge for a fancy wine-in-a-can kind of thing, and I was out the door.

It was colder than expected and I immediately regretted not putting on my flip-flops.

"No matter. In a moment, I'll be submerged in hot tubby hotness." I scooted across the expanse of the patio in the glowing golden lights and to one side of the long rectangular pool. No hot tub.

I peered across the yard toward the other end of the pool, which was cast in shadow. There was a darker depression off to one side. Maybe it was a very private hot tub. That seemed right.

I skittered my frozen toes across the icy pavement to the other side of the pool to find . . . a round garden bed. Not a hot tub.

"Where would I be if I were a hot tub?" I asked the frigid night air, which had begun to feel like it was poking me with icy fingers.

The yard was huge. It was very possible that the hot tub was up around a corner in a fancy gazebo or something. I'd just have to look. Only . . . shoes first.

I returned to the door after putting my fancy drink on a table outside so I could wrap the towel more firmly around myself and pulled the handle.

Which didn't move a lick.

"Oh no," I said, as if warning the universe not to even think about doing this to me.

I pulled on the door handle again. But unless I was willing to break down a glass door, it appeared I was locked out on the patio.

"Dammit." I muttered the word under my breath, which was possible since I could see my breath hanging in the air around me. "Okay. Don't panic."

I took stock. I had a towel. And a bikini. And champagne in a can.

I did not have a phone. Or shoes. Or any hope of getting this door open.

"Plan B, then." I followed the walkway from the patio around the side of the house and toward the front, taking note of any open windows along the way. It was January, though. There were no open windows.

The gate at the front of the yard posed only a minor hassle, since it held a small padlock that prevented me from opening it. I did recall something about that in the texts Teresa sent me. Which I could not check, since my phone and all my earthly belongings, and all the warmth in the universe, were inside.

The gate had a couple good places to put my feet as I climbed it while trying to keep the towel around me. It wasn't easy.

"Shit!" I landed on the other side with a hard thud onto concrete and a definitive splinter in my big toe. "Shit, shit, shit! What is even happening right now?"

I swallowed, pulled the towel tighter, and sprinted to the front door. Maybe I'd left it unlocked.

Naturally, I had not.

The garage had a code! Only . . . I could not for the life of me remember what it was. I had a key, which Teresa had sent by courier, along with the contract I'd signed and sent back to her. So why would I memorize the garage code?

The garage, naturally, was closed, the garage door secure, and when I catapulted myself back into the yard to check every single door and window, I learned that the house I'd agreed to house sit was every bit as secure as the White House must be. Minus helpful Secret Service guys to let the prez back in when he locked himself out.

I was well and truly fucked.

I squatted down on the patio next to the door, tucking my body into a towel-covered ball for warmth, and put my brain to work.

There were neighbors, of course. I could see if any of them had a key. Of course, in this neighborhood, they were not exactly just a foot or two away. And it was late. Like middle of the night late.

I'd never kept quite regular hours, and medical school had just cemented those unhealthy tendencies. Ironic, no?

It wouldn't be polite to wake any of Teresa's neighbors. But it would also be bad form to freeze to death on her patio.

I stared at the distant fence separating her backyard from the one next door. I could see the shape of a roof overhang in that yard. Maybe there was some kind of pool house or something I could sneak into for the night? I stood and moved closer, eventually pushing up on my tiptoes to see over the fence.

Another pool tarped over for winter. But this one? Had a hot tub right next to it. And I could see what I thought were hints of steam escaping from the edges of the lid. It could have been like a mirage, I supposed. But I was literally freezing to death. I needed to get warm. A quick sit in a neighbor's hot tub made perfect sense. I'd get warm and formulate my next plan. Or just wait until morning when it would be appropriate to bother neighbors for help.

I dragged a patio chair to the fence and climbed over, landing rather ungracefully in some kind of thorny bush.

"Ow, shit." Me and fences. Not a good combo. Not that I'd had a lot of occasions to learn that simple truth before now.

I glanced around the enormous yard, which had a built-in bar beneath that roof overhang I saw, and a couple couches under it too. No pool house in sight, though. And luckily, no guard dogs.

I tiptoed to the hot tub, like anyone would hear me out here if they hadn't already, and scooted the lid off enough to reveal half the tub. It was one of those in-ground types, had built-in lounger seats, and it was steamy and beautiful.

"Thank you, universe," I said, as I slipped off my towel and stepped in. Shit, that hurt. My feet were so cold that the hot water felt like spears against my skin. But after a few minutes?

It was bliss.

If only I'd remembered to bring my canned champagne.

Oh well. I'd figure out my next steps in a minute. For now?

I was alive. And better yet, I was warm.

CHAPTER 3
STEPHANO

FACE OFF WITH THE HOT TUB SQUATTER

I hadn't been able to sleep after talking with Mamma. It didn't make a lot of sense, but any time I knew I was going to see her, I worried.

I worried about not living up to her hopes, about letting her down. She'd raised me after my father died, though by then, I'd been as much the man of the house as he'd been at the end. But she'd taken care of my brothers and me even after my grandparents had lost everything and moved in. We'd had nothing. And Mamma had handled it all as if having us all under one roof was some great blessing to be celebrated.

Now I had more than anyone in my family had ever dreamed.

And somehow, it still felt like I was failing in some way.

I wandered my house, thinking about all that hockey had made possible for me, for my family. Even before the fire, when Nonna and Poppi had lost the vineyards and the legacy their family had built for more than two hundred years, no one in my family had lived like this.

It was a lot I knew. But after taking care of my family back home, I'd been able to take care of me for a change.

It was just that this house felt too quiet sometimes. Too empty. Too much.

That was why I entertained the team a lot, even though half my teammates behaved like they'd been raised in a backwoods shack. I liked having them here. I liked seeing them on my patio, in my pool. I liked seeing them inside my house a little less. But still.

I wandered by the back windows, staring out at the pool where my friends were all too happy to hang out when the weather was warm.

The hot tub didn't normally put out that much steam, did it?

Big billowing puffs of steam were rising from the tub next to the pool, and I wondered if I'd managed to forget to put the lid back on yesterday.

But no. That wasn't me. I didn't forget things.

Ever.

I squinted into the darkness beyond the patio lights. It was hard to see much more than the steam, but then something closer caught my eye.

Footprints.

There were wet footprints leading to the fridge behind my bar and then back out to the hot tub.

Was someone squatting in my yard? Using my hot tub? Drinking my beer?

I'd never heard of this kind of crime.

I glanced around for a weapon, though I wasn't sure I'd need to defend myself against a drunk hot tub criminal.

Still.

I picked up a hockey stick that was leaning near the buffet. It was a commemorative stick from a charity tournament last season —which we'd lost. I wasn't going to hang it or anything. I didn't know what to do with it, but maybe a good use would be to evict an intruder with it.

Quietly, I unlatched the patio door and stepped outside with the stick. Damn, it was cold. My bare feet stung on the cold concrete. I felt the familiar shift of adrenaline into my bloodstream.

I crept toward the edge of the patio, keeping the partition between me and the tub until the last possible moment. Just as I was about to spring around the corner, I paused.

Someone was humming.

The intruder?

It was hard to hear over the bubbles, but yes, she was definitely humming, and she had a pretty good voice for a nefarious hot tub squatting criminal. Was that Fleetwood Mac? I loved that song . . .

But it didn't matter.

Unless it was Stevie Nicks herself in my tub, this was in no way acceptable.

I stepped out around the partition, into clear view of the tub, holding the stick in a menacing way over one shoulder.

To no effect whatsoever.

The person enjoying my hospitality without an invitation was lounging comfortably, her head leaned back into the neck support of the far seat, her eyes shut as she continued to sing.

I stepped closer, confused.

Intrigued.

No, not intrigued.

Mad. I was mad.

"Hey," I said, focusing on mad and not on the very nice shoulders visible above the bubbling water line.

"Oh!" The intruder sat up, causing a little splash. Next to her was a can of the hard cider I kept in the outdoor fridge for Clara, Sly's fiancée. "Hi!"

"Hi?" That was not quite what I'd been expecting.

"Do you live here?"

"What?" I stared at her. She was looking up at me as if this was a completely normal conversation to be having. "Yes. This is my house. You are in my hot tub. Drinking Clara's cider."

"Clara's your wife?"

"No, she's Sly's—hang on just a minute. I don't have to explain myself to you."

"Sorry, just curious."

I lowered the stick, increasingly exasperated. I should have just gone to bed. "Who are you?"

"I'm Hillary Watters."

"Great." Who the hell was Hillary Watters? Why was she in my hot tub? What the hell was actually happening here? "Care to expand?"

"Sure. I'm thirty. From California originally. Was going to med school, but found I have a particular affinity for house sitting, so I'm doing that instead for a while."

I think my mouth might have dropped open. "This is not a conversation we're having. You get that, right?"

"Oh. You did ask." She took a sip of her cider and gave a little shrug.

I shook my head. "Do you understand that house sitting does not involve just showing up at people's houses and sitting in their hot tubs?"

She laughed, and the sound was a full-bodied, hearty kind of thing that would have been surprising if I had any further capacity to be surprised. "Yeah, I do know that. I didn't mean I was house sitting for you. What's your name?"

"Stephano." Why was I answering her questions? Why was this person still in my yard?

"Nice to meet you."

"No."

"Okay," she laughed again. "Not nice."

"Listen, I don't want to have to call the police here, but this is totally unacceptable. You're trespassing, and drinking my cider, and—"

"Clara's cider."

"Right."

She began getting out of the hot tub, steam rising off her skin as she extricated her very long golden limbs from the hot water and then covered them with a white, fluffy towel. "Sure, yeah, no. Don't call the cops, please."

I shook my head again, partially because she was the most confusing—and pretty—person I'd encountered recently, and because she wasn't putting the hot tub cover on right. "Here, I'll help."

Together, we re-covered the tub and then I stood there, staring at her.

"So here's the thing," she said, and strangely, I found myself very eager to hear exactly what the thing could possibly be. I needed to go to bed, to remove this stranger from my house, and get a good night's sleep for practice tomorrow. But instead, all I could do was wait for this odd person to tell me whatever it was she needed to tell me.

"I locked myself out." She chuckled, but I didn't. This still made no sense.

"Of my house?"

She laughed harder. "No, silly. I climbed the fence from over there."

"This isn't getting better."

She blew her lips out in a raspberry and tilted her head back, exposing the white column of her neck as she seemed to laugh at the stars above. "I know, I'm sorry. Let me back up." She fixed me in a dark-eyed gaze and slowly said, "I'm Hillary. I'm house sitting for Teresa next door." She pointed next door again. "I went out to see if she had a hot tub and locked myself out. And then I didn't know what to do since it was so late, and I was worried about freezing to death, and saw you had a hot tub, so I figured I could sit in it until it was a reasonable time to knock on your door and ask if you have a key, or if I could use the phone to call a locksmith or maybe Teresa to get the code for the garage again."

"That, uh . . . makes some sense, I guess."

"Totally."

I had no idea what the appropriate thing to do was in this situation. Did I ask her for ID? We couldn't exactly call Teresa to verify, since it was the middle of the night. I had met her, and I was pretty sure I had her cell somewhere.

"Okay, so . . ."

"So, can I use your phone?"

"To call a locksmith."

"Yes."

"At three o'clock in the morning?"

"A twenty-four-hour locksmith, I guess." She grinned and then she shivered, and I realized I was freezing too.

"Just come inside," I suggested, turning back to the house with the hockey stick I'd dropped on the couch on the patio.

"Oh, okay." She followed me and took a few seconds to towel herself off again before stepping onto the living room rug. "Oh my god, it's so warm in here."

"Thanks." What? That wasn't a compliment. What was wrong with me? "Heater." It was like I could not achieve normal in front of this bikini-clad stranger.

"Okay, so phone?" She was looking around her, as if I might have an old-fashioned landline hanging from the wall or sitting on a countertop.

I pulled my cell from my pocket and moved to sit on the couch. She didn't budge. "You can sit."

"I'm wet."

"Sit on the towel?"

That was the worst idea I'd ever had. She folded her towel neatly and then sat down, so now nothing was covering the exten-sive amounts of skin this perfect stranger was exhibiting. Skin covered with goosebumps.

"Here." I carried a soft throw over to her, one that usually did nothing better than drape the back of my couch. She wrapped it around herself.

"Thank you."

"Okay. Twenty-four-hour locksmiths." I sat opposite her and began searching for such a thing, but Wilcox was a pretty small town. Big enough for a hockey team, sure, but that didn't mean a whole lot if you went by some of the Canadian towns where we'd played. A thought struck me then. "I don't think a locksmith would open the house for you. Not without some kind of ID or proof that you have a right to open it."

"They'll open it for you?"

I shook my head. "We need to call Teresa. But it's the middle of the night."

Hillary sat perfectly still, waiting while I stared at my phone helplessly.

After another second, I dropped the phone to my side. "Okay, look. It's late. And you're probably not a criminal."

"You definitely don't know that."

"I think you're supposed to argue in the other direction." I took a breath, suddenly exhausted. "Here's the thing . . . I just, I think maybe we should both go to bed, and I'll help you call someone in the morning?"

"Bed?" Hillary glanced around. "I mean, I could just take this blanket outside, really. Those couches look comfortable. If you had, maybe, like some wool socks?"

"I'm not going to let you sleep outside. It's below freezing."

She frowned. "I'm not a criminal. I'm really not."

"Okay. Well, you can sleep in the guest room."

"Really?"

"Really."

I ushered her to a bedroom, telling myself this was a completely normal situation. Telling myself I didn't see her shimmering yellow-gold aura. Telling myself I could ignore the way something about this woman made my insides tangle up.

And that was how I ended up taking a perfect stranger into one of the spare bedrooms at my house and then putting myself to bed, feeling like something in the universe had just shifted. Maybe irreversibly.

CHAPTER 4
HILLARY

A BED THAT'S JUST RIGHT

I locked the bedroom door.

Technically, I was the potential criminal in this situation, but I still figured better safe than sorry was my best policy.

Stephano's guest room was big. And like Teresa's whole house, it was decorated as if the HGTV crew were on their way to film tomorrow. Huge fluffy duvet over the most luxurious mattress I'd ever flopped backward onto. And there was a chandelier. It was understated, if that was possible in a chandelier, but there it hung, over the bed.

The whole room was done in tones of dark navy and light dove gray, and it made me immediately feel wealthy and sleepy at the same time. I popped through the ensuite to rinse my mouth, and then tucked myself in.

And then my mind turned. Stephano . . .

He was pretty hot for a random guy whose house I was sleeping over at in a totally unplanned way.

"Hey," I whispered, popping my eyes open again to stare up at the ceiling blocking my view of the universe beyond. "Was this you?"

Only, I was pretty sure if the universe was going to deliver a guy, he would be slightly more . . . something. More easygoing? More fun?

Of course, many people were not at their best when wielding a hockey stick during a potential intruder scenario.

But Stephano was grumpy if I'd ever met grumpy. Even the rigid way he held himself told me from the second we'd met that he was on some kind of self-control kick. Plus, this house. Everything about it screamed "meticulous nature." Or "way too tidy."

And who looked that good at three in the morning? Not a hair out of place. A light scruff over his jaw. A collared shirt?

I didn't know who Stephano really was, but I was pretty sure he was uptight with an emphasis on the tight part.

Morning came with an irritating and repetitive thumping noise.

I sat up, startled, and then it took me a little while to remember where I was. And who could be thumping on the door like that.

"Goldilocks, you in there?"

Goldilocks?

I slid out of the bed, grabbed the throw I'd carried in here from the couch to wrap myself in, and pulled open the door. "Goldilocks? This is the only bed I tried out last night, Steph—" I met his eyes and the rest of his name hung there on the end of my tongue, forgotten.

If I'd thought he was handsome at three in the morning, I'd been mistaken. This guy, the one standing here shirtless and glistening with sweat, the hair still flawless—this guy was truly handsome.

"Good morning," he said. Then his eyes slid down my body, taking in the bare shoulders, the blanket pulled around me, and gliding down to my feet before popping back up. "Do you ever wear clothes?"

"When I am not locked out of the house where my clothes reside, yes."

"Oh, right. Should I get you some sweats, maybe?"

"That would be nice."

"I called Teresa. She confirmed that you are housesitting for her and gave me the garage code."

"Oh." Well, that was nice too. "Thank you."

He nodded. "Okay. Good. Stay there. Be right back."

A few minutes later, I was wearing a pair of oversized black sweatpants and a Wilcox Wombats hoodie and standing across from Stephano in his kitchen.

"Coffee?" he offered a cup across the black granite of his countertop. He'd put a shirt on. A Wilcox Wombats shirt.

"Sure. Thanks. You a big Wombats fan?"

He glanced at me again over his shoulder, a strange look on his face. "Uh, yeah. I am."

I nodded. "Never really gotten into hockey."

"That's too bad. Great game."

"Seems violent."

"The apparent violence is part of the strategy. Though it is definitely fast-moving and there are a few injuries on the ice, the players use the force and speed that looks like violence for one purpose only: delivering the puck."

"Thanks, Wikipedia."

Stephano frowned at me. "It's a serious sport."

"Do you play this sport?" I asked him, sensing there was something deeper going on here that I was not picking up.

He sniffed and put his cup down on the counter, then glanced around as if directing my attention to the walls of his living room.

I followed his gaze, noticing for the first time a few items that probably should have tipped me off in the first place. But it had been pretty late when I was in this room before.

A bunch of guys in a photo that was blown up and hung over

the dresser-thing in the living room. All wearing hockey gear. With a Wombats logo beneath them.

A couple plexiglass boxes in the built-in bookshelf that were lit from somewhere within. Holding hockey pucks.

Another picture, this one smaller, of a guy decked out in more pads than I would have thought possible, in front of a net. Hard to say who it might be, but I was putting my money on the guy frowning at me across the island.

I was about to give voice to my newly formed understanding, when his phone buzzed on the counter, and he picked it up.

"Yeah, just have to deal with something first. Be there soon." He put the phone back down. "Should we head over?"

"Over? Oh, the house."

"Let's head over there and you can show me something to prove to me that you're actually housesitting there."

"You seriously don't believe me? You talked to Teresa, right?"

"Just closing the loop, okay?"

I slurped down some of my coffee and put the cup down, grabbing my now-dry bikini on the way out Stephano's front door.

His house was a close rival for the opulence of Teresa's. Both sprawled the length of a football field, between the houses themselves and the manicured grounds surrounding them. Stephano opted to head down the walkway to the sidewalk and over to Teresa's instead of crossing either lawn.

I snickered. It would leave footprints. Couldn't have that.

I turned to face him in front of the garage keypad and he handed me the note where he'd written the code. I typed it in and the garage door slid open.

"Okay, so . . . proof?" I hesitated, feeling suddenly guilty of something, even though I was doing nothing wrong.

"Yes please. I'll wait here."

Bizarre as it was, I left him there at the door, and scurried off to get my bag, which I placed at his feet when I'd returned.

"A duffle bag."

"Pull anything out of it and I'll explain exactly what it is, where I got it, and even try it on for you, if you want."

"I was thinking more like a contract or agreement between you and the homeowner, along with some ID."

I'd already squatted down and pulled a pair of silky lace underwear out of the bag, intending to shove them aside. But now they were in my hand as I stood. "Oh. Yes, better plan."

I dropped the undies onto the duffle between us and went to the kitchen to get my phone off the counter. It had a charge, but barely. When I got back to the front door, Stephano's eyes were latched onto the soft pink lace panties, which had fallen to lay across the bag as if they'd been spread there that way purposely.

"So, here's the agreement." I said, and his eyes popped back up to mine, a slight rosy shade creeping over his skin. I held up a text chain for him to see.

"You made a legal agreement over text message?"

"I do everything via text."

"Are texts legally binding?"

"You're missing the point, detective. And she has the actual paper contract I signed. Look. Here is the homeowner's name. Teresa Palmer. Here is where she asks me to watch her house for the month—see the address? And here"—I scrolled down farther —"is where I agree."

"And you're Hillary."

I pulled out my driver's license. "Yep. As explained last night."

I could see that he really wanted some kind of paper contract to sift through to see that all the Ts were crossed and the Is dotted. But that wasn't going to happen. I didn't work that way.

"Okay," he said.

"Okay," I agreed, my underwear still laying between us like a third party to the conversation. "Do you still want me to try these on?" I asked, lifting the offending garment just to see him blush.

Stephano's skin immediately deepened to a glorious red. "No." He cleared his throat and pulled his eyes to the top of my head. "Not necessary."

I shrugged, laughing, and tucked the underwear back in the bag. "Okay then. That's all settled. I guess I'll be seeing you around?"

"Most likely not. Unless you lock yourself out again."

"Or if I go to a Wombats game?" I wanted to test my theory before the grumpy goalie disappeared from my life forever.

The tiniest smile lifted the sculpted corner of his full mouth. "Or that. And if you want to, I can probably get you tickets."

I grinned at him. "I'd like that. I can tell people I slept with the goalie."

"Don't tell people that."

"I'll get your sweats back to you," I told him. "Unless you want them right now." I started to fidget with the waistband.

His blush deepened.

I wiggled my eyebrows as he shook his head and turned away.

And oddly, when Stephano the Grumpy Goalie had departed, I missed him a tiny bit.

CHAPTER 5
STEPHANO

TURNS OUT HOCKEY IS HARD

John Samuels was annoying.

When I showed up for practice, which always started with coffee, breakfast, and a little jawing with the team and staff, he plopped himself down right next to me.

"Hey," he offered, the single word managing to grate.

"Hey," I said, feeling every minute of sleep I'd lost to the hot tub bandit the night before.

"So I wondered today if we could work some more on that top of crease drill Coach had us doing last week?"

I chewed the delicious bite of egg sandwich in my mouth, swallowing before I turned to look at him. "Yep. Should work on that."

"Right," he said, his boyish face breaking into a self-conscious smile. "I meant, like, you and me. Together."

Shit. I'd been planning to take it a bit easy at practice to nurse the hip that had been killing me lately. If I had to parade around, showing off for Samuels, there was a good chance I'd overexert and make it worse, because I couldn't help it. I hated the whole idea of being replaced. But really, I figured I needed two more years to round out the investment account I'd been putting together for my family. Something to get Mamma a new home of her own and see her through the rest of her life in comfort. The account was big, but with the markets fluctuating so much lately, I wanted a cushion. A big cushion. I'd been the first-string goaltender for the Wombats for a decade. Second strings came and went. This was the first one to have the skill and potential to replace me. Soon.

"Yeah, maybe."

I turned back to my sandwich, signaling that we were done here.

Samuels didn't take the hint.

"And the five hole, man . . . I don't know how you do it."

I slid him a look, then returned to my sandwich. "It's hard."

"No kidding." He chuckled and leaned back in his chair, relaxing again as if I'd just invited him to share his innermost thoughts with me. "There's just so fucking much to think about the whole time you're out there, right? And in college . . . the offense just wasn't as scary, I guess."

I turned to glare at him. "Don't ever admit to being scared. Not in front of our guys, not in front of another team."

"I'm not scared," he said, sitting up straighter. "Listen, I'm a great goalie. I just meant, when all the action's coming at you, it's a lot of pressure."

It was. And it was part of the reason the other second strings had been traded.

"It's a lot of pressure," I echoed, repeating it almost as if daring him to tell me he couldn't take it.

He was quiet a while, thankfully, and then he stood and said, "Good chat, Russ," and headed for the lockers.

That was the line we all used for a chat that had been . . . less than good. The movie was old, maybe, but sarcastic application of poignant quotes didn't age.

I knew I'd been rude. I was always rude to Samuels. I didn't like his puppy dog eyes, his eager-beaver mentality. He was so ready to step in and take the spot I'd spent a decade carving out for myself. When people thought about the Wombats, who did they picture?

Me. Stephano Mizzoni. One of the most successful goaltenders in the league.

The voice I used to remind myself of all this was quieter than it used to be inside my head, and I hated that it carried a little twinge of doubt along with it. I couldn't be that Stephano Mizzoni forever. I knew it, but I also knew I wasn't ready to be done.

I'd learned from experience that all good things ended. But this time, I wanted the end to come on my terms. A couple more years. And then I'd step away. But I didn't want to be traded, and I didn't want to fizzle. The Wombats were my home.

"How you doin, sweetheart?" Rock Stevens paused as he passed through the café, grinning at me.

"Go fuck yourself, Stevens."

"If only it were possible," he said, chuckling and heading off to the weight room.

I never showed up with a bright smile for all to see, but today, I found myself in a particularly shitty mood. I decided to blame it entirely on my new next-door neighbor.

Appearing in my yard in a bikini in the middle of the night and then ending up sleeping just down the hall—apparently naked, in my guest bed—well, I'd been thinking about it more than I should have. I knew it was a random, one-time thing.

So why did my mind insist on pulling up her smiling face, conjuring that perfect body, and replaying her whiskey and sunlight voice? It was exhausting.

Practice was blessedly brief, the meeting Samuels and I had with Coach Merit afterward, less so.

"And I need to see a little more time together during practice," he was saying. "Looking at you, Mizzoni."

I met his eyes, nodded. The coach's purple aura was darker than usual. Was he stressed about something? Or just about me?

"We were lucky enough to get this guy," he said, angling his head at Samuels but keeping his eyes locked on me. "Now you mold him into something we can use. Got it?"

I got it.

I was the dog about to be put down, watching my family fawn over a new puppy.

"Yeah. Got it."

"Good." Coach began to rise and then sank back down, giving a quick nod at Samuels. "See you tomorrow."

Samuels all but skipped out to the dressing room, and I sighed as Coach cleared his throat and aimed a steely gaze at me.

"Listen. I understand, Mizzoni. You think you're so stoic and reserved, but I can see exactly what's going on here."

Shit. "You can?"

"Yes. Clear as day."

"Okay."

"Let's get it out in the open."

"Sure. Yeah." He looked uncomfortable suddenly. Did he know about my hip?

"I know what the guys are saying, but he's not really paid more than you."

I sat up straighter. I hadn't even suspected that he might be. I was a ten-year vet. "Uh. Good."

"Yeah, I mean with the signing bonus, maybe he is this year, okay? But we value your loyalty, your dominance—you know all that. There's only one Stephano Mizzoni and we're lucky to have him."

That puppy was making more than me? I hadn't bothered to dig into his contract terms . . . why would I?

"Sure."

"We all square now?"

I did not think we were square, hexagonal, or triangular. I didn't know what we were, but I knew I felt like I'd just slipped a few handholds on this cliff I'd been trying to cling to.

"Yeah."

"Okay. Have the trainers take a look at your right hip. You're favoring it in practice."

Shit again. "Will do."

He rose and crossed the room before turning back around to look at me. "Everything okay? Everything else?"

I blew out a breath. "Yeah, Coach. Everything's fine."

"Good. See you tomorrow."

I finished my day in the weight room and took my time stretching, the knot of worry in my gut growing tighter every time I got a pang from my hip. A strain, I could nurse. A tear?

Well, I just had to hope it wasn't a tear. If it was . . .

I assured myself it just wasn't.

That afternoon I did as my mother suggested and spent some time in the kitchen. I'd had a gourmet kitchen put in when I'd built the house, but it didn't get used as often as I'd have liked. The side-by-side Wolf ovens had an eight-burner gas cooktop that still gleamed under the kitchen lights, and as I turned the knob to put some heat under my pan, a sense of calm focus wound its way through me.

I chopped and cooked, letting the natural rhythm of the movements take over, the speakers in the ceiling adding in the sound-track—one I'd never admit was mine. But hey, being able to listen to whatever the hell you wanted in the privacy of your own home was one of the perks of being me.

Soon, pasta was in the pot, and the scent of garlic and lemon was wafting through the space. I had my hands in a salad bowl when the doorbell rang.

It was most likely a delivery, in which case, the guy bringing whatever the thing was would be entirely accustomed to me not answering the door. He'd leave the item, and I'd go get it later.

I drizzled oil.

The doorbell rang again.

Did he need a signature? I wiped my hands on the apron I'd tied around my waist and headed for the door, pulling it open to find the last person I'd expected.

Hillary Watters.

Holding a plate of cookies in front of her.

"Hi!" Her voice was light and fresh, and she looked completely adorable in a soft white sweater and faded blue jeans, her blond hair wavy and flowing over her shoulders. Her feet were stuffed into big furry boots, and her cheeks were rosy from the cold.

"Uh." Too many seconds later, I managed, "hi."

"I wanted to thank you for last night," she said, the smile never faltering. "So I baked cookies. I don't know if you have allergies or anything, so I made macarons because they're gluten free and I made the filling dairy-free, so that avoids most concerns. Of course, if you're allergic to almonds, then we have an issue—"

"No."

She stopped, her lips parted mid-sentence.

Dammit. Too gruff. "No, I don't have allergies."

"Oh!" The smile was back. "Good! Okay then." She did a little gesture with the plate, offering it to me again and I took it from her.

"Thanks."

Hillary's eyes flashed and then she glanced past me into the house, and leaned in a bit. "Are you cooking? It smells like heaven right here."

"Oh, uh. Yeah."

"Italian? I'm getting garlic . . . and lemon?"

"My mom's recipe." I stepped back. At the mention of Mamma, I remembered my manners. "Thanks for the cookies. You didn't have to do that."

Hillary smiled up at me again, sending a snaky warmth through me. "I wanted to."

She did not seem to be anxious to depart. While I generally

cooked only for myself, it was beginning to feel exceptionally rude to let her continue to stand there without inviting her in. I didn't actually want her to come in, but I also wasn't an asshole.

"Want to come in?"

"If I'm not intruding," she said, stepping past me into the foyer and pulling off the big boots she wore. She let out a half sigh, half gasp and said, "I really do love your house."

I shut the front door and followed this whirlwind of woman through my living room as she continued talking. "And I did some Googling, hope you don't mind. I was so dense last night. I'm sorry for what I said about hockey. You're the goalie, right? For the Wombats."

"Yeah."

We'd reached the kitchen and I set the plate of macarons down just as the next song in my playlist fired up. And the timing could really not have been worse.

As the piano crescendo rose and then fell again, Hillary's mouth dropped open and her eyes widened. And then she swung her head around to stare at me in surprise as the first words of the solo female anthem left her lips in a low whisper, mouthing about how at first she was afraid . . .

I was petrified.

This was not exactly the image I tried to put out into the world.

But this song made me think of my mother, and every time Gloria Gaynor sang about being a strong single woman who didn't need a man, I remembered my mom back in Italy, taking over like a boss when Dad died.

Hillary hadn't missed a beat as the song continued, and as she danced through my kitchen, she picked up a whisk and began using it as a microphone, her voice belting out the chorus now.

Damn. She could sing.

Also, this was not the evening I'd planned. I was going to have a quiet meal, get my head back together, plan my family's trip, and proceed with business as usual.

Instead, I was watching a blond dynamo shimmy and twirl through my kitchen, singing at the top of her lungs, and I almost couldn't recall how the hell this had all happened.

She didn't seem bothered by my presence, or really, even to remember that I was here, so I moved back to the stove and drained the pasta. I continued putting the meal together as Hillary wound down, and when the song ended, she slid to my side at the island, watching me grind parmesan onto two plates.

"How much do you like?" I asked.

"Me?" Her big round eyes moved from the food to my face.

"You're here, you might as well eat."

"Oh!" That smile. It was the kind of smile that launched ships, that inspired battles between silly, weak-kneed men. I wished I was immune. "That's so nice. Yes, I'd love to have dinner with you, thank you. And yes to cheese. Always yes to cheese. There is really only one right answer when it comes to cheese."

She talked a lot. Which I guessed was good since I was not known for my verbosity. I carried both plates to the glass table by the window and waved her to sit.

"Wine?"

"Oh!" She said this often, and it was a sound of both surprise and pleasure, as if she'd never dreamed anyone might offer her wine with dinner. "That would be amazing!"

Amazing. Sure.

I poured her a glass of vermentino, setting a water before each of us too.

"You're not drinking?"

"Not during the season."

She pointed at me. "Right. Makes sense." Then she twirled a bite of pasta onto her fork and took an enormous bite, those bright eyes widening again as the flavors hit her.

"Mmmmmmhndd-aaaghn." She said something—It sounded very complimentary—around the bite.

"Thanks."

Once she'd swallowed and had a sip of wine, she leaned back

in her chair and shot me the smile that was suddenly feeling a lot like my personal kryptonite. "You are an incredible cook. This is possibly the best thing I've ever tasted. I could die right now and be happy."

"Please don't die in my house. It was enough trouble having you in my hot tub." It was a joke, but few people ever seemed to manage to pick up on my jokes.

The eyebrows lowered and she leaned forward. This woman was the most animated person I'd ever encountered. "I'm so sorry about that."

"No, it's fine."

She was shaking her head. "It was a huge inconvenience, I know. And now? Knowing what kind of cook you are? I kind of wonder if I should just take those cookies away before you taste one. I've been outclassed, I'm afraid."

"If it's any consolation, I can't bake at all." The cookies looked good. I did not want her to take them back.

The eyebrows rose again. "No?"

God, I could spend a lifetime just watching this woman's face change.

"No. My mom is a fantastic cook and baker, but I only got the one gene, I guess."

Taylor Swift was now singing loudly about sexy babies and monsters on the hill, and I saw the moment that Hillary registered the song.

"You, sir, are a tangled and fascinating twisty little knot of contradictions." She nodded, as if proclaiming herself correct.

"I am?" I couldn't help it. I was psychoanalyzed plenty by my mother and sometimes the team shrink, Agnes, but I wanted to know Hillary's opinion of me. Desperately.

"Oh yeah. It's seriously intriguing."

"It is?"

She nodded, a lock of hair falling forward and almost landing in her plate. She pulled it back, tucking it behind her ear and I was way too interested in that motion. Her hair looked soft. It glowed in the dim light of her champagne aura. Like the rest of her. I realized I wanted to touch her. I wanted her.

Shit.

"Totally. You've got this very stern, stoic exterior. I think you show the world only what you want them to see, right? Like, you're the tough guy, the league-leading goaltender, the veteran player, the boy who built an empire on nothing but grit and determination."

So she'd read the Wikipedia page.

"Yeah, but on the inside, you're a whole complex, mushy mess of feelings, swiftiness, and Martha Stewart."

"You think I'm Martha Stewart?" I wasn't sure I liked that.

"It's just a way to describe this whole homey vibe you've got going on. And the music selection? No one would ever guess you had a thing for Tay-tay. Not in a hundred million years." Her eyes glowed across the table, and she looked as excited as if she'd just uncovered some long-lost treasure like that thing supposedly hidden at that Colorado Resort I'd read about in some news article. But all she'd really found was the truth about me.

"Let's keep the music selections on the down low."

"Who am I going to tell?"

"Right."

We ended the meal with the macarons she'd made—which were perfect—and I was just about to usher her out so I could get a good night's sleep when my phone rang.

Mamma. Up at an insane hour, even for her.

I wasn't going to answer, but Hillary saw the screen and pushed my phone toward me. "Talk to your mom, I'll do dishes!" And before I had a choice, she was gathering plates and heading for the sink. I wouldn't have answered except for the time—I was worried something was wrong.

"Hi Mamma. Everything all right?"

"*Si, piccolo mio.* I'm just calling to tell you the dates we'll visit. Cristano cannot come because he is too busy sneaking around

Italy and keeping secrets from his family, but Luca and I will be there next Friday."

What was my brother up to? I made a mental note to call him later. "Did you buy tickets already? I haven't even had time to look, but you know I usually do that for you."

"Yes, with your credit card. Remember you gave me the number?"

I had. For emergencies. I wasn't angry at all, I just thought we'd had a plan and now she was changing it. Plus, this meant I had little control over the schedule. "Okay," I said, pushing down the irritation that always flared when plans changed on the fly. "Send me the flight info?"

"That's why I'm calling you, *sciocco.*"

"Hey Goalie!" Hillary whisper-shouted from the kitchen. I turned, wishing I didn't like seeing her at my counter with her hands lost in enormous plastic gloves as she scrubbed pots in my sink. "Where should I put this pot?" She held up the pasta pot.

"Island, far right cabinet," I told her, and then raised the phone back to my ear. "Okay, Mamma," I put her on speaker so I could put the information she sent into the phone. "Give me the flight info when you're ready."

"Is there a woman in your house?"

"What? No." I didn't need Mamma to revert back to her usual matchmaking ways, and if she suspected a woman was in my life, I'd never hear the end of it.

"Goalie!" Hillary called again.

I swung around to face her, wishing now that she'd just leave everything on the counter.

"Stephano!" Mom's voice shrieked from the phone.

"That goes below the island," I told Hillary in answer to the question I knew she was asking as she waved the strainer around in the air.

"Mamma."

"There IS a woman at your house. I heard her. Who is she?"

I sighed. "She's just a neighbor, Mamma. It's nothing."

I expected my mother to get excited about this discovery, maybe even to squeal, or at least to start choosing wedding dates and naming babies. She did not sound pleased for some reason. "And I'll get to meet her next week?"

That was definitely not happening. I just hoped Hillary couldn't hear my mother over the water in the sink.

"No," I said, harsher than intended. "I mean, sure, maybe. But Mamma, it's nothing serious."

"Good," my mother said, confusing me even more but sending a wave of relief through me at the same time. She gave me her information and said goodnight.

"Thanks for dinner," Hillary said, sweeping through the living room on her way back to the door.

"Thank you for the cookies."

She pushed her feet back into the enormous boots. It was dark out now, and through the transom window I could see snow falling lightly. "Should I walk you home?"

"It's not that far." She laughed and pushed a hand against my chest, her face dropping its gleeful expression and morphing into something far more serious as her fingers stayed there a beat longer than I'd expected.

"I'll watch then, to make sure you get in okay."

"I'll just pop into your hot tub if I'm locked out."

I tried to suppress the mental image. "Funny."

I watched as Hillary made her way across my grass and the lawn next door, produced a key and let herself inside, turning to me with a quick wave.

And then I stood there a moment longer, wishing she'd find some reason to come back.

CHAPTER 6
HILLARY

LAYIN' DOWN DOPE TRACKS, YO

It took me the full extent of the evening to digest all that had gone down in the hour I'd spent next door.

First of all, the music! It was like he'd cued up a list of my all-time favorite songs to sing and then dared me not to do it. Naturally, I'd been totally unable to resist that first one. "I Will Survive" is practically my mantra. Not because I'd had a man betray me or anything, but just because . . . well, doesn't everyone want to survive?

But then . . . the food!

I realized immediately that I'd be finding excuses to stumble next door around mealtime regularly if he was going to continue cooking. Teresa's personal chef might be good, but she was not in the same league as this guy. And I hadn't seen the woman, but I bet she didn't look as good in an apron, either.

I knew it was trouble spending too much time thinking about the grumpy goalie next door, but I couldn't seem to help it. It was like a personal challenge to see those pouty lips lift just a fraction into the barest hint of a smile, to get the faintest glimmer of humor to appear in those dark, dark eyes.

Generally speaking, I did not enjoy those who refused to see the fun in life. But there was something about Stephano. It was like he saw the fun but was trying to keep himself from acknowledging it. What would it be like to break a guy like that out of his shell?

"No, nope. Definitely not." I gave myself this reminder as I made my way down to Teresa's recording studio. "I've got much more important things to do than try to charm some grumpy guy who is dedicated to being uncharmed. He is not my problem."

But in truth, my interest in him was far from altruistic. It wasn't so much that I thought I needed to save him from a life of focus and boredom as I thought maybe I needed to save myself from a life of never knowing what it was like to kiss him.

"No kissing," I whispered to myself as I plopped down the laptop I'd brought that held a few of the tracks I'd been playing with.

I'd recorded myself in a closet before, but fate had dropped a real, actual recording studio in my lap, and I was going to take acoustic advantage. If this wasn't the universe speaking my name, I didn't know what was.

It took a little while to figure everything out—Teresa's equipment was way more high end than anything I'd messed around with before. But I'd never been too afraid of pushing buttons—on people or recording equipment—and soon the music was going and I pulled on some headphones and stepped behind the mic.

Damn, I sounded good in here.

I started with "I Will Survive" since I'd already practiced that one once tonight, and then moved through some of my other favorites. It felt good. It felt really fucking great, actually. Karaoke had always been a release for me, and lately I'd been mixing a bit of my own music, writing some lyrics and testing them out. It was fun, and it distracted me from the roiling mess of my somewhat non-existent future. And it drowned out Dad's voice in my head.

I was about to start one more song when my phone vibrated in my back pocket. I pulled it out and answered. "Hey Helly."

"Tell me what trouble you've gotten into since yesterday. I'm bored."

I wanted to be indignant, but my sister always knew what was going on. It was like we were connected on some deeper level. We almost didn't need the phone—I could feel it when she was bummed about something. I always knew when she needed a call.

"I'm not in trouble."

"What are you doing?"

"I'm laying down some tracks in this dope recording studio right now."

There was a pause. "There are so many things to unpack in that statement, I'm not sure where to start. Here, I've got it. Since when do you say 'dope' or 'laying down tracks,' Snoop Sis?"

I laughed and scooted onto a stool in the center of the room. "It felt wrong when I said it. But being in this space made me want to try something hip."

"Got it. Don't let it happen again."

"Yeah, I won't."

"Explain everything else you just said."

"The recording studio?"

"For starters," she said.

"I told you Teresa is a music producer. She has a seriously bussin' studio in her basement."

"Please stop using words you learned from teenagers on TikTok."

"Sorry."

"What exactly are you doing in her professional space?" I could hear the judgment in Hel's voice and I bristled.

"Being professional."

"In what way?"

"I'm just having fun, Hel. I'm singing." Helly knew I liked to sing. But I hadn't told her much else about it. Like that I had secret dreams that one day I'd be famous. I mean, I also had secret dreams that one day I'd be an airline pilot and that was surely not going to happen.

"Did you record it?"

"That is kind of the point of a recording studio."

"Are you any good? Let me hear something." She sounded poised to make fun of me, and I wasn't really in the mood for that. I knew Hel loved me, but sometimes the sisterly teasing felt like it was laced with truth.

"No, it's just for fun."

"Come on, please?"

Helena begged for a solid five minutes, and I finally agreed to send her a track when we hung up. I didn't want the real-time assessment of my little hobby.

"What else are you doing in your fancy house?"

Part of me wanted to keep Stephano all to myself, but another part of me hoped that if I let Hel tell me what a silly thing it was to have developed a crush on someone I barely knew, it would go away.

"I had dinner with the grumpy neighbor."

"Ew. Why?"

"What do you mean why?"

"Like an old 'get off my lawn' kind of guy?"

I laughed at that. Stephano was definitely not that kind of grumpy. "Uh, no. Like a hot professional hockey player kind of guy."

She was silent a moment. "Okay, now you gotta tell me everything."

"Well, I met him last night because I got locked out of the house and so I went into his hot tub—"

"I don't . . . Wha—you know what? Never mind. Okay, go on."

"So he came out and invited me in, and it was too late to call a locksmith, so I spent the night with him."

"You slept with a guy you'd barely met?"

"That's enough with the shock. I remember that frat party you confessed to with the ice luge and some guy named Frances."

"You swore we'd never speak of that again." Her voice was low and sad.

"You brought that on yourself."

"So you didn't sleep with him?"

"No!" I had thought about it, but the opportunity had not arisen. And while an occasional fling wasn't outside my rulebook, I wasn't looking for anything like that. "Of course not. I slept in the guest room." I told my sister the rest of the story, finishing with the dinner I'd just had with him tonight.

"Holy shit. So what now?"

"What do you mean?"

"Don't play coy. You're going back over there. I'd bet you'll find a reason to head on over in the morning."

"I will not." Unless the scent of bacon was wafting across the yard . . .

"Maybe you should," she suggested, her voice going all funny.

"Think that through. What could possibly happen if I did?" Odd how the tables had turned. Why was I being reasonable suddenly?

"I can think of a few things, and so can you."

"I'm old enough to know that flings are worthless. And there's no chance of anything more with a guy who lives next door to a house I do not live in for real."

"What have you done with my sister, the princess of impermanence? Flings are fun."

"Yeah. I know. I've just been thinking that maybe it's time to grow up a bit. Figure out what I'm really doing. Pay off my loans." I cleared my throat trying to soften the edge on my words, hoping to hide my hurt.

"Hill," my sister said. "I didn't mean anything. You're doing good, right? You're okay."

"Yeah. I am. But you were right last night. I need a plan. A real one."

"Maybe you just hang out with the hockey player until you figure it out?"

It was not a plan. But it was tempting.

I woke the following morning to a renewed sense of purpose. I didn't need to settle down, per se, but I needed a steady income. I'd heard recently about a girl from our high school who had found herself homeless. The situation was totally different—she'd also had some legal issues and substance misuse had been reported, but it got me thinking. The only real difference between us was that the universe had been really kind to me. Maybe karma wouldn't hold out forever. And while I had been working, I hadn't exactly been molding myself into the image of a responsible adult—as evidenced by the repeated calls I was now getting from the loan people.

A steady income would be a start. Then at least I'd know I could rent a room somewhere if I needed to and start making payments for the loans. Since I didn't have a permanent home base, I decided that an online business was clearly the right answer. But there were so many options.

An Etsy store or selling actual things didn't really work since I didn't have a place to store inventory.

I considered as I sipped coffee and stared out Teresa's big back windows.

Courses? I was not an expert in anything, really.

Want to spend most of your parents' money on a medical degree you'll never finish and get yourself into crippling debt? I can show you how!

Didn't seem like a big seller.

Consulting?

Again . . . probably wouldn't work.

I paced the living room, my mind whirring in circles as my feet pushed through the thick fluffy pile of the living room rug.

Nothing was coming to me immediately, and I hated the feeling that was rising inside me. Kind of a rush of overwhelming self-doubt, capped off with a heap of regret and just a splash of the guilt that haunted me whenever I let I my guard down.

I shook my head hard. Nope. I wasn't going there.

The only recourse was action.

Clothes on, hair on top of my head, lip gloss applied, I headed next door.

Stephano's doorbell had a very melodic ring, I thought as I pressed it a second time. Either he wasn't home, or he was ignoring me. I chose to believe the latter rather than the former.

So he was not going to distract me . . .

I turned and headed to my car. A little tour, then. I just needed to get out of the house to escape the dangers that lay within my own mind. There was a craft mall in downtown Wilcox I'd been dying to go see. Today was the perfect day.

For a second, I wondered what day it actually was. When you worked a non-standard job, it was easy to lose track.

Wednesday? Sure, I'd go with that.

I pulled up outside the enormous barn-like structure and headed inside through the scant snow piled up on the sidewalks. And the second I walked through the door, I was enveloped in the scents of candles and soap, and giddiness lifted my spirits as I scanned stall after stall of handmade items and useless knick-knacks. I could spend hours here.

And I did, eventually returning to my car with my arms full of things no one really needed but everyone would undoubtedly love when I sent them as gifts. Of course, my generosity did not help in the cash department.

When I found myself at loose ends once again, I poured a glass of wine and flipped on the television in Teresa's cozy den, laughing to myself at the coincidence as a hockey game appeared.

I watched, intending to flip away from the channel, but then realized it was the Wombats playing. And there, covered in thick pads and hovering in front of the net, was my next-door neighbor.

I'd never watched a whole game before. Everything flew. The puck, the players, the time. It was like a complicated dance across the enormous rink, and every time the puck got close to Stephano, I found myself holding my breath.

He moved as if the pads were nothing, like he was on a trampoline rather than an ice rink, bending and stretching and making himself exactly the right shape and size to block every single shot the other team—the Tsunami—sent his way. It was incredible. I wished I could see more of his face, but I already knew the expression he'd be wearing the whole time—that same grumpy, determined, jaw-locked look I was seeing in my dreams.

He might be grumpy, but Stephano Mizzoni was really fucking good.

What would it be like to know you were so good at your chosen profession? To even have a chosen profession?

I envied him as much as I admired him.

Maybe there was something to be learned from Stephano.

Maybe that was why the universe had sent him to me.

I went to bed feeling slightly better. The universe had a plan for me so maybe I didn't need one of my own. And the universe's plan included the grumpy goalie next door.

CHAPTER 7
STEPHANO
BECAUSE. WELL, BIGFOOT.

The flight home from the Tsunami game was exhausting. And not because it was a four-hour flight that had me crawling into bed after two when I finally arrived home.

It was exhausting because Coach had pushed me to sit next to puppy dog, and I spent most of the flight reviewing the game with him verbally. On top of that, I had a message from Shotz, my agent, who irritatingly was also puppy's agent. He suggested I help Samuels get more time on the ice if I could. Which I couldn't, and he knew it.

"You know we'll have time to do this back at the rink. With tape?"

"Yeah, but it's fresh in my head," he said, grinning. "Talk to me about that last block. It came at you so fast, and you were back at the trapezoid . . ."

"I remember," I told him, leaning back and closing my eyes. "I was there."

"It was gold, man."

It should have been nice, I guessed. Having the unmitigated adoration of the puppy. But Samuels didn't seem to read social cues, and my cues were clearly stating that he should fuck off and take a nap.

"Thanks."

"Tired?"

"I played the entire game. So, yeah."

"Yeah." Now he sounded sad.

I didn't blame him. He'd been dressed and ready to shift, but the Tsunami was up by one until the last five minutes of play. And Coach kept me in.

Good for me. Bad for John Samuels. And not great for my hip.

I forced my eyes back open and sat up, turning to face him. "Look, Samuels. You're a good goalie. You're a smart player. You'll get your time, trust me. Maybe sooner than you think."

His face cleared, and he looked surprised at this sudden rush of words from a guy who'd been mostly grunts and avoidance before.

Shit, I was a dick.

"But for me, this is like the final flash of glory, you know? And having you right there, ready to step in . . . It's just a mindset shift. This is my team. My life."

He nodded. "I know."

"I'll help you," I added, settling back into my seat. "Because it's what the Wombats need. But you've gotta back off a bit." I crossed my arms, tilted my cap down, and closed my eyes.

"Yeah," he whispered. "Okay, Mizzoni."

And for the last hour of the flight, it'd been blissfully silent.

We had a short practice Thursday, and it was easy, giving us some time to rest up from the game and get our heads right for the home game Saturday.

Of course, my head wasn't right at all.

Mamma and Luca were arriving sometime after noon on Friday. And while neither would expect to be presented with a printed itinerary of activities and events, I owed my mother more than an exhausted, injured dude who just wanted to take a nap.

The house was clean, so I wasn't worried about that. But Mamma would want to cook.

Lots of people made themselves at home by unpacking suitcases into drawers or hanging their things in a closet. Mamma did it by settling into my kitchen and using every pot, pan, and tin I had to turn my house into the best Italian restaurant in town.

Maybe the cooking Italian mamma was cliché, but there was a reason for that. Her name was Lucia Mizzoni.

Thursday evening I settled on the couch to review some of the tape from the Tsunami game, paying special attention to the plays in the trapezoid. I was a good puck handler, but getting distracted back there or getting caught up left the net open, and I was always trying to walk the line on that.

I let the game run on the big screen over the fireplace and flipped through the house cam footage on my phone. I didn't have a fancy system with alerts for movement in the back yard or anything, but I liked to scroll what did appear there. Usually birds, the occasional intrepid raccoon, or deer. One time I'd scanned the backyard footage and seen something traipse through my yard. It was too far out to see what it was exactly, something that walked like a man, lumbering and huge, though. And it had crossed through the camera angle, then disappeared. It could have been Cade Simpson, but he denied it vehemently.

Part of me sort of thought it was Bigfoot, but I was never bringing it up again in public because the team already caught wind of it and hadn't let me live it down. Still, I checked. Just in case.

Because. Well, Bigfoot.

And when I came to the footage from the other night, where Hillary wandered into the frame, draped in a towel, and then sank into my hot tub . . . I froze it there. She was gorgeous, that was for sure. And there was something about her. The steam coming from the tub amplified her glow, her brightness.

It matched what I knew of her personality. Light, effervescent.

I sighed and made myself delete the footage, and then switched to the doorbell.

There she was again. Standing on my front step, hair piled atop her head, looking around. I chuckled when she pressed the bell a second time and did a little dance to the chimes before turning and walking away.

She'd stopped by. Why did that make something low in my chest warm up? Why did I find myself concocting reasons to go next door suddenly?

Dammit. This was bad.

I did not need any kind of next-door-neighbor intrigue. I didn't have time for distractions during the season. Not when I was nursing this injury with Samuels salivating over my job, and not when my mom was already in flight and heading this way.

Despite Mamma's strange hesitation on the phone about the mention of a woman in my life, I had no doubt she was planning to continue her years-long effort to get me settled down. She did it every time she was here. Waitresses, checkout girls, random women on the sidewalk. Everyone we met was a potential target for her meddling.

I knew she had my best interests in mind . . . but last time she visited I'd caught her quizzing my cleaning lady Hester about whether she was single and still fertile. Hester was nearing sixty, I figured. Not really in the sweet spot of marriage potential, if I were to be consulted.

I'd just have to keep her away from Hillary. She'd take one look at that bubbly next-door blonde and see wedding rings and round-cheeked babies.

I leaned forward on the couch, stretching my hip and thinking. Why did the idea of avoiding Hillary rub me the wrong way? Why couldn't I just decide something and have it be?

I picked up the phone and dialed.

It was late, but I knew he'd be up. "Hello?"

"Hey, Uncle Julius."

"Stephano. How are you?"

"I'm good. Bothering you?"

"Never. You played well last night."

"Thanks." His praise always felt good. "Mamma is visiting tomorrow."

"Che bello! You'll bring her to the rink?"

"She'll be here for Saturday's game," I told him, picturing Mamma the last time she'd been at a game, cringing and covering her face half the time and screaming at the other team the other half. "You won't miss her."

"It will be nice to see her. Thanks for letting me know."

"I'm sure we'll have you over for dinner too."

"Wonderful." My uncle stretched the word, and I had the feeling he knew I had something else on my mind.

"Yeah, that's not the only reason I called, Uncle Julius."

"A woman, then?"

I hesitated. "I mean . . . yeah. But also hockey."

"The ultimate combination, Stephano."

"There's this woman next door. I've kind of gotten to know her a little, and—"

"You'd like to know her more? You are a pro hockey player. I can't imagine there's a problem. She knows who you are?"

"Yeah, but I don't think she cares about that." Which seemed like a distinct point in her favor.

"Even better."

"No. I mean, well, that's the thing. I barely know her. But Mamma's going to come and get busy trying to set me up left and right with bank tellers and parking cops and mimes, and—"

"Are there mimes in Wilcox now?"

"No, it was just an expression."

"That's not an expression."

"Fine, no mimes. But you know Mamma."

"I know Lucia, yes. She worries about you."

"Right. And her worry is demonstrated through humiliation in front of anything upright with breasts."

"Yes." Uncle Julius chuckled. "How can I help?"

"I don't know . . . I was just thinking, I should probably keep her away from Mamma, right?"

"Do you want Lucia to go next door to meet this girl and wrangle her to your house, explaining that you'd like to marry her and impregnate her immediately?"

"I'd prefer that didn't happen."

"Then I wouldn't mention the girl at all."

So Mamma's visit would mean ignoring this little niggling desire to see Hillary again. Which I should probably ignore anyway, but now? Being told I should stay away from her? I knew I was not going to.

"You're right. But maybe there's one more solution."

"Find someone to marry before Lucia arrives tomorrow." Uncle Julius laughed at his own joke.

"Kind of. Maybe."

"Stephano . . ."

"Thanks. You gave me an idea." A probably really terrible idea, but Hillary seemed like the kind of woman who might go for it. If I could work up the nerve to try.

"Okay," my uncle said. "See you at the game Saturday." Uncle Julius drove the Zamboni. But his hockey history went much further back than that. And his history with my family? Well, he was the reason I played for the Wombats.

I put down the phone, feeling the calm wash through me as it always had when Uncle Julius talked to me. It had worked back in the day, when Dad had died, and it worked now. If I couldn't have my dad, it was nice having his stepbrother nearby.

This idea, though . . .

I decided to sleep on it. I wasn't the kind of guy who jumped on impulse. And this was potentially the most impulsive thing I'd ever considered doing.

CHAPTER 8
HILLARY

A BAD IDEA WE SHOULD DEFINITELY CONSIDER

I'd barely rolled out of bed the next morning when the doorbell rang. I didn't have friends in Wilcox, and I hadn't invited anyone over, so I figured it must be someone looking for Teresa. She had one of those doorbell cams, but told me it showed on her phone, so that didn't help me much.

I gargled a sip of water, pulled my wild hair back into an elastic and scuffled to the door. I'd already pulled it open when I caught a glance of myself in the mirror just inside the hall. The well-smudged mascara and ragged South Bay Sharks T-shirt really completed my DGAF look this morning.

Only, as soon as I saw who was at the door, I realized I should have given just a tiny bit more of a fuck.

Stephano.

"Hey, Goalie."

"Hi Goldilocks," he said. One eyebrow climbed high as he gave me a once over. "Rough night?"

I did my best to look offended, bringing one hand to the pearl-clutching position. "I would never answer the door like this if you visited at a decent hour. It's only"—I pulled my arm up to look at the time. Damn. It was noon. "It's barely noon."

He let a tiny smile lift one side of his face. "Want me to come back later? What's a decent time in the world you live in?"

"You can come in if you'll give me five minutes to put myself together." I really hated the thought of him seeing me look all disheveled, though I wasn't sure why. Because he was hot? Or because I had a goalie-sized crush?

"Sure," he said, stepping inside and shutting the door behind himself. "Take seven if you need it."

"I'll be back in three." Why did something about him make me feel all wired and competitive?

I zipped back to the bedroom and put on a bra and a shirt that wasn't full of holes, and then tugged on a pair of leggings before passing through the bathroom to clean up. The hair was a lost cause, so I left it up, but a quick rinse of my face, and some mascara and lip gloss, and I looked halfway decent.

I was back in four minutes to find Stephano wandering around the kitchen.

"I've never been over here," he said. "It's really nice. Kind of trendy-cool, huh?"

"Totally. Teresa's a producer, so I think she's on a whole other level of cool that I can only visit by house sitting."

He smiled at me then and stopped pacing. "I have something to ask you."

I pulled up a stool at the counter across from him. "Oh yeah?" I watched him watching me as I spoke. His eyes were deep, intense. The kind of eyes you wanted focused on only you . . .

"Yeah. Why were you at my house yesterday?"

Oh. Disappointment surprised me. What did I think, that he was going to propose? "Oh, ah . . . no real reason. I was bored, and my head was getting a little out of control. I needed a distraction."

That tiny smile flickered, but then shifted away and his face became stern again. "Ah. Okay."

I waited, thinking he was going to ask something else, but he just stood there, his eyes on the countertop and his face like stone. Had he frozen there? Was he having some kind of mini stroke? I'd heard about those, where you just kind of stop moving, stop talking.

I poked his hand with my finger, and he whipped it away, and looked up at me in surprise.

"Sorry," I said quickly. "I thought maybe there was something wrong."

"So you poked me with your talon?"

I lifted the bright pink nail he was referring to. "Yeah. Sorry. Not sure I like this whole pointy nail trend."

He rubbed his hand. "I definitely do not."

"Okay." I watched him, the tension becoming increasingly awkward. "Hey, do you want . . . not a beer. Maybe . . ."

"A beer would be great."

"You don't drink during the season. And it's only . . .noon."

"I do drink if I have to ask something that I'm having a hard time finding words to ask."

Maybe he *was* going to propose. That would be exceptionally weird, since we had met twice before this. What was the universe thinking?

"Ah . . . okay. Sure. There's also this champagne in a can . . ."

"Beer please."

I pulled two beers from the refrigerator and popped off the tops, handing him a bottle. "Do you want to sit down while you contemplate the mysterious question you are going to ask me someday when you decide you're ready?"

"Good idea."

We moved to the couch and sat at the corner facing each other at an angle, our knees nearly touching.

I swear a full five minutes passed. And he did. Not. Say. A. Word.

"You're killing me," I whispered.

Stephano put down his beer on the coffee table and turned fully to face me. "Yeah, sorry. I mean . . . the thing is, I just am generally not impulsive. And I am nearly certain this is a terrible idea, but I think I'm going to ask anyway."

"I think it's way too early to get married." I was joking, but his eyebrows climbed so high that I wondered if it was altogether the wrong joke for this situation. "I'm kidding!"

"I know, I just—" he let out a huge sigh, and I was inspired to distract him, as much as I wanted to know what the thing was.

"I saw you play last night."

"You did? In Oregon?" His tone warmed.

"I was not in Oregon, actually. You do know they show those games on television, right? I watched it here."

"Oh, yeah." The flicker of a smile again, the slightest twinkle of his deep chocolate eyes when they met mine. "But you said you don't watch hockey."

"I don't. I mean, I didn't mean to. I turned on the television, and there you were."

"So are you a hockey fan now?"

"I'm a Goalie fan." The words were out before I had time to plan them, and I cringed. I did have a little crush—I mean, the guy was glorious on the ice and even better in person. But I wasn't trying to embarrass myself.

"Thanks." He smiled then, and I could see that the compliment hadn't been lost on him. He looked a little smug, even.

"It was a good game," I said, having no idea what a good game in hockey looked like.

"It was good," he said, nodding. He checked his watch, glanced at the window next to the front door. "Okay, listen. I'm just going to ask. This is crazy and I know that, and you should say no because it's a terrible idea and I don't even know why I'm asking."

The description he'd just dropped gave me no choice. "I'll do it."

"What? You have no idea what it is."

"I am known for terrible impulsive ideas," I told him. "At least I am now. I didn't used to be." I swallowed hard, not really meaning to bring up the past.

The eyebrow rose again. "Maybe I should tell you the thing first?"

"Sure. Go ahead." I waved my hand before me, inviting him to speak.

"My mother is coming today." He nodded as if I'd have any idea how to take this news. "With my little brother Luca. And she is the most important person in my life. She raised my brothers and me on her own after Dad died, and she saved money and worked so I could play hockey and move here. She's my everything."

"That's amazing," I said, very unsure now what I'd agreed to.

"She's wonderful. But she is terrible."

I leaned in, frowning at him. "Say what? You lost me."

"She wants grandbabies. And I'm the oldest. And she thinks I should have been married years ago, so she spends all her time scouting for appropriate and marriageable women."

"Oh." My stomach churned a bit. I was about as far from marriageable as one could get without leaving the planet.

"I don't want her to do that."

"No, of course not."

"I'm not marrying a random security guard at the mall or a mime."

"Okay. Yeah, no mimes. Good." Where were we going with this? Universe? "Is there a question here?"

"Yes." He took a deep breath and then continued. "Is there any chance you would be willing to pretend that we are dating? Just while Mamma's here?"

Dating. Stephano. My body sang out an immediate yesssss. But my brain, for once, was cautious.

"Well, hang on. How long is she going to be staying?"

"A few weeks. Maybe a month." He sounded somewhat miserable at that.

"You want to fake date for a month?" I still wanted to scream yes, but there were concerns. Namely—could I fake it with him? Or would I fall devastatingly in love and end up heartbroken?

Also, I was supposed to be getting more responsible. This did not seem responsible.

He made a sickly face, as if he was rethinking this whole chat. Or had eaten bad tuna. "Never mind. It's a stupid idea. You have better things to do."

"It's not stupid, it's just . . ." Hadn't I just decided that it was time to settle into some kind of steadier life, procure an actual income? Saying yes impulsively would be something yesterday-Hillary would be completely fine with. But today-Hillary was supposed to be turning over a new leaf. "I would totally do it, but I'm supposed be like . . . finding a job, an income to pay off these loans."

"I could pay you." As soon as he said these words, his eyes slammed shut and he braced his forehead with a hand. "That sounded awful. I didn't mean—"

"Can I think about it?" He just offered to pay me to be his fake girlfriend, and honestly, I wasn't offended. It almost felt like the universe had just delivered me the solution to my problem. But did this make me a prostitute? Taking money to live in other people's houses was one thing. Taking money to live in other people's lives? I wasn't so sure.

He looked sad for a split second, and then the mask slid into place. "Of course. But I mean, we can just forget I mentioned it. I don't know what I was thinking. Mamma wouldn't be fooled anyway, and this was a lot to ask a friend, let alone someone I barely know—"

"It's fine," I assured him. "And I think we are friends. And maybe it would be kind of an employee and employer kind of relationship . . ." I needed to think. Alone.

"Um. Yeah, maybe. Or, you know? Really just forget I said anything. This was crazy."

"Crazy is kind of my forte."

"Well . . . " He scrubbed a hand down his face and stood, paused for a deep breath, and headed for the door.

Now things were awkward. I hated that. What could I do to fix it?

I stepped close and hugged him, trying to eliminate the uncomfortable tension between us. He stiffened, making the hard blocks of solid muscle under my hands feel more like stone, but then he relaxed and hugged me back, his strong arms encircling me. I tried to ignore the way he smelled, like aftershave and wintertime, and closed my eyes for a second. It was nice, being in his arms, being held at all.

He let go, stepping away and scrubbing a hand over his jaw. "Well, okay," he said.

"Okay," I told him. "Give me your number," I suggested.

He looked wary, but we exchanged phone numbers.

"So when I decide, I can just . . . text you?"

"Really, let's just forget it. I'm embarrassed I suggested it now." He stepped across the threshold and took two more steps, but then turned. "Hillary?"

I waited for whatever he was going to say, my body still longing to be held again. "Yeah?"

"Mamma will make a ridiculous amount of food this weekend. Come for dinner Sunday? As a friend."

"Oh, um. Sure, yeah."

"Yes?"

I nodded. "Okay. Thanks."

When I closed the door behind him, my brain whirled at double-time. I didn't want to think about it. I wanted to chase after him and say yes to being his girlfriend, even if it was fake. But I didn't like the part about the money. Or how badly I actually needed it.

CHAPTER 9
STEPHANO

OPEN MOUTH. INSERT FEET.

I was a moron.

Why had I gone over there? Why had I asked her to pretend to be my girlfriend? Not only was it a crazy plan, but now she thought I was desperate. And I'd doubled down on crazy when I'd offered to pay her. The part of me that actually wanted her to like me did not want her to think I had a hard time getting women or that I typically paid them to spend time with me.

I didn't have a hard time with women.

I just didn't normally like the kind of women that were easy to get.

Shit. What the hell was wrong with me?

I checked my watch. Mamma and Luca would arrive in an hour. That gave me enough time to put together something for dinner and be at least partially recovered from my humiliation before the driver delivered them to my door.

I was nearly done putting together the meal I'd started prepping that morning, and almost past the humiliation of the conversation with Hillary, when the doorbell rang.

I wiped my hands, switched off the playlist I had going, and went to greet my family.

Only it wasn't them. Confusion quickly replaced the anticipation I'd felt.

Hillary stood on my doorstep, her long legs in black leggings and her hair down and wet. "Hi."

I glanced past her, expecting to see the Town Car pulling down the street any second. "Hi."

I didn't want to be rude, but having her here when Mamma arrived would just confuse everything. Mamma would jump to conclusions and Hillary would get roped into a situation she clearly didn't want to be part of.

"Can I come in a minute?"

"Um, sure." We went inside after I shut the door.

"You're cooking again." She took a deep breath and let her eyes fall shut, and I tried not to imagine her making that face anywhere else. Like maybe lying across my bed.

Dammit. Her eyes popped open and she gave me a suspicious look, her animated face lighting up like she knew exactly what I'd been thinking. "No Taylor Swift this time?"

"Just turned her off, actually. A little too much 'Lavender Haze' for my mother." I really didn't have time for this. I needed her to leave before Mamma showed up.

"Not here yet, then?"

"No, but she will be—" and before I could finish the thought, the doorbell rang again. "Now." Shit.

Hillary clapped her hands and grinned, but my stomach was twisting up inside me. If Hillary didn't want to pretend to be my girlfriend, she'd need to be ready to be forced on me like there was no tomorrow. Mamma would take one look at her and assume things. This was going to be bad.

I pulled open the door, feeling Hillary squeezing to my side in the open space, and did my best to appear normal. Despite the trepidation sizzling in my veins, warmth rushed through me to see my family. Luca was at least a foot taller than the last time I'd seen him—he practically looked like a man now. And Mamma was the same, small, compact, and smiling broadly at me as our eyes met.

"Mamma," I said, opening my arms to hug her. "Come in out of the cold. Hi, Luca." I pulled my little brother into a hug, helped pull their bags in, and waved the driver off. When the door was shut, Mamma and Luca both grinned at Hillary expectantly.

"Good flight?" I asked, reaching for her coat. My mother was not a tall woman. She was four foot ten inches on a good day. How she'd managed to create my brothers and me, all of whom were over six feet with Luca's sudden growth spurt, I didn't know. Except that my father had been very tall. Now, I bent down to help her out of her coat, and hoped maybe Hillary would somehow just disappear or something.

But it wasn't to be.

Mamma's eyes were big and round as she turned to me and whispered dramatically in a very loud voice, *"chi è questo?"* Who is this?

I swallowed hard, opening my mouth to introduce Hillary, but she beat me.

"Hello!" Hillary said.

"Hi," Luca gushed, clearly already in love with the blond beauty from next door.

"Hillary Watters, meet my mother, Lucia Mizzoni, and my little brother, Luca."

"It's so nice to meet you," Hillary said, leaning down to hug my mother and then pulling my brother in for a hug that I thought might cause him to pass out from sheer proximity to her beauty. Or from her breasts pressed up against his seventeen-year-old chest.

"And you as well," my mother said, not bothering to hide her curiosity or her suspicions in the look she passed from Hillary to me. I told myself it would be fine. She was my neighbor, that was all.

"Come in," I suggested. "I'll take your bags back to your rooms in a bit. Unless you want to go lie down for a bit or clean up? I know it's a long flight."

"I am not tired at all," Mamma said, glancing at Hillary to make sure she was coming with us toward the living room. "I would love a glass of wine, and then you tell me everything." Mamma was using her very best English, something she rarely bothered with unless we had company she cared to impress. I could practically hear the matchmaking wheels turning.

Soon, we were all seated in the living room, Hillary still at my side, and I realized she hadn't told me why she'd come over and now she was trapped entertaining my family.

"How was the flight?" she asked them.

"Oh, you know," Mamma said, waving her hand to dismiss this.

"No Wi-Fi," Luca told her, holding his phone up. "Stephano, password?"

"Oh, Luca, we have just arrived. For five minutes, let's just talk to your brother and his . . . Hillary," Mamma chided, a strange note in her voice as she indicated Hillary.

Luca dropped his phone a bit lower, pretending not to be looking at it.

"Hillary, did you want to speak with me?" I turned to the pretty blonde at my side who seemed to be perfectly comfortable despite the cold sweat covering my back.

"Umm, no. It can wait." She chuckled and bumped her shoulder against mine. This little move worried me even more. It was like she thought we were sharing a secret. But were we? She hadn't really given me an answer, and if I introduced her as my girlfriend but then she'd just come over here to tell me she didn't want to do it, it would be a disaster.

"Oh. Well, can I talk to you? In the kitchen, maybe?" I rose.

Hillary nodded and looked at Mamma. "Be right back."

Once we were out of earshot, I said, "sorry you got dragged into that. You can go."

"I—" Hillary's face fell, like she was surprised at my words.

"Stephano?" Mamma appeared around the corner. My stomach clenched.

"Yes, Mamma?"

"I know this is not polite, but I have been waiting for a proper introduction. Hillary is . . ." She reached out a hand, indicating we should complete the sentence.

"His . . ." Hillary began.

"My . . ." I tried.

"Neighbor," I said at the same time as she said, "Girlfriend."

Mamma looked confused, and I didn't blame her. But the word "girlfriend" lingered, and now her attention was fully focused on Hillary.

I slid my eyes to Hillary, relief washing through me.

"I'm Stephano's girlfriend," she said smoothly, sliding her arm around my waist. "And I live next door."

Mamma nodded, but didn't erupt in cheers or throw herself to her knees to thank the lord as I'd always suspected she would when I finally introduced her to a woman. What was going on here?

She actually said almost nothing for a long, uncomfortable moment. And then she nodded, her lips pressed together, and finally said, "I see."

Not the reaction I'd expected. Had we gone through all this for nothing? Had Mamma given up trying to force me into producing grandchildren?

I sighed. There was no going back now.

CHAPTER 10
HILLARY

DAMN, I'M A GOOD COOK

Timing had never been my strong suit. And the way Stephano was staring at me right now told me he was a guy who didn't do well with surprises.

I was guessing that if I'd said yes earlier, we would have spent the next hour creating a spreadsheet or something, mapping out how we first met, what our first fake date had looked like, and what the rules of engagement for fake dating were supposed to be.

Now, as I sat on the couch at his side, a glass of white wine in my hand and his mother and brother across from me, I wondered what exactly he'd had in mind.

Touching?

Hand holding?

Kissing?

What would his family expect to see? What was Stephano Mizzoni like when he dated someone?

I had no context at all. In my Google research, I'd seen that some of his teammates were photographed a lot, out and about in their bespoke suits with women on their arms. But my online searches hadn't come up with anything like that for Stephano. All the photos I found of him had him looking solo, stern, and so very serious. His trademark expression.

We were sitting close on his couch now, and the heat from his dark denim-clad thigh was radiating through the thin leggings I wore. Never one to do things halfway (with the exception of med school, of course), I decided to go all in. With a glance up at him, I slid a hand over that muscular thigh, letting it come to rest on his knee.

Wow. Holy muscle. The guy was built like a block of stone. Or ice.

But maybe that was just because he'd frozen when my hand had landed on his leg, his explanation to his family of the next week's schedule bumping to a stuttering stop.

"Ah, what was I saying?"

"You were telling us every detail of your calendar," Luca said, sounding bored. "You have a gaming system, bro?" Teenagers. It seemed like they had a shared culture regardless of their country of origin.

"Yeah, but maybe wait until after dinner?"

Luca let out a dramatic sigh and fell back against the couch, as Stephano shot me a questioning look. I smiled and shrugged.

"So Mrs. Mizzoni, tell me about the place you live, where Stephano grew up," I suggested, giving the hard knee under my hand a squeeze. I hoped the familiar touch would look like something we did all the time, make this fake relationship seem more real.

I liked touching him, being close to him. But part of it could have been that I really hadn't been close to anyone in a long time.

"We are from a small village," she said, glancing at me but directing her words at her son. "Where there is much history. You have been to Italy?"

"No, never," I said, my voice carrying the longing I felt.

"We live in Veneto," she said. "A little village called Fumane." She wore a dreamy look that gave me the impression that she was seeing the years of her family's history in the place she spoke of.

"A place where there is little to do and no one to meet," Luca added before his mother swatted his leg.

"And Stephano said your family was in . . ." I trailed off, realizing the spreadsheet might actually have been helpful.

"Wine," Stephano finished. "But not anymore."

His mother clucked. "Actually," she said, "that is not true. And that is part of what I wanted to visit to discuss."

I felt Stephano stiffen again beneath me. "Okay," he said carefully. "What's going on?"

"I think after your game tomorrow."

"Because whatever you are going to say is going to upset me," he predicted. "But now I will worry about it instead."

"We've only just arrived, *Mimmo*. Tell me what you've been cooking." Stephano's mom said this, but then stilled as if a thought had just struck her and she swung her gaze to me. "You cook, Hillary?"

"Ahhhh," I looked to Stephano in case there was a wrong answer to this sudden and imperative question. "Not—"

Stephano interrupted me by grabbing my hand and pulling me to my feet. "Not only does she cook, she spent all day yesterday and this morning making some specialties from our region. Come see what she's made us," he said. As he tugged me into the kitchen, he leaned in close, sending a surprising shiver through my chest as his breath tickled my neck. "Sorry, but the only answer to that is yes, unless you want to spend the next month stuck in the kitchen under Mamma's stern eye."

Having Stephano whispering in my ear had me thinking of other things I might spend the next month stuck under—namely him—but I pushed away the fluttering wisps of attraction vying for my attention and nodded. "Got it."

"*Luccio alla gardesana*," Stephano said. "*Ovi e sparasi, pappardelle al ragu bianco di anatra*, and *fondi di carciofo*." He waved his arms around various pans and dishes that were on the stove and counter, and reached into the oven for more.

Hearing Stephano speak Italian was painfully sexy, but I desperately hoped Mrs. Mizzoni wasn't going to ask about my methods or any of the ingredients. I could cook Rice Krispy treats and toast, and that was about it.

"All my favorites," his mother said approvingly. "Stephano must've helped. How would you know?"

"Oh, yes," I agreed. "He helped a lot."

"And I was just hoping for a burger," Luca said in a low voice, sliding onto a stool in front of the island and surveying the ridiculous feast with something like disgust.

Stephano put down the plates he was holding on the counter and moved toward his brother. He was calm and his face was placid, but I could feel the storm gathering beneath the surface. "Luca," he said, his voice like a storm about to break. "My beautiful girlfriend Hillary has cooked for you. To welcome you." Then Stephano slipped into Italian, his voice dropping even lower and deeper, and whatever he said had his younger brother sitting up straighter and taller, his entire frame becoming stiffer with each uttered word.

"This smells delicious," Luca said as Stephano turned back to the food. "Is there anything I can do to help?"

"Yes," Stephano said. "Wash up and then come carry some dishes to the table."

Luca dutifully slid from the stool and disappeared down the hallway, and I gave Stephano an admiring look. I'd seen him stern. I'd seen him kind. But this fatherly discipline was a whole new side that had previously untapped regions of my anatomy suddenly taking notice. He was hotter than I'd thought possible.

I didn't have much time to appreciate this new side of him though, because Mrs. Mizzoni was already talking again. "I'm sorry. He is tired from the trip. But you'll see—this pappardelle is his very favorite. He is just being grumpy because someone told him teenagers are supposed to act that way." She shrugged and turned away from me, moving to help Stephano again. She was polite, but not exceedingly happy about my presence, from what I could tell. I wondered briefly if I'd rubbed her the wrong way somehow, or if I just didn't meet her standards for women who might be attached to Stephano.

How would my own parents react if I suddenly told them I had a serious boyfriend? If they visited, and he was just . . . there?

It was almost impossible to imagine since they'd met exactly one of my boyfriends ever, and that had not gone especially well. Dad didn't think I should be dating during med school. In the end, maybe he'd been right.

I shook off the memory, taking the dish Stephano handed me. "This is the *fondi di carciofo*," he said quietly, and I pushed down the tingles that erupted deep inside whenever he spoke Italian in that low, sexy voice. "Artichoke bottoms fried in herbs and oil."

"Yum," I said, staring at the dish in my hands with new appreciation. "I'm a really good cook, huh?"

Stephano winked at me, and it made me happy, sharing this secret with him. Soon, we were all sitting around the broad table next to the wall of glass that separated his dining room from the enormous patio outside.

"If it was warmer, we'd be outside," Stephano told his family. "But I promise, we'll grill burgers while you're here."

Luca gave him a sheepish smile, and then turned to me. "Hillary, the food is incredible."

It was. Every bite was a new experience, and I tried hard to pretend like I expected the tender surprise of the duck or the crisp delicious flavor of the asparagus. My favorite part of the meal was the polenta that sat beneath the little filets of white fish, and I made a mental note to ask Stephano to teach me how to make it when his mother wasn't around.

"This is amazing," I gushed, my mouth full of polenta. I turned to Stephano to offer more compliments, but his wide eyes and the firm line of his mouth reminded me of my mistake. I swallowed quickly and turned to his mother. "Having you both here," I mean. "It's so nice that you could visit."

"Where is your family, Hillary?" Lucia asked.

"I grew up in California," I told her. "Near San Francisco. But my parents live near Los Angeles now. Pasadena."

She nodded, her eyes assessing and cool.

"That must have been amazing," Luca said, and I wondered what he'd heard about the Bay Area or California to make him think so. Not that I disagreed.

I nodded. "It was nice. But I like it here better."

"Really?" Stephano asked. "Why?"

I looked up from the bread I was using to sop up every last bit of the delicious meal and met his eyes, stunned for a second by the intensity of his gaze. "Well, you're here," I told him, wishing my voice was more than a whisper.

I could feel Lucia's attention on us, but it barely registered because Stephano's eyes had heated, and he held my stare, that split second communicating something like a promise that sent my blood sizzling through my veins.

"How do you have time to do so much cooking on a weekday, Hillary? What do you do for work?" Lucia asked now, pulling my attention.

"Oh, I uh—" Suddenly 'house sitter' didn't feel like enough, though 'professional fake girlfriend' wasn't going to work either. I froze.

"She's a musician," Stephano told his mother, sending my mind speeding in confusion. "She has a beautiful voice."

His praise surprised me, and also sent a spark of pride through me.

Lucia seemed to think about this answer, and she made a little "ah" sound as I shot the goalie a questioning look. He shrugged and smiled at me.

"What kind of music?" Luca asked.

"You name it, really," I told him. "But I write a few of my own songs, and those are kind of a rock and roll, folksy pop mix, I guess."

"Huh." Luca wasn't impressed and I tried not to take it personally.

"Maybe an example?" Stephano suggested.

I took a sip of water and turned to him. "You want me to sing at the table?"

Those lips pulled into a brief smile, and he shook his head. "I meant maybe you could name a few bands that are similar? Something we might know?"

Of course. "Oh," I laughed. "I guess maybe Fleetwood Mac would be close? Or Tom Petty. Maybe Dire Straits or the Eagles? Like those all mixed up together. With Taylor Swift added in. And a bit of The Wknd and Harry Styles." I could have gone on for hours, but forced myself to stop.

Stephano's face held an expression I couldn't quite read as he looked at me, and I wasn't sure what to make of it.

"You sing for a band?" Lucia asked, and my mind spun, looking for the right answer.

"I'm more of a solo artist," I hedged.

Stephano reached over and gave my hand a reassuring squeeze, sending my heart skittering around inside me, and then stood. "Let's get dessert."

Stephano's mother waved away the idea. "Stephano, no, I can't." She looked tired, suddenly, her whole form sinking into the dining chair. "The day is catching up with me."

"Of course, Mamma," Stephano said, going to help her from her chair. "I'll help you get settled. Hillary, I'll be right back."

"I'll clean up," I told him, rising to collect plates.

Luca stood too, dutifully helping carry things to the kitchen.

As the younger Mizzoni son and I cleaned up the kitchen, I could feel his interested gaze following me around. Finally I turned to face him, and the question he'd clearly been holding all night flew from his lips.

"Are you going to marry my brother?"

CHAPTER 11
STEPHANO

SAVED BY X-BOX

I returned to the kitchen just in time to find my brother quizzing Hillary about her intentions toward me, something I found both charming and irritating.

"I, uh . . " Hillary's face cleared when she spotted me.

"Luca," I told him. "It's not polite to ask questions like that."

"Just curious," he said with a shrug. "I mean, we've never even heard of her, and now she's here, cooking in your house, and—do you live here?" he asked her.

"I live next door," she said, her eyes moving from my brother to me.

I didn't understand quite what was going on, but it was clear there was something Luca didn't like about Hillary's presence, and I wasn't in the mood to sort through it right then. Hillary and I had things to figure out.

"I have an X-Box," I told him, interrupting the awkward conversation.

"Yessss," he said, slamming his hands together in front of him and forgetting that he'd been in the middle of interrogating my fake girlfriend for a moment.

"It's in the den," I said. "I'll show you."

We left Hillary alone for a moment and I walked my brother to the den. "Please be polite to my guests," I suggested, working to keep any hint of anger from my voice.

My brother raised his hands, slipping into Italian. "Just curious."

I set my brother up with headphones and the gaming system and showed him where his room was, and then returned to the kitchen.

Hillary was just finishing with the pots on the stove.

"Sorry, I meant to help . . ."

"It's the least I could do," she said, hanging the dishtowel back up to dry and turning to face me. "Even though, I mean, I did do all the cooking."

She looked up at me, those big brown eyes full of questions as she seemed to realize at the same moment I did that we were standing just inches apart. If I'd taken a step, my chest would be pressed against hers. If I reached out, she'd be in my arms.

My body vibrated with tension. I wanted to touch her, but now that we had no audience, there was no reason to.

I forced out a breath and stepped back, breaking her hold on me.

"Uh, we should probably talk," I said, glancing over my shoulder to make sure Mamma and Luca were nowhere around.

"Yes," she agreed. "Walk me home?"

"Sure."

We headed out the front door into the frigid chill, our boots crunching on the days-old snow frozen to the ground. Hillary's arms went immediately around her body, fighting the cold.

"You didn't have a coat?"

She shook her head, all the blond hair flying around her shoulders, caught in the breeze.

"Can I grab you a coat?" I moved back toward my front door.

"Don't be silly. It's only a few feet to my door," she said, taking off at a brisk pace.

I felt useless, like I'd failed somehow, but she was right and I tried to shake it off. But I hated seeing her shiver.

Soon, we were stepping into the warmth of her house, taking off our boots again. The business of arriving ate up only a minute or two, and then that same anxious tension filled me.

"Come sit?" Hillary suggested, gesturing toward the living room. Teresa's house was filled with unique items, a cow hide across the floor, abstract metal sculptures reaching skyward from her coffee table toward the exposed pipe light fixture hanging over it.

"Sure."

We settled on the couch, but as soon as Hillary had curled up next to me, her feet tucked beneath her, she popped up again. "This is going to require wine."

I nodded, though I made a mental note to cut myself off with a glass. I had a game the next day, and needed to get back to my usual in-season regimen.

She returned with a bottle of red and two glasses, pouring a healthy glassful for each of us. I accepted the glass she handed me, and we settled back, facing one another. I was nervous, but I wasn't sure why.

"So," she said, raising the glass and then taking a long drink. I watched her swallow, doing my best to ignore the way the wine stained her adorably puffy upper lip and how her sweatshirt had the tendency to slide down one shoulder, revealing golden skin that made my fingers itch to touch it.

"You surprised me," I told her.

"But a good surprise, right?" She tilted her head, her eyes gleaming.

I thought about that. It had been my idea. And there was no going back now. "I guess so. I just—"

"You don't like surprises."

"Not traditionally."

She shook her head. "That's too bad. But I do get that I might have sprung that on you before you could find time for us to review the spreadsheet or whatever."

Now she was speaking in code. "What spreadsheet?"

"The one I thought you probably made with all the fake details of our fake relationship. And the rules."

"Wow. You think I'm that tightly wound?" Her and everyone else on earth.

She raised an eyebrow and took another sip.

In reality, I was exactly that tightly wound. But something about Hillary made me want to appear just a little more fun, spontaneous.

"There is no spreadsheet, Hillary, but I do think we should probably get a few things straight."

"Agreed."

I was about to pull out my phone so I could begin making some notes about things like how we met, when our first date was, and what her favorite color might be. But unsurprisingly, Hillary surprised me.

"We met exactly how we met—the fewer lies the better," she said. "And it can be new—that explains why you haven't mentioned me."

"I already stretched the truth a bit, I guess. With the cooking and the career."

She dropped my gaze, her eyes holding fast to her wine glass for a long beat, then she let out a sigh that sounded sad. "Yeah. I wish I had something a little better for you to offer. Like, I wish I really was a doctor, or an accountant or something."

I caught her gaze when she glanced up again. "Do you really wish that?"

Hillary looked almost wistful, something I hadn't seen in her before. Her mouth was pressed into a line, and her eyes had lost their usual playful glint. Worst of all, her light dimmed and her animated eyebrows were low, as if they were trying to hide her from me. "No, not really. I just wish . . . I don't know. It's not a lot to impress someone's family with. Yours or mine."

"What's not? The arbitrary facts you can spew about a job? Those things don't really matter." Mamma had traditionally been more interested in a woman's likelihood to bear tiny Mizzonis than anything else.

"Says the guy who is a pro hockey goalie for a team that almost won the league last year."

"You've been doing more research." The knowledge made me unreasonably happy.

"I'm a Wombats fan now. No going back." She winked, and the jolt of desire that shot through me was almost enough to make me spill my wine.

"You don't really think that what you do for a living has anything to do with who you are as a person, do you?"

Hillary leaned forward, putting her half-empty glass on the table. And then she sat back and sighed, her eyes on the strange light fixture hanging before us. "I don't know. I didn't used to think so. Of course, that was when I was going to be a doctor, and that was all anyone—including me—cared about."

I nodded but didn't speak, sensing that the thought wasn't complete.

"But back then," she went on, "life just felt so scripted. I did what I was supposed to do. College, med school. The right credentials and accolades. I was just following the path that had been put in front of me. I didn't really question it for a long time."

"But then you did?"

She glanced at me, her face wearing a look of apology or regret. One side of her mouth lifted, and her eyes squeezed shut for a second. "Yeah. Then I did. Everything changed."

There was clearly something else there. Despite the late hour, the fact I'd had more wine than I should have, and my family potentially needing me back at my house, there was absolutely nothing more important than hearing the next words from this gorgeous woman's mouth. What had affected her life so deeply?

But the words didn't come.

To my shock, instead, a single fat tear was rolling down Hillary's cheek as she stared at me.

Neither of us moved as it tracked along the fair skin of her face, veering sideways as it hit her top lip and then trailing down her jaw. She wiped it away with her sleeve, sniffing and breaking eye contact.

Why was she crying? Oh god, no. "What?" I asked, my voice coming out as a whisper.

She reached for her glass, taking a healthy slug and then replacing it on the table. I watched her take a deep breath, and then she turned back to me, the sadness replaced by a defiant smile. "I learned how short and unpredictable life can be, even when you've got it all planned out. And I decided not to follow the plan."

She wasn't going to tell me. Whatever the thing was that had dramatically shifted her life, her mindset . . . she wasn't going to trust me with it. Disappointment surprised me.

Why would she? We were practically strangers.

"Okay." I said, sensing a definite change in the air. That door had closed. "Well, let's hammer out whatever details we need to."

"Yep. First date?" I sensed Hillary was pasting on a happy attitude, but didn't want to push her.

"Uh, dinner?"

She shook her head. "You're dating me. I don't do dinner for a first date."

"What do you do? Skydiving?"

A terrifying grin lit her face and her eyebrows jumped. "Great idea! But no, not in wintertime. We probably went to this karaoke club in town that I just read about. I mean, if we were actually going on a date, that's where I'd want to go."

"Okay. So we went to listen to some people sing cheesy songs in a dark club."

"Nope. We went to sing."

"Right. Of course." Would anyone believe I sang with this woman in a club where anyone might see me? As I watched her thinking, I realized if we really were dating, I probably would. I'd do just about anything to never see her cry again.

"You sang 'Call Me Maybe,' I sang 'The Gambler,' and then we did a duet."

"Can't wait to hear what this one was."

"There's only one real option," she said, tilting her head and leaning in. "You sure you don't know what it is?"

I shook my head.

"'Islands in the Stream.' Duh." I'd been in the US long enough to have heard this extremely cheesy song.

"Duh." I laughed, feeling surprisingly light and happy, given the complicated situation I'd found myself in suddenly. "And we need to decide what you'd like to be paid."

Hillary blanched and dropped my gaze. "No, that's okay."

"I'm asking for your time. You should be compensated." I didn't want her to feel awkward, though this was potentially the most awkward thing I'd ever had to propose to someone. I meant it. She deserved to be paid for her time.

"It's just . . . isn't that weird? Doesn't that make me . . ." she trailed off, but the word prostitute hung in the air.

"Absolutely not." How could I explain that suddenly I wanted more than sex from her? Sex would be nice, of course, but this was a chance to actually get to know her. To spend time with a woman who didn't dive into sex because she thought it would help secure me to her, improve her image, or realize her dreams of dating a sports star?

"I don't know."

"You're playing a part. Acting. I'm paying you to act." When she risked a look back up at my face, I went on. "Actors can be pretty well paid, too."

Hillary's face was turning pink. "This feels wrong."

"It's not. And I insist." I typed a number into the calculator on my phone. "How's this?" I turned the phone toward her.

The pink turned to red. "That's way too much! No, forget it! I won't take your money."

The last thing I wanted was to embarrass her further. So I put the phone away and agreed. But in the end, I'd pay her. There was no way I could feel right about this otherwise. I had time to convince her. "Okay, I won't push."

"Okay." I was happy to see her color fading a bit. "Where do you think our first kiss happened?" she asked.

"You really think they'll ask that?" My mother might, actually. I tried not to think too hard about what it would be like to kiss Hillary. Would it be as wild and unpredictable as she was proving to be?

"Better to be prepared and not asked than to never be prepared at all." She held up one finger while she delivered this little nugget of wisdom.

"You know that is not a famous quote, right?"

"I think when you say it all serious like that and hold up a finger, it gives it the same impact, though. In fact, it really sounds like something Steve Jobs or Gandhi might say."

"Both dead. Probably not saying much at this point."

"You know what I mean," she said, laughing.

"I do," I told her, holding up one finger and saying it in a very serious voice.

She reached out and grabbed my finger, laughing and pulling me toward her with the motion. I was laughing too, but suddenly, I was bracing myself with my other arm on the back of the couch, just inches from her.

Hillary smelled sweet and fresh, like clean laundry and green fields. The scent made me want to close my eyes and just breathe, but the way her gaze was lingering on my face had me frozen there, eyes wide open. Those coffee brown eyes dropped to my lips then, and I remembered suddenly that we were talking about a first kiss.

Moving slowly, she released my hand, but before my chest could deflate with disappointment, she reached for me, her cool long fingers landing on the back of my neck.

Time slid by at a fraction of its usual pace as I considered her, centimeters from me now. She was beautiful—light and free, with a layer of trouble just below the surface and another layer of complex and mysterious unknowable things under that. My eyes dropped to her lips—ripe and plump.

Her fingers tightened on my neck, and she tugged me closer, and in the next second, my lips found hers. I brushed against them lightly at first, relishing the sensation. Her mouth was yielding, whisper soft. And then I leaned in, moving the hand on the back of the couch to her back, pulling her into me.

A second later, she was in my arms, and the kiss had morphed into something else, something like breathing and aching combined into one. I gave, I took, I yearned in a way I wasn't sure I'd ever done before, and then too soon, it ended. I remembered who and where I was, and I set her back on the couch. Away from me.

My mind went into overdrive. What did I do? What did this mean? Shit. Shit. SHIT!

"Well, there you go. Now we have a first kiss story." She delivered this line in her normal voice, pushing a loose lock of hair from her face.

I stared, trying to get my life back together. She was unaffected, and I felt like I'd just unpacked every single thing I owned and scattered it around us, and now had to scoop it all back into a suitcase much too small to fit it all.

"You okay?" she laughed.

"Yeah," I said, doing my best to sound as completely unaffected as she clearly was.

"Okay." She picked up her wine and finished it. "So. Rules?"

My brain was still turning uselessly over things I needed to shove aside. "What?"

"Rules of fake engagement. Or fake dating."

"Right."

"Clearly, touching and kissing are on the table."

"Right." I'd become a robot.

"And do you think your mom will think it's weird if I don't sleep over? Or if you don't?"

The thought of Hillary in my bed made it necessary to shift my weight a bit to accommodate certain parts of me that perked up at this suggestion. Heat rose in my chest as I pushed down the idea. "Mamma is pretty traditional. She'd expect us to at least pretend that we're not sleeping together until marriage."

"Oh, good. That makes that easy."

"Right." Why did I feel disappointed? What was wrong with me?

"And so, you have a game tomorrow, right?"

"Yeah."

"Should I come?"

"Uh. Yeah." I tried to imagine her in the stands with my mother. A recipe for massive distraction. But if we were really dating, she'd be there, right? Mamma would wonder why she wasn't.

"Okay. Good."

"Good."

"Think that's enough for now?"

I needed to get myself out of her atmosphere and figure out what was wrong with me. It'd been a while since I'd kissed anyone, but in the past I hadn't been completely non-functional afterward. "Yeah."

She was squinting at me now, her head tilted in that way that seemed to mean she was figuring something out. Those lips twisted. "You okay?"

I rose, brushing myself off and turning to look around me, as if searching for that damned suitcase I'd just unpacked in here. "Yeah. Good. I'm gonna, uh . . . " I moved toward the door. "I'm gonna head out."

"Okay." She rose and followed me to the door, where I was trying to put my boots back on.

She watched me struggle, and when I was upright again, she said, "so tomorrow?"

"Tomorrow?"

"What's the plan?"

"I've gotta head to practice in the morning, but I'll be back around noon. I'll probably grab a nap, then I'll head over around two? I've got a car taking Mamma and Luca to the rink. You can go with them?" I wished I didn't have a game. I wasn't feeling quite right.

"Sounds good."

The next thing I knew, I was on the porch, and the winter wind was waking me up from whatever coma I'd been in for the last ten minutes.

Shit.

One thing was certain. I could not kiss Hillary again. It messed with my brain.

And yet, the thought of never kissing her again suddenly felt like the saddest I'd ever had.

CHAPTER 12

HILLARY

BURNING DOWN THE HOUSE

Holy shit, that kiss.

I'd had to stop it before my clothes melted from my body.

And what had been with the guy afterward? It was like I'd kissed all the personality right out of him.

Had he liked it? He'd kissed me like he liked it.

But that reaction . . .

I wasn't sure what to make of it, but one thing was clear to me. I needed to kiss Stephano Mizzoni again. For science. And because it was the hottest kiss I'd ever experienced.

When I'd recovered myself enough to peel my body from the door he'd just escaped through, I went back to the couch and promptly shotgunned the rest of his wine.

And then I scooped up my laptop and headed down to the recording studio.

I felt pretty confident this time, flipping switches and pressing buttons. I'd figured out how to integrate my laptop so I could download tracks from there and manipulate them on the board in Teresa's studio.

A teeny part of me wondered if she'd mind me being in here, but then I reassured myself. This equipment was no different from a television or a piano upstairs. At least, not if you knew how to use it. And I did. I wasn't hurting anything.

When I got everything set up, I moved into the recording room, pulling on the headphones and testing the microphone. And then, I let loose. Maybe it was the wine, maybe it was the kiss. Maybe it was the brief moment when I'd let myself relive the end of my medical school career there on the couch. But there was something inside me that night that screamed to be let out.

I started with my familiar favorites. "Landslide" and "Gypsy," "Fast Car" and "Since U Been Gone." But then I shifted, pulling up the piano riff I'd been playing with and rearranging it a bit. Finally, I sang one of my own songs, and the lyrics I'd been working on fell from my lips like the truth I'd been afraid to tell Stephano.

> There's no clarity in this world for girls like me
> They feed us lies from infancy
> Tripping blind through a mouse's maze
> Seeking solace in an approving gaze.
>
> Glass houses were built to break
> Tender hearts were made to ache
> This whole world is just a fake
> But now I see the truth. Truth.
> Chaos is the truth.
>
> We read the books and take the tests
> Drive ourselves, we don't need rest
> Accolades, houses grand
> Building shrines that never stand
>
> Our glass house was bound to break
> My foolish heart was made to ache
> Everything I knew was fake
> The truth now is you're gone. Gone.

Only chaos. Chaos and truth.

The legacy they hide from us
Is anarchy and randomness
The world is wide; wicked and wild
Not at all what I learned as a child

Eyes open wide, I step through glass
Into a life that moves too fast
No guardrails, no rules in place, society's fabric has
    finally slipped
I move through chaos at my own risk

The house is gone, I'm on my own
At least the truth is clear.
I learned it all before I'd grown
Our lives are carved from fear.

I leap from glass into the truth, I'm trying not to
    drown
Keep my head up and kick my feet
Keep moving cuz I can't stay here.

Keep moving cuz we can't stay here
Keep moving cuz you can't stay here

As I belted the last line, I physically sagged. I felt spent, exhausted. I could barely stay upright as I hauled myself through the booth, shutting everything down and heading up to fall into bed.

I woke in the morning to the buzzing of my phone, which was conveniently positioned just beneath my left boob, smashed between my body and the mattress. I'd slept on my face again. Not good for future Hillary's chances with the wrinkles.

Oh well.

Who called people at this hour? I wondered as I dragged the phone out and peered at it.

Teresa.

Oh.

I sat up suddenly, making my head pound violently, and cleared my throat, and then accepted the call.

"Hi," I croaked. Shit, I should have tested my voice first.

"Did I wake you?" Teresa's voice was bright, full of smiles.

"Ah, I could lie and say no, but you'd know I was lying."

"Sorry," she said with a laugh.

"So good news," I told her, my voice sounding more normal with each word. "The house is not on fire. I haven't broken anything, and I haven't had a single party."

"You sure about that last one?"

Oh oh. What? "Uh, yeah. I'm sure. Why?"

"Well, that's why I'm calling."

Oh shit. Had asleep Hillary done something? "Oh."

"Yeah, I mean. No big deal, nothing wrong at all. Just . . . I had a few tracks hit my drive this morning that I was kind of surprised to see."

"Tracks?" My mind flashed back to the recording studio. Adrenaline shot through me. What had I done?

"Yeah. I've got the studio set up to cloud sync to my drive, and you must've recorded some stuff in there yesterday?"

"Ohhh. Shit. Yeah. I'm sorry, I'll stay out of there. I sing as a hobby, and—" Oh god, I was going to lose this job and then I'd be even more screwed. And I'd just agreed to be Stephano's fake unpaid girlfriend. Oh god.

"Hillary?" Teresa interrupted me.

"Yeah?" I was cringing, literally trying to shrink into the bed. I just hoped I hadn't broken anything. She didn't sound especially pissed off, though.

"There was one track that was really good. Something I hadn't heard before."

I uncrumpled slightly. "There was?"

"Yeah. A little dystopian kinda rock thing with a pop beat? Very Stevie Nicks meets Taylor Swift."

"Oh." Oh god. I'd sent one of the biggest names in music a bunch of karaoke-level tracks by accident? And she'd listened to them? Humiliation stung my cheeks and made me want to sink through the bed directly into the place super humiliated people disappeared.

"I like your take on that old Kenny Rogers song too."

"Oh god." My cheeks were burning. Was she going to tell me to keep out of the studio? Or toss me out of her house?

"Yeah, listen. That chaos song. I was thinking . . . could you do it again, but try tweaking the EQ a bit, cut some of the low mids to give them more clarity and cut through the mix better?"

Shock twisted my stomach into a knot. Were we . . . collaborating? "Uh, sure, yeah."

"And the vocals are fire, but let's experiment with a little layering. Maybe try some doubling or harmony?"

"Yeah, I can do that." When I was able to catch my breath, I found that ideas were already percolating in my mind as I imagined how I might mix another layer.

"Awesome. I'd like to add a bridge too, to break it up a bit, add some dynamic contrast? I think we can do it with that last bit, but we can work on that later."

"We can?" I couldn't help it. What was happening here? I bounced up and down on the bed to try to expel some energy. Was I dreaming maybe?

Teresa laughed. "Yeah, sorry, I know this is totally random, but I didn't expect to wake up to this track and it's just got my mind humming. I wish I was there to work on it, but you seem to have a pretty good feel for the equipment."

"Trial and error," I admitted, warming with the compliment.

"Okay, well mess around with it a bit and send me some new ideas if you want."

"Yeah," I said, pulling up the bravery to ask the question in my head. "But Teresa? Why?"

"Why what?"

"Why do you want me to work on it? I mean . . . why do you care?"

She laughed again, sounding strangely approachable and down to earth. "Sorry, yeah. I'm totally ahead of myself." She paused, and then said, "Well, it's really good, Hillary. Fresh. And if you're up for it, I thought I might play it around for a few folks while I'm out here. See if there's any interest. You have other songs, right?"

"Yeah," I said, my voice soft. "But what would happen if there was interest?"

"You name it," she said. "I mean, one song doesn't make a career, but it's a start."

A career? "Oh. Okay." I was afraid to get ahead of myself, but elation was lurking just around the corner. Could I really have a career in music?

"Is it okay? I mean, I'm getting that you didn't mean to send me this."

"No, I would never do that on purpose! I totally don't want you to think I was like, 'I'm sure Teresa has nothing better to do.'"

She laughed at the other end of the line, and my nerves unspooled just a bit.

I was going to work with Teresa Palmer? "But, yeah, it's okay. I mean, it's actually really exciting. Just . . . I'm surprised."

"That's what the song is about, right? Life is full of surprises."

"It is." I blew out a breath, trying to convince myself this was my reality.

"Okay, well, send whatever you want when you're ready!"

"I will."

"And please don't burn down the house."

"I won't." I hung up the phone, feeling like I'd woken up on a different planet than the one I'd gone to sleep on. Everything looked just a little different suddenly. I stared at the phone with unseeing eyes as the call replayed in my head.

And then I focused and saw that it was after noon. I needed to pull myself together to be presentable for my fake boyfriend and his family. There was a hockey game to attend!

CHAPTER 13
STEPHANO

JET FUEL AND CONVERSATION

I went to bed worried. And woke up worried. (More worried than usual.)

Mamma's warning that we needed to talk was fizzing in the back of my head like some kind of slow-release, bad-news bomb, and then there was my neighbor.

This thing with Hillary had all kinds of potential to go sideways. She was a bit unpredictable. And Mamma was like a dog with a bone when she thought I might be dating someone.

And it had been my idea. I finished brushing my teeth and combing my hair, and picked up my practice bag, carrying it out toward the garage.

"There you are, Stephano!" Mamma called loudly from the kitchen, nearly giving me a heart attack. Why had I thought she and my brother might sleep in?

"Morning, Mamma."

I dropped my bag in the living room and walked into Mamma's arms. She squeezed me tightly and I gave her a kiss on the cheek.

"Luca still sleeping?"

"Teenagers," she said, shrugging. "Sit down. I will make breakfast."

It looked like she'd already been busy. There were pots and pans everywhere, and the house smelled like pastry and garlic. "Eggs?" she asked, holding a spatula aloft as her dark eyes found mine.

"Just coffee for now. I eat with the guys before practice." I knew that turning down my mother's food would be perceived as an insult, but I wasn't about to break my routine on game day.

She sniffed and put the spatula down a bit more dramatically than was necessary, and moved to pull a coffee cup from the cabinet. Either she remembered where things were from her last trip two years ago, or she'd been up a while and had already familiarized herself with where I kept everything. I wasn't complaining. It was nice to have someone take care of you a little, even if it was just a cup of coffee in your own kitchen.

Mamma poured me a cup of coffee—which was about three times darker than any American would make it—and then poured herself a cup and came to sit next to me at the island. She looked so tiny perched on the stool. Sometimes I was struck by the diminutive size of the woman who held such a huge space in my life. She had always glowed a tiny bit red—I remembered it even from when I was small. But now her light was muddy.

"What did you want to talk about, Mamma?"

"Tell me about Hillary." Mamma sipped her coffee and waited. I'd hoped she would tell me whatever the thing was that had brought her out here, had made her act strangely. But this topic was inevitable too.

"What would you like to know?"

"Everything."

"Do you like her?"

Mamma lifted a shoulder. Noncommittal. It would take more than one dinner to win her, even as eager as she was to see me married off. In the past though, she was the one pushing women at me. This was new. "She is pretty."

"She is," I agreed, trying to keep my mind from the conversation—and the kiss—on her couch. She was so easy and comfortable, everything about her settling naturally into any situation. There was so much appeal in that. "She's a good person," I added.

"A singer, though." Mamma clicked her tongue and stared down into her coffee.

"Why is that a problem?"

"She is ambitious, Stephano."

I watched Mamma, surprised at this resistance. I'd supposed pretty much any woman would fit into the space in my life that she perceived as empty. "Yeah," I said, prodding her to continue.

"The music world," she said, lifting her coffee and sipping. "Very competitive. Male dominated, no?"

I waited. She was clearly going somewhere.

"A pretty girl trying to accomplish something big in a world run by men . . ."

"I don't think I like what you're implying. Hillary's not like that." At least I didn't think so. She wouldn't even accept my money when I'd offered to pay her. Besides, Hillary wasn't really in that world, and this wasn't a real relationship—of course, Mamma knew none of that.

"Maybe not." Mamma tsked and sipped her coffee again, clearly not convinced.

"How's Cristiano?" I asked, eager to change the subject.

Mamma glared into her coffee for a moment. "There was a time all I wanted was for you boys to meet women and build families. But I thought you would do it at home. Nearby."

"Is Cris dating someone?"

"Yes. And now he keeps secrets. Runs off to Milan for weeks and goes on mysterious trips to islands where tourists spend too much money."

That didn't sound like my brother. "What? What's going on?"

"He says he will tell me when the time is right. But yes, there is a woman." Mamma didn't deliver this news in anything close to the gleeful tone I would have expected. Something was definitely up, but I needed to get to practice.

"Good for Cris, I guess," I said, trying to picture the woman who'd managed to wrangle my stylish and carefree brother into a relationship.

"But he's not the only one keeping secrets, is he? When are you going to tell me what you came to talk about? Something about the family winery?"

Those sharp eyes jumped to mine, and Mamma stiffened a bit. "It can wait."

I didn't like surprises, and there was clearly something going on that Mamma didn't want to tell me. "Or you could just tell me now so I'm not worried." As if it would make a difference.

"No, *Mimmo.* You go play hockey. We will talk after."

I sighed. I didn't have time to get into anything right now anyway. "Uncle Julius wants to see you."

Mamma's face darkened, but only for a flicker of a second. "It will be nice to see him again." The words were right, but I knew any reminder of Dad was tough for her. And Uncle Julius was so much like my father—even if they were not related by blood.

I checked my watch and then stood, slugging the rest of the rocket fuel Mamma had made. "I better go." I scooted my chair back under the counter. "I'll be back around noon for lunch. Then I'll probably get a nap before I head back for the game."

"What time is the game?"

"It's at six. I've got a car coming at five twenty to take you and Hillary to the rink. I'll bring you home."

"It will be nice to spend more time with the woman you love." Her simple statement sent a chill down my spine. I hoped she wouldn't be too difficult or ask too many questions when they were alone.

"I mean—" I caught myself before I protested too much. "It's new, Mamma. We're not at the love part yet."

"Maybe that's good. We'll see."

I kissed her goodbye and headed to the rink, my gut swirling with a weird mix of anxiety over whatever Mamma needed to talk to me about and what might transpire between her and Hillary when I was away, focused on the game.

It didn't help that the first person I saw when I pulled into the lot was Samuels.

"Mizzoni!"

"Hey," I said, trying not to sound like an asshole. And failing.

"Feeling good?" he asked. I gave him a sideways glance as we headed into the café, suspicious that he somehow knew I was not, in fact, feeling great.

"Never better," I lied. Puppy didn't need to know I wasn't one hundred percent.

"Excellent." He gave me what some people probably considered a winning smile, but to me it just looked predatory. He was here to oust me. And if the pain in my hip had anything to say about it, it was going to happen sooner than later.

"'Sup Mizzoni?" Cade Simpson sat at one of the long tables in the café, three egg sandwiches on the plate before him.

"One of those for me, or does your beard need its own sandwich?" Simpson had a beard that could have had its own zip code. It was the same deep mahogany as his hair, and was the reason the fans and commentators referred to him as The Viking. In reality, Cade was a teddy bear. Nothing like a Viking. But the moniker worked for publicity.

"Get your own," Cade said, throwing a protective arm around his plate, prison style.

A few minutes later, the puppy and I were seated across from him, and Corny and Klaus Arndt, our second and third left wingers, were pulling up chairs.

"Heard the Ocelots are pretty good this season since they got those new guys," Corny said.

"One of those new guys is one of our old guys," I reminded him. "Hawkins." He'd joined the Ocelots when it had become clear he wasn't playing here. He was a good goalie, unfortunately. I wasn't worried though. I was better.

"Right," Arndt said, as if he'd just remembered this.

"Goalie, right?" Puppy asked, his eyes shining and bright.

Ugh.

"Yeah. He's the old you," I told him.

Samuels nodded, accepting this.

And if I wasn't better at making him feel part of the team here, he'd be the next one out the door to defend against us.

"Except you're staying," I added, catching an open-mouthed stare from Simpson.

"Are you being nice to young John here, then?" he asked, grinning.

"I'm always nice," I told him.

Corny spit out the coffee he'd just sipped and Arndt slapped him on the back.

I didn't look at Samuels to see his assessment of my statement. Maybe I wasn't nice, exactly.

"I think your aura's off today, Mizzoni," Corny laughed.

"Shut it," I told them. This was the way we talked, and I pretended to hate it, but this was a huge part of why I loved playing for the Wombats. For ten years, this place, this team had been my family. This was my home, and these crazy bastards were my brothers as much as Cris and Luca were.

"Hey, any Bigfoot sightings lately?" Simpson asked, his beard mostly hiding his grin.

"Funny." I focused on my food. I had enough swirling around inside my head that I didn't need any evaluations of my personality, my aura, or my belief in Sasquatch today.

"See you in there," I told the guys, stuffing down the last few bites and rising to clear my plate.

"See you," Corny called back.

"Stephano." Uncle Julius was just coming down the hall. Uncle Julius was shorter than me, balding, and he wore the worries of his life in lines around his eyes and mouth. I felt a rush of affection for the man who'd looked out for me for so long.

"Hey," I said, greeting him.

"Lucia is here?" he smiled broadly, and I thought again about Mamma's reaction to me saying his name. He reminded us all of my dad in the way he thought of others first, cared for his family.

"She is. Looking forward to seeing you tonight."

"Good. I hope to have some time to catch up. It's been a while."

"It has."

"And the other thing? Everything is okay?"

"Hillary. Yeah. Kind of."

"Kind of okay is not okay."

I chuckled. That was an understatement. "She'll be at the game tonight with Mamma."

Uncle Julius raised an eyebrow. "I see."

"It's complicated."

He nodded.

"I'll see you later."

He watched as I strode past him, but called to me again just before I headed into the dressing room. "You hurt?"

Shit. Was I favoring the hip? "Nope. I'm good."

I didn't wait to see his reaction, and headed inside to stretch and ice. I didn't want to mention the pain to the trainers, but maybe it was time. I knew there was a chance they'd send me for evaluation, and if that happened, Coach would be informed. I decided to downplay it. Get a few more tips on stretching, maybe.

I went home feeling good about my play, despite the pain that niggled at me. I was ready for the game. I got home to find the house empty and still. Just as I wondered where my family was, my phone buzzed with a text.

Goldilocks: Took your family out to check out the town. Meet us for lunch?

I sank down onto the couch. I needed to take a nap to be ready for the game. But I also wasn't sure what might be going on between Hillary and Mamma without me there. It wasn't that I didn't trust Hillary—though Mamma would catch her in a lie if she wasn't careful. Mamma raised three sons. She could sniff out something fishy without trying too hard. The feeling I had when I thought about the three of them out together was much closer to one I wasn't used to at all. Envy. I was missing out on something.

For a guy who was not historically a joiner, it was an odd sensation.

> **Me: Sure. Tell me where and when.**

> **Goldilocks: Diner in Boomsmack. Twelve-thirty?**

Boomsmack was the next little town over from Wilcox. And the diner was pretty good. I looked at my watch. If I left now, I'd make it. Maybe there'd be time to sleep when we got back.

> **Me: See you there.**

I stood back up and headed for the garage again, telling myself that the little flare of excitement I felt at the idea of seeing Hillary was nothing important. More annoying than anything else.

But as I pulled into the parking lot at the diner, it burned just a little brighter.

CHAPTER 14
HILLARY

ONE THING MUST BE CLEAR: MILKSHAKE OR MALT?

After the talk with Teresa this morning, I'd been unable to focus on anything. I'd told Stephano I would pop over around five, but knowing his family was there without him gave me the idea to go kidnap them and show them around.

Wasn't that what a real girlfriend would do?

Lucia was not exceptionally excited about the idea, but Luca seemed to like it, so together we cajoled her into agreeing. I took them to the craft market I loved, drove them along the main drag of Wilcox, and cruised past the arena where the game would be tonight.

"You know we've been here before, right?" Luca reminded me as I pointed out the little town center with its brick and ivy buildings in the middle of town.

I had forgotten that, actually. And Lucia had been quiet during my little tour. I thought she'd been soaking in the sights, but maybe she'd been more focused on me, actually.

I glanced at her as we pulled into the diner parking lot, glad to know Stephano would be meeting us here. So far, I'd managed to bore and annoy his brother, and his mother was beginning to freak me out with her assessing stare.

We entered the diner, which was cozy and smelled like maple syrup, and slid into a corner booth to wait for Stephano to show. Lucia continued watching me with that strange impassive look on her face.

I pointed out the old-fashioned soda fountain and went on a nervous rant about the difference between milkshakes and malts before she finally interrupted me.

"You know that hockey ruined our family once before?"

Well, that was a strange place to begin. Was hockey ruining their family now?

"Ah, no," I said.

"Mamma, don't start," Luca suggested, rolling his eyes.

I waited, and Lucia folded her small hands atop the menu in front of her. "It is true. My husband's stepbrother. He fell in love with a woman."

I was beginning to wonder if there was actually a thread of logic in this story or if Lucia was just stating random facts about the Mizzoni family. Was this guy a hockey player?

"That's nice," I said, hoping that was the right answer.

She ignored me, finally continuing. "Julius was my husband's stepbrother and closest friend. He practically lived with us when Stephano was small. He was like a second father to him."

I nodded, eager to hear about Stephano as a kid. He couldn't have always been so serious, could he?

"But Julius was younger than my husband. Wilder. And he was a hockey player. A good one."

"So it runs in the family," I pointed out.

Lucia nodded. "Julius is not blood." She let that sit and then continued. "Julius was engaged when my husband died. To a wonderful woman who would have been a good wife. But he made all the wrong choices."

I tilted my head. "Like what?"

"At that time, many things were going wrong." She waved a hand as if I already know about this, but then added, "The winery . . . failed. My husband's parents lost the business and the land. My husband was also lost." She paused, offering no more explanation than that. Maybe she thought I knew what she was talking about already.

I glanced at Luca, but he was absorbed in his phone.

"By then, Stephano was almost a man," Lucia went on. "And it was very hard on him, losing his father."

"Of course."

"Julius could have been there for him."

"He wasn't?"

She shook her head. "Soon after, he had the chance to come to America to play hockey. It was a lot of money, and he thought he could rebuild the business. Maybe buy back the land. So he left."

I thought about that. I didn't know Julius, but it sounded like a reasonable choice. Though leaving your family when they were struggling would be so hard. "And what about his fiancée? She left too?"

"No. She couldn't. Her family needed her. So he promised he would come back."

Luca sighed, clearly having heard this story before.

"What happened?" I asked.

"Julius sent money. Enough to feed us and keep us housed, but not enough to buy back the land." She glanced down at her hands. "His fiancée married someone else. She wanted a family, not a famous American hockey star who visited a couple times a year."

"That makes sense," I said, feeling like Julius got the raw end of the deal in this story.

"And our family lost a good man."

Wait, was he dead? "Did he . . . did he die?" I asked, risking a glance into Lucia's stern eyes.

She sat up straighter, her lips pressing into a line before she scoffed. "What? No. He lives here. You miss the point."

I was about to take a stab at what the point of her story was, but was saved from the effort by the appearance of a broad-shouldered, devastatingly good-looking man sliding into the booth next to me. He smelled clean, and his big body pressed into mine as he scooted in close.

"Hey," Stephano said, kissing my cheek and smiling across at his mother and brother. A little riot of dragons erupted inside me.

"Hi," I said bumping his shoulder with mine. "How was practice?"

"Good," he said, his eyes catching mine and lighting for a split second with heat. "Did I walk into the middle of something?" He looked between his mother and brother.

"Mamma was reciting ancient history," Luca picked up his menu again and then peered over it at me. "So a malt is better?"

"Definitely," I said, happy to have veered away from the topic of families being split up by ice-based games with sticks. "I mean, you really can't go wrong with a shake—they both have ice cream, right? But there's this whole cult coming up around malts, and even just the nomenclature of the thing. People have been calling milkshakes malts erroneously forever, and I'm guessing all those folks from the fifties are probably up in arms over it all. It's really a smear on diner culture as a whole, and—"

"Hillary?" Stephano's voice was low and husky.

I turned to look at him. "Yes?"

"Are you getting a malt?"

I blew out a raspberry. "Is there even a question?"

Luca laughed and some of the tension at the table lessened a bit. I scanned the menu, relishing the nearness of Stephano at my side. There was a lot of uncertainty swirling around in my head after the call with Teresa this morning, and on the heels of Lucia's strange story about hockey and her family. But Stephano felt like something sure. He was solid and good and strong, and I liked having him next to me.

When his hand dropped onto my knee under the table, I realized something else. I liked having him touching me. I'd been trying very hard to keep my mind off the previous night's kiss, but now it flooded back to me—all that intensity focused just on me. It had been heady.

I glanced up at him, studying the side of his face. His jaw was square, the lines exact, and it was stubbled with dark hair. His lips —the ones that so often wore a frown—were full and sculpted beneath his prominent nose, deep observant eyes and dark brows. He was more than just handsome, but I wasn't sure what the right term for my goalie was.

His eyes pulled away from his menu and he gave me an amused look. "You're staring at me."

"You're handsome," I said, my honestly surprising even me.

His fingers on my leg tightened slightly and a bolt of want shot through me.

"Where will we sit at the game?" Lucia asked, breaking my growing focus on just where I'd like the goalie to place all of his intensity.

"Just behind the team," Stephano said.

"Were there no seats farther back?"

I laughed, thinking she was joking, but stopped when Stephano gave me a warning squeeze.

"Mamma thinks hockey is violent and scary."

"It's not an opinion. It is a fact." Lucia put her menu down and looked around, clearly ready to order. I wondered if I'd made a mistake, forcing her into spending time with me. She definitely seemed riled up.

"I like being close," Luca said. "You can really see what's going on in the fights. Sometimes there's blood."

I wasn't sure I wanted to see blood. Not up close. And not if it might be Stephano's.

"I've never been to a hockey game," I said before my brain caught up to my mouth.

The squeeze came again as Lucia's brows lowered in confusion and her mouth dropped open to ask the obvious question.

"You mean, you've only been to Wombats games," Stephano said quickly.

"Right," I laughed. "I meant I haven't been to other hockey games."

"Oh," Lucia said, but the suspicion on her face didn't fade.

"What can I get for you?" asked the waitress, appearing just in the nick of time. She was young and blond, and as soon as Luca laid eyes on her, everything about his posture changed.

"I hear that malts are the best thing on the menu," he said, a flirtatious edge in his voice.

The waitress was clearly picking up what he was laying down. "Oh, they are. You have to try one."

"What flavor is your favorite?" he asked, leaving no room for confusion about whether he was flirting. I was charmed by his clear intentions.

"Strawberry," the waitress said, batting her eyes.

Luca glanced around at us, as if just remembering that he had an audience. "Maybe I can buy you one when you're done working?"

"You have a hockey game to attend," Stephano reminded him.

The waitress's gaze left Luca and landed on Stephano, and stayed there. Her eyes widened slightly, and a faint blush climbed her cheeks. "Oh my gosh, are you Stephano Mizzoni?"

"Yeah, hi. Nice to meet you."

"Oh my gosh," she said again, gushing now. "My dad is not going to believe I met you. I mean, we knew you lived around here, but. Oh wow. What can I get you?" She held up her little order tablet suddenly, ready to put in an order for the famous goalie.

Just then, a sharp kick caught my shin under the table.

"Ow!" I yelped without thinking.

Every head turned to stare at me and my cheeks flooded with heat.

"Sorry," Luca whispered.

"Did you kick her?" Stephano asked, incredulous.

"It was meant for you."

Lucia whacked her younger son's shoulder.

Finally, we'd put in an order, the star-struck waitress departed, and Lucia dropped the bombshell ending of her story.

"My point is this: Stephano is not going to do what Julius did. He'll finish the season, come back to Italy where he belongs, and marry someone there." She nodded. "So I hope this isn't serious between you."

Stephano's jaw dropped in unison with mine.

CHAPTER 15
STEPHANO
AURA OF MUD

Mamma's proclamation hung in the air and all the pieces began assembling themselves in my mind. Mamma had spent most of my lifetime trying to foist me off any marriageable woman within ten feet. Now she was going to be geographically picky?

Her muddy aura had me wondering when she'd first arrived, but her hints about the wine business seemed to explain it. But now?

"Where's this coming from, Mamma?"

My mother straightened and an indignant look made her eyes squint and her lips purse. "It is coming from me. Your mother. I am tired of the men in this family running away and leaving me to handle everything."

I glanced at Luca, who was rolling his eyes as if he'd heard this one before.

"It's not like I just left. I've been here ten years," I pointed out. "And I've been gone this whole time for a reason. To build savings. For you. My family." This was what drove me. It was why I couldn't be done with hockey yet.

"Long enough, I think." She folded her arms across her chest and shifted her angry look to Hillary. "Especially now that Cristiano has fluttered away from us."

I was regretting dragging my neighbor into this situation.

"Malts!" the waitress sang, delivering two towering glasses topped with whipped cream and cherries to my brother and Hillary. They exchanged a little smile, like they didn't want to look too happy on the heels of what my mother had just said.

The rest of the meal was awkward, Mamma's stiff silence speaking louder than any words I could think to say, though Hillary made several valiant attempts. First, she headed off on a ramble about the wonder of dill pickles, and then, as the check was delivered, she loudly meandered around the linguistic ambiguities surrounding the words "check" and "bill" in restaurants and inquired about these words in Italian (*controllo* and *conto*). Mamma was not amused.

But I was.

Hillary had a way of diverting difficult conversations, lightening the atmosphere, and distracting. I saw how it could be perceived as tone deaf or even annoying, but I sensed there was something much more to it. She was taking the bullet, basically. When everyone else was wrapped up in some kind of tough emotion, she forged ahead, ensuring that we tried to move past it, working on everyone's behalf to get back to a more comfortable emotional state.

As we left the diner, I took her hand—because I thought Mamma and Luca probably expected it. But also, because I wanted to.

"Thanks for trying," I told her in a low voice.

She shot me a weak smile. "It's okay."

It wasn't okay. "Was she like that all day?"

Hillary shook her head, sending her soft hair dancing around her shoulders as we strolled to the parking lot. "Not until we sat down. Then it was all warnings about the way hockey ruins families."

"She told you about Uncle Julius."

"Yeah."

"You know he drives the Zamboni at the rink?"

"Seriously?"

It was kind of an open secret. Uncle Julius had played out in Washington but had never achieved the kind of fame that would follow him, despite having had a great career. When he quit playing, I was on my way to Virginia, and he met me there. Shotz had helped him find a way to involve himself so he could keep an eye on me.

I thought his Zamboni driving and proximity were an apology to Mamma of sorts.

But it was also a way for him to serve some kind of penance for choosing the game over love, I suspected. The Zamboni was his proverbial boulder.

"Yeah. You'll meet him tonight."

Hillary squeezed my hand as we arrived at her car. I'd parked my truck in the next spot over.

"Mamma, how about you ride with me? Luca, go with Hillary." Maybe I could explain to Mamma that I'd be home in a couple years. Maybe. And that Hillary didn't need all the details of Uncle Julius's life.

Luca grinned at the prospect of time alone with a pretty woman, and Mamma frowned at my truck. I could see the wheels spinning in her head. The truck was big, and she wasn't a tall woman.

"I'll help you in. You get a better view from up there. And it's safer," I told her.

"I will ride with you," she said, as if she'd had this idea herself.

The ride home was quiet at first, but my confusion and annoyance with the way Mamma had treated Hillary got the better of me.

"That wasn't very nice, Mamma. Hillary is a good person. You should be happy we're together."

"Is she a good person who wants to move to Italy?"

I glanced at her to see how serious she was. This sudden pressure to move home was new, and I had no idea where it was coming from. "I don't know. We just started dating. It's a little early to talk about international moves." I thought for a moment about what my mother wanted so suddenly. "Mamma, I don't even know if I want to move back to Italy."

My mother sucked in a sudden breath and let out a tiny "oh."

I shook my head. It wasn't like her to be dramatic.

"What is going on? What is this thing you're not telling me? Why the sudden focus on me coming home? Are you sick?"

"It is nothing. We will talk after the game."

"If you don't want to worry me, it's a little late." I could already feel the anxiety and concern burrowing deep into my brain. I was far from my best self and hoped it wouldn't affect my ability to block the net. Between my injury, which I still hoped was not a big deal, and John's eagerness to take my spot, my future with the Wombats was anything but certain. And I was so close to my goal. Once I had the money, I could buy the land next to our old vineyards and give it back to my family. I knew it wouldn't erase the tragedies of the past, but at least it would allow them to build a future.

"We will talk after the game."

I sighed. "Fine. But you'll be nice to Hillary tonight, right?"

"I will."

"And then you'll tell me whatever this great mystery thing is."

"Yes."

Mamma went straight to her room when we got home, and I caught Hillary after she dropped off Luca.

"I'll see you tonight?" I asked her.

She nodded. "Do you think your mom will be okay going with me?"

"She'll be fine. Luca will be a good buffer. He loves you."

Her face twisted into a comical expression. "He does? He's barely said three words to me."

"You introduced him to the malt. You're on his hero board now."

She shrugged and smiled. "Ice cream solves everything."

"I wish it could," I said, thinking about the strange situation with my mom just as a throb of pain shot through my hip, making me flinch.

"You okay?" she asked, taking my hand and looking up at me as we stood in front of her door.

Something about the way she asked made me realize I actually wasn't doing great. I was stressed and worried, and my hip hurt. But none if it felt as bad now that she'd asked. "Yeah, I'll be okay. I'm gonna take a nap and then head back to the arena. I'll see you there. Tickets are at the window for you. My name."

Hillary smiled up at me. "Okay, Goalie. Get a good rest."

"See you later, Goldilocks."

Our hands stayed connected as I stepped away, and I let go of her soft fingers only when I had to, the feel of them leaving a warm imprint on my palm that radiated through me.

Shotz called as I was on my way to warmups. I answered, assuming he was going to wish me good luck in the game. Shotz had been with me my whole career. We were pretty close to friends.

"Hey, how's it going?" he asked.

"Good, man. Sorry I haven't called you back. My mother is in town."

He laughed. My agent had met my mother, so he had some vague idea what I might be dealing with, I guessed. "No worries at all. I'm just checking in on the situation with Samuels."

"The situation?"

"The one where I sent you the best backup I could possibly find and Coach Merit won't give him a second of play."

"He's backup. That means most of the time we don't need

him." I knew this wasn't the right attitude, but I couldn't help myself. I hated everything about the idea of giving up my position to a younger guy. I hated thinking about what it meant for my own future.

"No, that means you play him strategically to help lengthen the years you get to be on the ice. I know Merit agrees, I just can't figure out why he isn't doing it." And this was where being friends with my agent—who was also my backup's agent—got tricky. I had no control over how much Samuels played, not really. But I could let the coach know I understood, and so far, I hadn't done that.

"He doesn't want to piss you off, but that's gotta change, Stephano. You're the best, no doubt. But you're part of a team. And Merit needs to start thinking about preserving you for a couple more years by taking off some pressure."

Preserving me. Like a mummy. Because I was old.

Sigh.

"Yeah." I'd told myself the same thing. Why was it so hard for me to accept when I knew it was right?

"Talk to you after the game. Think about it. Talk to Merit maybe."

"Yeah."

"Good luck tonight. You're a legend. You'll do great."

"Thanks. Talk to you later."

I checked in at the arena with plenty of time to spare, hoping to get a few extra minutes with the trainers to loosen up my hip.

"This been bothering you a while?" Frank asked me as he pushed and pulled at me.

"Nah, it's nothing really," I said, partly because Samuels was on the next table over. "Just a little ping now and then."

"Feels a little swollen in here," Frank said, prodding me in a way that would've made a less controlled man yelp. "That hurt?"

"No. Feels fine," I lied. If he decided it was serious, odds were good I wouldn't play tonight. And I was going to play. Mamma and Hillary were here to see me.

"Should get you in for an MRI just in case maybe. You okay for the game tonight?"

"It's fine, Frank. I just wanted to check."

"Sending you for an MRI Monday, though." He did not look satisfied, and I wondered what he could possibly have figured out from poking me and moving me around. It couldn't be good. But he wasn't saying I couldn't play, so it also couldn't be that bad.

"Fine. But it's pointless." I knew it wasn't. I also knew that whatever they'd find would probably mean a few games off. And if I was out, Samuels was in. And if he did well? I might be coming back to play backup. Or it could even end the season for me. Possibly my career. I needed to avoid the MRI if possible.

I glanced over at Samuels as I stalked from the room. He had headphones on, so hopefully he hadn't picked up on any of that. The last thing I needed was him or Frank telling the coach.

I geared up and took the ice with the team for introductions, letting the rush of the crowd and the buzzing atmosphere fill me up. I loved it out here—this was why I played.

The crowd was shouting "Rock It! Rock It!" like they always did when Stevens was called. For the few minutes before face off, I let my eyes scan the crowd behind the bench.

Mamma and Luca were there—Luca standing and yelling, and Mamma looking small and out of place huddled in her seat. On the other side of Luca was Hillary, and the sight of her made my heart ping just a bit quicker. She looked gorgeous, her hair flowing over her shoulders and a huge smile on her face as those bright eyes of hers found mine.

A zing snapped through me at the connection, and I felt myself relax and tense all at once.

I had a thing for my neighbor, I realized. I was into her.

There was no time to consider the gravity of this realization, because the Ocelots were driving down the ice.

As the puck flew, Elks and Simpson stood before me. My body and mind clicked as one. Into action. Away from Mamma, my hot neighbor, away from the throbbing pain in my hip. All that mattered was this. Now. Defending the crease, keeping the Ocelots out.

My body vibrated, matching the intensity in the air, and I shuffled across the crease, anticipating every move as the game went on.

We scored first, Stevens sending a scathing slap past their goalie and causing the arena to erupt in more screams of "Rock It!" The second shift flew out and the game went on with an intensity that would be exhausting as soon as it was over, but which felt like the greatest high I'd ever experienced until then. Somewhere in the back of my thoughts was the knowledge that Hillary was here. Watching me.

"Get there!" Rubio and Craft were talking, but they couldn't move in time to block the shot the opposing team's winger let loose. I pushed a leg out and threw my glove up, bracing for impact, but the puck snapped past, catching the edge of my glove before dropping.

"Shit!" The goal light buzzed and my gut sank.

"It's okay," Rubio said as he flew past.

The score was tied.

I tapped the posts with my stick, rolled my shoulders and reset. That was the one goal I'd allow tonight.

In the end, I ended up letting in one more, but it didn't matter because our offense never quit. We finished two ahead, and when the final buzzer went, the whole place exploded in celebration.

I couldn't pretend it didn't feel good. Hell, it felt great. I lived for this feeling. And when I spotted Hillary waving her arms and screaming, Luca jumping up and down, and even Mamma standing and clapping, it felt even better.

Back in the dressing room, there was more celebrating, and Uncle Julius flagged me down on my way to the showers.

"Your mother is here?"

"Yeah, just behind the bench."

Uncle Julius smiled widely. "I'll go entertain her while you shower?"

"That would be great," I said, relieved I wouldn't have to rush through the coach's talks and media interviews. "She's in a weird mood today though, just a warning."

"Weird how?"

"A lot of talk about hockey ruining our family."

Uncle Julius's smile dropped. "Well, then, this should be fun."

"Luca's out there too. And Hillary."

"Hillary?"

I clamped my mouth shut as the word 'girlfriend' tried to escape. She wasn't my girlfriend. Hell, we were barely friends. But for now, we were trying to make people believe we were together —though I'd practically forgotten why.

"Ah," Uncle Julius said, saving me from having to lie to him. "The woman you mentioned."

"Yes." I didn't want to explain everything to my uncle and left it at that.

"I can't wait to meet her."

"Thanks," I said. "And if you want to come over this weekend, Mamma's cooking Sunday dinner."

He hesitated. Uncle Julius tended to keep to himself, especially if my teammates were around. He didn't like to advertise the family connection for whatever reason, and only a few of the guys had picked up on it. "Maybe," he said, giving my shoulder a squeeze. "Great game tonight."

"Thanks."

"We'll meet you in the family lounge."

"Okay."

I showered, lingering under the hot water as long as I could, and when I returned to dress, John Samuels was waiting for me.

"Great game," he said.

"Hey, you played too," I reminded him. Coach had put him in during the second period, but pulled him when he missed a save, putting the other team even with us.

He nodded, looking glum.

"What?" I asked him. "I let a couple in too. It happens. That's part of the position."

"Yeah, it's not that."

I was impatient, knowing that everyone was waiting for me, but I stood still, letting the puppy form whatever thought he needed to come up with.

"It's just . . . . What does my future look like here? You're amazing. You do it all. You're a one-man show. The Wombats don't need me, no matter what Shotz keeps saying." He threw his hands to his sides, looking completely defeated.

I shook my head. "You know that isn't true. Every team needs a backup."

He sputtered, making a noise in the back of his throat, and when he lifted his head, I saw a defiance in his eyes I'd never seen there before. "Yeah. Backup. The thing is, Mizzoni? Before I came here, I'd never been anyone's backup. I was it. I was the Stephano Mizzoni of every team I've ever been on."

I blew out a breath. "I get it. But—"

"Yeah, we all start somewhere. I know." The anger in his tone dissipated. "It's hard to play second fiddle."

"Good for the ego though?"

He chuckled; a mirthless sound that actually made me feel sorry for the guy.

"Hey," I said, catching his eye again. "Let's run some drills Monday, okay? You and me. I was thinking about talking to Coach about using you more."

His chin popped up at that. "Yeah?"

"Yeah."

"Using me ever."

"Right." Shotz's words were sinking in. If I had a chance at a couple more years, I needed to take whatever breaks I could get. Even if it hurt my ego.

He stood there a minute, as if processing this new development, and then he grinned. "Yeah, okay. Thanks, Mizzoni. Good game tonight."

"You too," I told him.

Then I picked up my bag and headed out to see my family. But it was Hillary I was most excited to greet.

CHAPTER 16

HILLARY

MAMMA DROPS A BOMB

L ive hockey was not something I ever would have expected to enjoy, but the experience had been incredible. The rush of the game, the sound of the crowd, and the unique scent that wafted around us—like beer and popcorn mixed with the inside of a freezer stuffed with leather—it was intoxicating.

And then there was the goalie.

Watching him crouched in front of the Wombats goal, sheer determination telegraphed in every line of his body. Well, if I'd thought he was hot before, I was a goner now.

My fake boyfriend was the hottest man I'd ever been near.

And as we waited for him in the area his uncle Julius had shown us to near the dressing room, nerves began to jangle in my chest. I wanted to spend more time with him. I wanted to be close to him. I'd developed a huge crush on my goalie, and while we'd agreed on rules, I was pretty sure we'd never talked about real feelings.

Lucia had dropped some of the icy demeanor she'd had earlier as the game went on. She spent most of the action shielding her face and wincing, but she also popped out of her seat and yelled every time Stephano stopped a goal. She might not have been a huge supporter of his hockey career, but she was still clearly his biggest fan.

"That was incredible." Luca was still on a high as we waited in the lounge. "Stephano is ridiculous. He's so good."

"He is good," Lucia agreed.

"So you're going to stop pressuring him to come home?" Luca asked, impressing me with his willingness to hit the issue head on. Lucia could be intimidating, but Luca wasn't pulling any punches.

"There are other reasons we need your brother at home." Lucia glanced at me as she said this and gave me a half-smile. "Nothing personal, of course. Family matters."

"Of course," I said, but the way she'd excluded me still stung a bit. I busied myself eating M&M's, and eventually Stephano emerged, looking freshly showered and handsome.

"Hey," he said, moving to kiss his mother on the cheek.

"Dude!" Luca said, his exuberance making him loud. "That was amazing."

"Congratulations," I said, slipping an arm around his waist as a little thrill flew through me at the contact.

"Thanks," he said, his eyes snagging on mine and heat flinging between us. "You guys ready to head home?"

"You don't want to go out? Celebrate?" I asked him.

"We should go home," Lucia said. "We have things to talk about."

Stephano's mouth shut in a grim line, and he gave a quick nod. "Okay, well," he turned to me. I'd ridden with his mother and brother to the arena, but they could obviously ride home with him. "Let's go."

I wasn't sure why I'd expected to be left to find my own ride home, but Stephano was a gentleman. He looked out for people and took care of them, and it was comforting being part of that. Even if it was only for a bit.

We all climbed into the big truck, Lucia taking the seat up front while I sat in back with Luca. And soon, we were pulling into my driveway.

"I'll call you tomorrow?" Stephano said.

"Okay. Good night." Longing filled me as I watched the truck pull away and then pull in next door. As I closed the door and went inside, the big house felt quiet and lonely.

I imagined Stephano and Lucia would soon be deep in conversation about whatever it was she was holding back on telling him.

I wondered what it was.

Not that any of it had any impact on me.

I had my own issues to consider. Like the surprising phone call from Teresa. I wanted to tell Stephano about it but wasn't sure why. If he really was my boyfriend, it would make sense. But he wasn't. And why would he want to know?

I knew I should head down to the studio and try to implement Teresa's suggestions, but my head was fuzzy around the whole thing. What did it mean? What if she played my music for someone and they liked it? What then?

I didn't see myself moving to LA. I wasn't exactly a full-fledged performer. They couldn't book me in at the Whiskey or anything.

Beyond what success might mean or look like, I was having a tough time understanding what I even wanted. I considered calling my sister, but the situation would take a fair amount of explaining. Plus, I'd probably tell her about the arrangement with Stephano, and that was a whole other can of worms. She'd tell me it was a terrible idea. I had a habit of getting attached when I let myself. And I knew I'd already gotten too close to my goalie for an easy goodbye.

Why was it so hard to figure out what I really wanted?

Besides the hot guy who lived next door. But like everything in my life, that situation was temporary.

By design.

I'd put on some comfy leggings and a big sweatshirt when I'd arrived home from the game, and now I tucked myself into Teresa's enormous couch and sipped a cup of hot cocoa, trying to let my mind sort itself out. I sipped the chocolate and let a Netflix movie play on the flat screen, but my heart wasn't in it, and I wasn't making an effort to follow the plot. I was tired, and soon I had drifted off, the comforting background noise of the movie lulling me to sleep.

I had no idea what time it was when the doorbell rang, but it startled me out of a deep sleep. I wiped at the side of my mouth, giving the pillow I'd been hugging a quick drool check, and then staggered to my feet. There was only one person who could be at the door—or at least I hoped that was true.

Before opening the door—It was pretty late, after all—I glanced out the side window. There, standing in the porch light in the soft snow that had begun to drift down, was Stephano. My heart gave an extra little thump in my chest, which I tried to ignore, but I couldn't ignore how sad he looked standing out there.

"Hey Goalie," I said, pulling the door open and trying to play off the sudden tangle of nerves jumbling around inside me.

"Goldilocks. Sorry it's so late."

"That's okay," I said, waving him in.

He wore a look I didn't recognize. Uncertainty, maybe? He usually looked so sure of everything, so pulled together. The flicker of indecision as he glanced around the living room made me want to reach for him, reassure him.

"You want a drink or something?" I asked.

"Water, maybe."

He followed me to the kitchen and paused at the counter as I poured two glasses of water from the pitcher in the fridge. I handed him one and then looked up into his face again as we stood at the edge of the kitchen island. "You okay?" I asked, restraining myself from reaching up to press away the furrow between his brows. He wasn't mine to touch. Not like that.

But still, he was here . . .

"Yeah." He sipped his water. "No. I don't know."

A little laugh escaped me. "This is the first time I've heard you anything but completely certain about something. Except when you were asking me to be your fake girlfriend. You're not about to ask me to be your fake fiancée, are you?"

I was kidding, but as soon as the words were out, I knew they were wrong. His face drew into a frown, and he let out a breath, like he'd been holding it. "No. Let's sit."

"It was a joke," I said, following him to the couch.

"Yeah. I know. Sorry." He put the water on the table and shook his head, clearly out of sorts.

"What's going on?"

"Mamma dropped a bomb tonight."

What could she have said? She'd hinted around at something, maybe to do with the wine business, but I didn't know what could make Stephano look like this.

"Okay," I said slowly, trying to give him a chance to tell me only what he wanted to.

We faced each other, only inches between my bent leg and his knee, his strong hands resting there. I reached forward and took his hand, surprising us both.

His eyes met mine and heated, but he blew out a breath as if reminding himself why he'd come. To talk, I guessed.

"You knew that my family had a winery? When I was just a little boy."

"Right. Your mother said they lost it?"

He nodded. "There was a fire. It took everything—the vines, the structures. My father."

My hands flew to my face. That was awful. "I'm so sorry." Lucia had definitely not made that clear.

"My grandparents moved in with us after." Stephano's face was stony and pale, as if he'd steeled himself against any emotion while he recounted the terrible way his family had lost his dad.

I nodded, not wanting to interrupt even though my heart was shredding in sympathy.

"There was a cellar on the land, under the main structure. It was obscured by the detritus of the fire, and my grandparents didn't have the heart to try to dig it out. The firefighters assured them everything in it had burned or melted to nothing anyway, and so they sold what was left of the land and forgot all about it."

I frowned, wondering why they hadn't checked, but then I remembered that they'd lost their son in the fire. Of course they hadn't wanted to go back and dig through the ashes.

"The man who bought the land understood the loss my family had suffered. He never built anything on it. He was a family friend, really, and now that I'm older I understand he bought the land as a way to help my family. And recently, he died."

I shook my head lightly. So much loss. But where was this going?

"He willed the land back to my mother. And my brother Cristiano uncovered the cellar."

I leaned in, taking Stephano's hand as I whispered, "What did he find?"

A sad smile flickered across Stephano's face and he squeezed my fingers and then took my hand, turning it over to trace a line across my palm. "He found wine."

"Not really a shock, I guess."

"It's a very rare wine, and the vintage was a celebrated one in the region."

"What kind of wine did your family make?" I was no wine expert, but this was getting interesting.

"Amarone. It's a special wine—very difficult to make well. And my family was famous for it. When the winery closed, it was a tragedy for many. So to find a cellar full of the *Tenuta Mizzoni dell'Amarone* . . . " he trailed off, his eyes finding mine. A warmth passed between us in that connection, and I leaned in.

"Valuable, huh?"

He nodded.

"Why did your mother hesitate to tell you this, though? How does it affect you?"

"She wants me to come home." I bit my tongue. I didn't want him to go.

He shook his head. It was pretty clear he didn't want to go either. "With the land and the value of the wine she holds now, there is significant interest in investment to rebuild."

Stephano was still holding my hand, his big thumb tracing absent circles on my palm now. Heat pooled within me, but it suddenly felt imperative that he finish the story. Was he planning to leave? Maybe it wouldn't matter. It definitely shouldn't matter to me. Our arrangement was short-term anyway. I'd need to get back to figuring out my life when it was over.

"Can't your brothers help?"

"Yes, and they will, but . . . " His dark eyes were cloudy, troubled. "The investor wants me. My name, my fame."

"Can't you give him all that without physically going there?"

"He wants me physically present to be involved in promotion, to be the name and the face of the new winery. Mamma wants to agree, to see the winery restored to honor my father. She wants me to come home."

He didn't sound opposed, and worry spiked within me but I couldn't explain to myself why. Not rationally, anyway.

"Are you considering it?"

He released my hand, dropping my gaze. "I have to."

"Do you, though?" I'd been pushed plenty by my family, and ended up making my own choices in the end. "You're an adult. You decide."

Something flickered in his eyes as he looked back up at me. "When hockey is your life, sometimes the decision is out of your hands."

I stared at him, trying to decipher the meaning behind his words. I didn't know what he was alluding to, and as I contemplated how to ask, Stephano pushed a lock of hair behind my ear, his fingers lingering there along my jaw. I watched him, holding my breath. I wanted him to kiss me again, more than anything.

But I also knew that it would complicate things between us even more.

And I found I didn't care.

I closed the small gap between us, pressing my mouth to his as my hands found his shoulders. For a split second, he froze, and then with a grunt that I felt all the way in my core, he wrapped his hand around the back of my neck and pulled me closer.

Stephano's other hand slid around my waist, and he angled his head, deepening the kiss. The tension and worry inside me unspooled, replaced with a thrumming beat of desire. As the goalie's rough fingers found their way under the hem of my sweatshirt, tracking a firm fiery line up my back, I heard myself moan.

Our tongues touched and teased, and I pressed myself into his arms, seeking more contact, more heat.

Stephano's other hand lifted my top, breaking our kiss for a moment and pausing to ask my permission with his hot gaze.

I nodded, and a second later, my sweatshirt was on the floor next to the couch, and Stephano was pushing me back to lie beneath him along the leather surface.

His lips moved along my jaw, down to my collarbone, as his hands slid up the exposed skin of my torso. Every lick and nip and touch felt so good, I was intensely focused on the sensation, trying to memorize every second of it to replay later.

My hands pulled at his shirt, and he sat up for a second to remove it, exposing the most perfectly chiseled chest I'd ever laid eyes on. There was a scattering of hair across the top of his chest, and every muscle was cut in deep relief, all the way down to the solid vee disappearing into his jeans.

"God, you're hot," I murmured, not meaning to speak the thought out loud.

A tiny smile flickered across Stephano's face, and then he leaned down again, planting kisses along my ribs as one arm wrapped around me, and his other hand cupped my breast. He teased and caressed, and my nipple pebbled beneath his fingers, sending heady shots of want straight through me. When his mouth found the peak of my breast, I let out a whimper. It was so much sensation—and not nearly enough.

I moved my hands from the hard expanse of his back to the waistband of his pants, working the button until it released. Without a word, without lifting his head from my body, Stephano worked off his pants and then peeled off my leggings. When they had been removed, he sat back and looked at me, his eyes glowing.

"You're perfect," he told me. "So fucking beautiful."

His hands ran up the length of my legs, leaving a trail of heat in their wake, and then he took my mouth again, shifting to lay beside me on the wide couch. One of his hands traced my stomach and then teased the line of my underwear, toying with the fabric at my hip.

I couldn't take anymore, and I pushed his hand where I wanted it, his fingers immediately going to work as he let out a little chuckle into my mouth. He kissed me as his fingers moved, and I felt the hardness of him at my hip. Knowing he was as turned on as I was spurred me on, and I writhed beneath his touch, wanting him. Wanting more.

CHAPTER 17

STEPHANO

THE BUTTERFLY EFFECT

Hillary and I were in a different place, having departed the earth the moment I touched her soft, smooth skin. Time paused and shifted around us, and as I stroked the satin skin of her pussy with my fingers, finding the bundle of nerves at her center and pressing, I didn't care about anything else.

All that mattered were the breathy little moans she was making, the way her mouth devoured my own, the way her body responded as I touched her.

I wanted to make her come. I wanted her to scream my name. I wanted the release that would come from watching her unravel, knowing I'd done it.

But Hillary wanted more.

Her hand slipped beneath the waist of my briefs and a second later it was wrapped around me, forcing a groan from my lips.

We worked together, each of us pushing the other harder, further. Her hand slid up and down my length, her grip tightening here and there in a way that made me yearn to be inside her, to feel her wet heat gripping me, milking me. But I wasn't going to force it. This was more than enough.

"Fuck," I groaned, pulling myself back into control as Hillary panted out a breath beneath me.

"Condom," she gasped. "Now."

I did have one—I'd gotten in the habit of keeping one in my wallet, but usually ended up giving it to one of the other guys when we were all out. I just wanted to make sure this was the right thing. I pulled myself back, and her hand slipped away. "You sure?" I asked her.

Hillary's face was flushed, and her eyes were heavy-lidded. She looked so fucking hot it took everything I had to be a gentleman, to wait and ensure we weren't making rash decisions in the heat of the moment.

"Goalie," she growled. "Put on the condom."

There was no misconstruing her words or the way she reached for my cock again as she pushed my boxer briefs from my hips.

A moment later, I sat astride her, looking down at her and rolling on the condom. I'd pulled her panties from her gorgeous hips, and now she was naked before me, and it was the most incredible view I'd ever had.

"You're so fucking beautiful," I whispered, wondering how I had gotten so lucky that this woman had just appeared in my life this way. She glowed—her aura was sparkly and practically gold—but everything about her emanated warmth and beauty. She was unlike anyone I'd ever met.

As I sank into her, she hissed out a breath.

"Okay?" I asked, hoping it was, because now that I was here, it might take an army to pull me back.

"So good," she moaned. "So full."

I sank the rest of the way in, and for a moment I froze there, every nerve in my body focused on the hot tight space where she held me, the way she pulsed slightly around me, the way her breath came in hard gasps like she was teetering on the very edge of control.

I began to move, slowly, relishing every last sensation, and I could feel her tightening even more around me.

"Oh god," she moaned. "Fuck, that's so good."

I sank into her again, over and over, holding myself back as I watched her move closer and closer to the edge. Her body was shaking, and her grip on my shoulders was like a vise. She was matching me now, rising to meet me and crying out with each thrust, until finally I slid home and she locked me there, gasping and moaning, keeping me inside her with her legs around me. And I felt it--every shudder, every pulse of her body as she cried out and tipped over the edge of her release.

"Fuck that was hot," I whispered, burying my face in her neck, breathing in the soft scent of her as I tried to wait it out. But she bucked beneath me, and that was it--I reared back and drove home once more, my own release pouring out of me in a shuddering orgasm that seemed to last forever. Until finally, we were still, only our haggard breathing moving between us as we each regained ourselves.

"Holy shit, Goalie," she laughed finally. I liked her laugh—and her admiration.

Gradually, her arms loosened, and soon I shifted to her side again. After a few moments, I reached for the throw tossed over the back of the couch and pulled it over us. The house was warm, but winter in Virginia held a certain inescapable chill when you laid around on couches naked.

"That didn't feel fake," Hillary whispered.

"No," I agreed. "That was pretty real."

Hillary's head rested on my chest now, and I took a lock of soft hair between my fingers, marveling at the softness of the strands, the sheer brightness of the color.

"So you're going back to Italy?"

The distraction had been a good one, but it had done nothing to solve the problem I faced. I didn't want to return to Italy—my life was here. Even if my career ended tomorrow, I had the house, my friends. I lived here now. But the way Mamma had phrased her request . . . "If you come home, it will be the greatest honor you could offer your father."

"I don't want to," I told her honestly. If I agreed to go, let my contract end this year and didn't seek to renew it, part of me would be relieved. My hockey career would come to its natural end that way. And if I agreed to this investment, my reasons for continuing my career even when my body was telling me it was time to stop disappeared. The money I was saving wasn't my family's last hope. It was just a nice addition to the investment in the winery. But I didn't want to go. And part of the reason, I realized, was here in my arms.

"Then don't."

I shook my head, resettling her weight against my side. "It's not that simple. Haven't you ever felt pushed to do something for your family? Because you owed them something?"

Hillary let out a little sigh. "Yeah, but I blew up that bridge a long time ago. Now they just sit around at family events joking about what ridiculous thing I might do next and discussing my credit."

I pulled my head back to see her face. "Why do you say that?" I didn't like hearing her put herself down. And her credit? Was the beautiful girl in my arms in financial trouble?

She met my eyes, searching for something there, her irises bright and assessing. Then she wrapped an arm tightly around me. "When I was growing up, I was on a very specific path. And it wasn't one I chose, not really. My parents expected certain things. A certain level of performance. So I performed. The grades, the extracurriculars, the college acceptance. It was all just stuff I did because I'd never really been given any other choice."

"I get it," I said softly, knowing there was more.

"Med school was the same," she said. "Only, once I was there, I stepped off the path."

"What do you mean?"

Another soft sigh that tickled the hair on my chest. "I fell in love. And my parents were not supportive of that choice. But it hadn't really felt like a choice. It just happened."

I stayed quiet, waiting for the rest and ignoring the prick of jealousy I felt at the thought of Hillary being in love.

"Still, I focused and worked. For them. Maybe I even worked harder, knowing they didn't approve of my relationship. Like, I had to be even more perfect to compensate for falling in love without their explicit approval."

"That makes sense."

"So when all my friends were going downtown one night, I didn't go. I had to work. I had to study. I had to make my parents proud. So Marcus and all our friends took off to go see this band on Sunset . . . " Hillary's voice broke, startling me.

I lifted my chin, angling my head to meet her eyes, surprised to find they were full of tears. I didn't want her to cry. In fact, I felt like I'd do almost anything to see her smile again. "Goldilocks . . . shh, you don't have to tell me."

She shook her head a little and sniffed. "It's okay. It was a long time ago." She blew out a breath and went on. "There was an accident. Marcus and our friend Sue were killed. Drunk driver."

"Oh god. I'm so sorry."

"I should have been with them."

"Then you might have died too."

She shook her head and sat up, reaching for her bra and beginning to dress again as she spoke. "You've heard of the butterfly effect."

"Yeah."

"If I'd gone, I can almost guarantee those two cars would not have been in that exact spot at that exact moment in time. The accident probably would never have happened. My presence would have changed tiny things—a split second longer to get into the car, a couple more minutes at the club waiting for me to use the bathroom..."

"You don't know that. You can't think it was in any way your fault."

She stood, picking up her leggings and then sitting again at my feet to pull them on. "If I hadn't been forcing myself to meet expectations that I didn't even share, I could have prevented the whole thing."

I couldn't argue with her, but I felt like her logic was seriously flawed. I did understand it though. How many times had I wondered if I could have prevented the fire that killed my dad just by doing one little thing different that day? Or maybe I could have at least prevented his death in the fire. But I knew it did no good to let myself contemplate the what ifs in life.

Hillary continued. "And so I stepped off the path. For good. I'll never follow someone else's plan again. I'm never going to try to make all the people happy. I go with my gut. I do what seems right in the moment, what the universe suggests."

"You don't make plans? Ever?"

She stared at me, her brows lowering for a second over those glowing eyes. "Not if I can help it." She nodded, as if reaffirming this idea for herself. "But one hundred percent certain—I don't let other people dictate my plans."

I thought about that, sensing some inherent issues in that thinking, but understanding that they were coming from a place of pain. Hillary was scared of not controlling her life. It made sense. And in a way, her experience just confirmed what I'd already learned—the great things in life were easily lost.

My father.

My hockey career.

My life in Virginia . . . it was all just the tick of the clock, a split-second decision . . . and everything would burn down.

I rose and went to clean up. When I returned, Hillary was fully dressed. I reached for my pants. "Dinner tomorrow at my house? A lot of the team is coming. Mamma's probably already started cooking."

"Sure," she said in a quiet voice. "Do you think she'll mind though? I sense that I'm part of the problem. She thinks I'm keeping you here."

I pulled on my shirt and looked at her, adorably mussed and

beautiful. It wasn't the easiest thing to admit to myself, but she was part of the reason I didn't like to think of leaving.

"Hey, that thing you said . . . about your credit. Is everything okay? I meant it when I said I'd pay you. I'd feel better if you'd let me."

Her face paled slightly and she dropped my gaze.

"I'm not going to lie and say everything is great," she said. "But I'm also not taking your money."

I didn't like that answer. It felt wrong, letting her worry about something I could help with.

"I want to help."

She shook her head, her eyes meeting mine again. "Doesn't feel right."

"What will you do when you're done house sitting?" I asked her, realizing as her eyebrows flew up that the question was sudden and kind of out of left field.

"I have no clue," she said. "Maybe go back to Los Angeles. There's a chance I could sing for a bit . . ."

I wondered if it was that simple, though Hillary had an incredible voice. She'd never mentioned any plans to pursue music. Though it wasn't like we'd known each other long.

"I don't really know," she said. "The universe will guide me."

"The universe?"

She nodded. "I leave all the important decisions to the universe."

"Sounds risky."

Hillary smiled and lifted a shoulder. "It's worked out so far. The universe brought me to you."

I was tired, and her words weren't giving me a warm fuzzy feeling about anything, they were just giving me more to think about. To worry about. "It's late," I said. "I'll see you tomorrow, okay?"

"Okay, Goalie. I'll walk you out." Her smile warmed her voice and some part of my chest. But I knew it was a mistake to get attached. Hillary's 'universe' did not seem to intend for us to be together long.

She followed me to the door, and a second later, I was out in the snow, leaving footprints between her door and mine. As I climbed my front steps to look back, the footprints were already fading, being erased by the falling snow and the gentle wind.

CHAPTER 18

HILLARY

COCKBLOCKED BY KATIE

When Stephano left, I wandered Teresa's house like a ghost for hours, trying to figure out what the universe had in mind for me. First the phone call from Teresa about my music . . . and now sex with Stephano?

One of those things seemed to be screaming, "look at the world, look how much there still is for you to do and explore!"

But the other was a quieter murmur. Something about how nice it would be to love someone again, to let myself be loved, to stop the frenzied dash of my life and be still enough to stand next to someone else for a while.

The universe wasn't making any sense, and pacing through the rooms of this house wasn't making things any clearer. Eventually, I pulled the warm throw from the back of the couch and snuggled into it, drifting to sleep while trying to absorb some of the warmth Stephano had left behind.

The thing about going to sleep in the living room in front of a wall of plate glass was that it was pretty likely you were going to be up with the sun. And having drifted off somewhere around three, that meant my night had not been quite as long as most sleep experts would suggest it ought to be. But I was young. I could roll on less than four hours of sleep.

I yawned and stretched and made a huge pot of coffee, which I poured into an enormous Yeti cup I found in Teresa's cupboard. And then, before I could overthink it, I went down into the studio and replayed the tracks I'd accidentally sent her.

I listened to the one she liked at least ten times, making notes for myself and imagining the bridge she'd suggested, along with the other changes. The Yeti cup was at least two thirds of the way empty when I'd managed to pound out some new lyrics for the bridge and decided how to rearrange the first part.

By the time most of the world was scratching their naughty bits and rolling out of bed, I'd recorded two new versions of the song.

Maybe I couldn't control what happened between me and the goalie. Maybe I was going to be homeless and broke soon. And maybe I didn't dictate much of what would happen once I'd sent these new tracks off . . . but I could control how I approached things. I could control the part I played.

I drained the last of the coffee, switched off the lights downstairs and went back up to the kitchen, glad to see it was now a respectable time to be awake.

"There you go, Universe," I called out. "Happy? I took what you sent me and did something with it."

I was answered by the jangling of my phone from the coffee table where I'd left it charging overnight. As I headed to answer it, I half expected the screen to read "Universe," but it was just Helena. I hadn't called my sister since things had gotten sticky with the goalie, and now I wasn't sure I wanted to get into it. But I couldn't ignore her either. She'd send a SWAT team to make sure I was okay.

"Hey!" she sang when I answered. "You're alive!"

"I'm alive," I confirmed.

"You sound like maybe you're only half alive. What's wrong?"

"I'm one hundred percent fine," I told her. "There's just been a lot happening."

"In a huge house in a town where you know no one, there's a

lot happening?" I hated the skeptical tone in her voice. My sister loved me, but like my parents, she seemed to think I was trapped in some permanent childhood and needed guidance.

"Actually, there is." I couldn't help the indignant sniff or the hoity-toity tone that delivered this statement.

"Do tell."

I plopped back down into the corner of the couch and tucked my legs up under me.

"Well, I'm in a relationship, for one thing." The words were out before I considered the wisdom of them, but I was tired of everyone assuming I was flighty and incapable of any kind of commitment at all.

"What?" Helena sounded legitimately shocked by this. "With whom?"

"He's kind of famous, actually."

"The hockey player?" Now my sister's voice had gone an entire octave higher and I was a little worried about the glass face of my phone. "I told you to have a fling, not get into a relationship! What's his name?"

"Stephano Mizzoni."

I heard furious keyboard abuse on my sister's end of the phone and then a gasp. "Stephano Mizzoni, ten-year veteran of the league and one of the leading goalies in the FHL."

"Goalie," I said in a near-whisper as an image of Stephano's face floated before me. I snuggled deeper into the couch.

"Holy goalie," Helena giggled. "He's really hot, Hill."

"Yep."

"And how did this happen? You went back after the hot tub incident to borrow a cup of sugar?"

"No, he came here actually."

"Oh my god, it's like a Hallmark movie. He actually came to borrow sugar?" She was gushing with enthusiasm, and I decided that not telling her the whole thing was supposed to be fake was the right move. The truth would only cement her impression that I made poor decisions. Because really, wasn't that what this was?

"There was no sugar involved." Plus, was it still fake? And it didn't seem like Stephano's mom wanted to set him up with anyone unless they lived in Italy, so maybe he'd want to call it off? My stomach dropped at that thought.

No, he'd been here—right here—last night. I could still smell him on the blanket I'd wrapped around myself.

"No? Flour, maybe?"

"I took him some cookies after he helped me with the whole locked-out situation."

"That's still romantic. So much better than how Anson and I met."

"Swipe right," I said.

"Yep," she agreed. "And the rest is history." She and Anson had been dating three years before they got engaged. He was a good guy, but I wasn't a fan of app dating. It seemed a little contrived. Did the universe work in 5G?

"Okay, so tell me everything. Is it serious?"

"It's new, so no."

"Have you been to his games? Are you like, the recognized girlfriend?"

"I've been to one. And no, I don't think he's told anyone." I paused. "I mean, except his mom. Who is visiting from Italy right now."

"You've met his family? So this is totally serious!"

"I think you're making more of it than it is." His mother's stern face flashed across my mind. Lucia would definitely not support this being serious.

"Mom meeting is definitely on the top-ten list for ways to know a relationship is serious."

"What else is on that list?" I asked, curious now what my sister thought indicated next-level in a relationship.

"Toiletry exchange," she said. "Like if your toothbrush is at his place."

"Hmm."

"The presentation of a drawer or a space on the hanging rack in the closet, a house key, discontinuing the practice of making actual plans because it is just assumed that you'll be together . . ."

"Okay, well we don't have most of those things. So not serious." My heart gave a little squeeze in protest as I said this.

"Hmm," Helly sounded like she wasn't worried about this. "How's his mom? Nice?"

His mom wasn't quite what I'd call nice. She didn't seem to like me much, but I didn't think it was personal. "Not sure she loves me, actually."

"That's not good."

"Why? I'm not dating her." I was starting to feel a little judged in general. Like the whole relationship was under a spotlight it just didn't need.

Helly sighed. "You know, with guys, what their mothers think means a lot."

I thought about that. Marcus had introduced me to his family, and they'd liked me. But of course, they drank the same Kool-Aid my own parents did, and were fans of anyone who was sacrificing freedom, happiness, and experience of the world in the name of doing impressive things that society considered important.

"I'm also working on a song with Teresa Palmer."

"What? What does that mean?"

I explained that I'd sent her a track—not mentioning that it had been an accident—and that Teresa had liked it and wanted to shop it around out in LA. Saying it out loud made it kind of scary and I hoped I hadn't jinxed myself somehow.

"Damn, girl." There. Now my sister sounded sufficiently impressed. More importantly, I'd distracted her from any further dissection of the situation with Goalie. "Well, let me know what happens there." She sighed. "Your life sounds so exciting."

"Yours isn't?"

"I mean . . . it's just the same. Work, come home to Anson. Dinner with Mom and Dad on Thursdays . . . "

It did sound repetitive. But also . . . reliable. Comforting, in a way. But that was only because Helly followed her expected path and Mom and Dad were proud of her. Facing them every week would be rough for me, which was part of why I wasn't there.

"But it's good, right? You're happy? It's what you wanted."

"It's what I wanted. Just a little boring sometimes."

"I get it." Why did boring sound nice suddenly?

"What's the next exciting thing in your life? I need vicarious stimulation."

"Well, I'm supposed to be heading over to Stephano's soon. His mom is cooking and I think the whole team is coming over." Which, by the way, was a little terrifying.

"Holy goalie," she said again. "Get pics."

"Ummm, I'll try." I would not try. That would be weird. "Love you."

"Love you too. Stay out of trouble."

"You too."

I hung up and breathed deeply, nestling myself into the spot where I'd lain with Stephano just hours before. If I closed my eyes and breathed deeply enough, I could almost feel him still there, his essence imbued in the fibers of the blanket, the pillows of the couch.

It turned out that working hard to inhale someone's essence was exhausting. Or maybe it was getting only a few hours of sleep that tired one out. Either way, I conked out and didn't regain consciousness until almost five o'clock. The afternoon sun was slanting through the trees on the far side of the yard, painting the snow a soft gold.

And I needed to shower and head next door.

Fifteen minutes later, I was walking up Stephano's front walk, which he'd clearly shoveled for the evening's festivities. (Seeing that from my doorstep was what convinced me to be a proper lady and use the sidewalk instead of traipsing across the lawn.) There were five big shiny cars parked in his driveway, and more on the street. Hockey players liked fancy cars, I guessed. Nerves bubbled within me at the idea of meeting the entire Wombats team. What had Stephano told them about us?

When I reached the door, I could hear the faint din of masculine voices inside, and I stood there a moment listening for Stephano's. But as I heard someone shout out something that sounded like "Banana pudding," I realized that Goalie wasn't typically loud. I wondered if he was different around his team? But his mother was inside too. I couldn't imagine him yelling about pudding with his mom there. I was about to push the doorbell button when the door swung open.

At first I was confused by what appeared to be an empty doorway, but then I lowered my gaze a couple feet to find a small blond girl holding the door open and staring up at me, suspicion in her narrowed gaze.

"You don't play hockey," she told me.

"Nope."

"And you don't live here."

"Ah, no. Next door."

"I live next door to Sillllvester's family."

I did not know who Silllvester was, but this announcement seemed to come with the expectation that I would be impressed by this news.

"That's great," I told her. "I guess we all live next door to someone, huh?"

She lifted a hand to her little face and tilted her head as she considered this. "Not if you're an ogre and you live in a cave out in the woods with no one around for miles."

"Well, yeah, maybe not then."

We stood there for what felt like a long time, the little person blocking my entrance and considering me. It was beginning to snow again.

"How'd you know I was out here?" I asked her.

"I didn't. I wanted to see the snow."

"Oh, well, do you think I can come in?"

"There's a lot of people here. It might be a bad time." She glanced over her shoulder like a bouncer guarding a velvet rope in front of a club.

Did I need to bribe her or something? I didn't think showing cleavage would work in this particular situation.

"I was invited," I told her.

"By who?"

"By Stephano."

She shook her head. "Don't know him." She stepped back and began to shut the door, and irritation mingled with the cold that was beginning to seep through my body. Was I seriously being cockblocked by a five-year-old? I decided that as soon as she shut the door I'd ring the bell, hopefully attracting some grown-up attention. But there was no need. Just before the door shut all the way, a meaty hand wrapped the edge of it and it opened again.

There, with one hand on the little person's shoulder, was one of Stephano's teammates. And he looked far friendlier than the tiny doorperson.

"Hey," he said, his voice full of humor. "Did Katie give you the third degree?"

"I think she'd just decided not to allow me in," I told him. "I'm Hillary. I live next door."

The guy's smile broadened. "Saw you at the game," he said. "Between you and me, we're all rooting for you and Mizzoni. Maybe you can lighten him up a bit, show him there's more to life than perfectly ironed briefs."

"He irons his underwear?"

The guy shrugged. "I mean, probably." He stepped back and opened the door, his hand pulling the small blond person back with him. "I'm Sly," he said. "Come on in."

"This is Silllllvester," the little girl said, as if I should have known this all along.

"Thanks." I stepped past the little girl and brushed the snow from my shoulders. "Nice to meet you."

"This is Katie," Sly told me, looking down fondly at the little girl. "Her mom and I are engaged."

My heart did a little flip. "Oh, that's great," I told him. I loved love. At least for other people. It was so much less complicated when I wasn't actually involved. I hoped it would all work out for them.

We moved into the living room, which looked smaller than it had previously, since now it was filled with a variety of enormous men covering every surface.

"Hillary, meet the Wombats." Sly gestured around and then ushered me toward the couch. "This is Corny, Simpson, and Elks," he told me, gesturing at three guys who all turned to smile up at me.

"Tyler, Cade, and Freddy," the first one—Corny—said. "We do have first names, Sly."

"News to me," Sly laughed.

"Hello," I told him. "Nice to meet you guys."

"Nice to meet you," Cade said as the other guy smiled and then they returned their attention to the hockey game on the television.

Sly continued his introductions. "That over there is Rock Stevens, and next to him is Samuels."

"Rock is his real, actual name," Katie told me in a high-pitched voice. Then she burst into a fit of giggles.

A pretty woman with a blond ponytail crossed the room, clearly alerted by Katie's giggles, and stopped in front of me. "Hi, I'm Clara. This one belongs to me." She put a hand on Katie's head.

"So does this one," said Sly stepping closer to her and looking exceptionally pleased about it when she put a hand on him too.

"I'm Hillary," I told her. "It's nice to meet you."

"You too," she said with a smile.

"I think I drank some of your cider," I told her. "I'll replace it."

Clara looked confused, but before she could respond, Luca appeared at my side then. "Hi Hillary. It's nice to see you. Want to play Super Smash Bros?"

Just then Stephano came around the corner from the kitchen. "Luca, she didn't come over to hide in the den with you playing video games."

"Later," I whispered to Luca.

He grinned and headed for the kitchen, with Clara, Katie, and Sly just behind him, and Stephano leaned in and kissed my cheek, a faint blush climbing his stubbled jaw. "Glad you made it."

A loud cheer came from the couch as something important happened in the game, and Stephano steered me toward the kitchen, seating me at the counter between two other women.

"Hillary, meet Drea Coppersmith." He gestured toward the dark-haired woman to my right.

"I'm married to Rock," she said. "If you're trying to figure everything out. It's overwhelming at first."

"Nice to meet you," I told her.

"And this is Sarah Houstein." He indicated the woman on my left, who held a baby in her arms and gave me a weary smile.

"I go with Chris," she said, gesturing across the counter at yet another big guy.

"Okay," I said. "It'll take me a while to remember everyone, but I'm happy to meet you."

"I get it," Drea said, smiling at me. "These men are a lot."

"Ah, you are here." This was directed at me from across the counter. Stephano's mother. She wore an apron and had a mitt on one of her hands, which she removed and practically threw at me. "Lasagna needs to come out of the oven."

"Mamma," Stephano said, his voice full of warning.

"She can help," his mother said, giving me a meaningful look.

I slid off my stool and fetched the lasagna, setting it on a hot pad on the counter.

"You can finish the antipasto," she said, suddenly at my side.

"Okay." I glanced around. I did not know how to finish the

antipasto. I wasn't sure what antipasto was, but it seemed like a poor time to admit this to Signora Mizzoni.

"Here." A strong hand was on my back, and a moment later, Stephano and I were shoulder to shoulder at the opposite counter. "Just roll a few of these." He showed me how to roll the meat and place it along the edge of the little platter. "Back home, the antipasto would be mainly seafood—cured salmon and anchovies, octopus . . . "

He handed me a little jar of pepperoncini and a fork.

"But here, we're using what I could get at the gourmet market."

"Looks good," I said, surveying the spread of olives and cheese, meat, and pickled veggies.

It should only have taken a moment or two to arrange the little platter, but I lingered, enjoying the warmth of Stephano's calm presence at my side. It felt like maybe he was drawing it out too, and I did my best to stop my spinning mind. It didn't matter what it meant or didn't mean. It felt nice to be near him. I'd hold on to that.

"Ah, good. Stephano, I need you here." Lucia pushed herself between us, breaking the moment. "Hillary, the trash is very full."

I was being put in my place, I sensed, but I didn't mind. Lucia had a lot on her mind, clearly, and I was standing in the way of what she wanted, which was for her son to come home. If I needed to take out the trash to keep the peace, I'd do it.

"I got it," came another deep voice from my left.

I turned to find one of the guys from the living room—Samuels, was it?—at my side.

"Oh, thanks," I said. I helped him wrestle the bag from the tall can. "I'll find a new bag."

He grinned at me, holding the stuffed trash bag up. "Any idea where this goes?"

"Garage?" I suggested.

We stared at each other a second longer, neither of us knowing where the garage might be, and then Stephano was back.

"I'll take that." He practically ripped the bag out of the other man's hands and disappeared through a side door.

"Well okay," I laughed. "It's John Samuels, right?"

"Yeah," the guy said, giving me a bright smile as we both moved to the sink to wash our hands. "Not Stephano's favorite teammate."

I frowned at him as I waited for the water. He was soaping his hands and still looked cheerful despite his words.

"Why not?"

"I think he believes I was brought here to replace him."

"You're a goalie."

"Right."

"Got it," I said, scrubbing my own hands as he dried his. "So he feels threatened."

"I do not feel threatened by the puppy." Stephano appeared behind us, and he did not look especially happy to find us chatting about him.

"Puppy?" John and I said at the same time.

Stephano let out a heavy sigh. "Never mind." He turned away. My eyes followed him back to his teammates on the couch, a little tinge of worry seeping into my mind.

"You might be right," I told the other man. "But he'll probably come around."

John shrugged and headed back for the living room just as Stephano's mother appeared, shoving a pile of plates into my hands. "Put these on the end of the counter there."

She was setting up a kind of buffet on the counter, and the sheer quantity of dishes appearing from various parts of the kitchen was impressive.

"Did you cook all night?" I asked her.

"I rose early." She sniffed this, and I felt the judgment aimed directly at me.

The hair rose on my neck in defense. "I'm sorry I wasn't here to help."

"No matter now. At least you'll be here to clean."

It was clear I couldn't win here. If I had come early, I was certain I would have been made to feel I was in the way. Maybe this was easier.

Too much scrutiny would only reveal one of two things:

- That Stephano and I were only pretending to date, or
- That I was starting to wish it was all real.

CHAPTER 19
STEPHANO

THE ONE WHERE ROCK STEVENS EATS LASAGNA

As predicted, Mamma made enough food to feed an army. Or a hockey team. And the guys were not complaining. I watched Sly Remington single-handedly demolish half the pan of lasagna. Luckily, Mamma made three.

It was nice, actually. I liked sitting back with my own plate in my own house and seeing it full of life and chatter. Full of people who mattered to me. There were groups of people in every corner of my usually empty house, and while it wasn't as tidy as I liked it, I found I preferred it this way. Alive. I didn't even say anything when Simpson put a piece of garlic bread down on the coffee table on only a napkin. I'd have to spray that spot later to cut the grease, but it was going to be okay.

And it was nice having Hillary here, at my side. No one on the team had asked too many questions yet, and that was fine with me. It was hard enough lying to my mother, and I was only managing that because she was so distracted with the offer on the winery and her plans to drag me home whether I liked it or not.

The guys? I couldn't lie to them. Most of them, however, weren't looking for declarations of my intentions about anything beyond the game. If I wanted to bring a different girl to every party? Well, actually, that was something we had a rule against, thanks to Rock Stevens and his previous puck bunny proclivities. But no one would confuse Hillary for one of the girls Rock had once been fond of. She wasn't hanging all over me, for one thing. She wasn't flirting with my teammates, either. Her clothes fit appropriately, and she knew so little about hockey, there was no chance I was just some part of a master plan to land a hockey player.

Instead, she was at my side, and had drawn John Samuels into conversation about music somehow. I didn't know the guy had an interest in anything beyond taking my spot on the team, but I supposed I hadn't really asked him. Now I listened as she worked her magic, getting him to tell her things he probably didn't tell his own girlfriend. I shoved down my annoyance and did my best to think of him as a teammate, not a rival.

"I mean," he was saying. "I've always wanted to play pro hockey. But I was going to be a lawyer."

"That's incredible," she said, and the golden glow around her seemed to burn even brighter. "Don't most guys who want to go pro focus totally on that?"

"I think a lot do," Samuels said. "But for most of those guys, it's not a realistic goal, right? So I just figured I'd better have a backup plan. And by the time I was in college, things worked out in ways I couldn't have predicted. Hockey was just something I got lucky enough to be good at."

"Okay, but you can't just be good to go pro. You have to be amazing. You must've known you had a shot."

Samuels chuckled. "I guess that's just my personality, though. I don't want to count my chickens and all that. I was doing my best to focus on what I could control—which didn't mean I wasn't working at hockey. But I came up watching guys like Mizzoni here . . . " he trailed off as our eyes met, his head shaking slightly back and forth. "How could I hope to match him?" The sincerity in his voice surprised me.

Hillary glanced at me then, her eyebrows high on her pretty

face. I had the sense she was trying to get me to say something, but as usual, I didn't have anything to say to the puppy.

"I think that's even better, then," she told him. "You're humble. You know what you have."

He did this bashful head nod thing and wrapped a hand around the back of his neck and then shot her a smile I was pretty sure lots of girls found charming. My hand landed on Hillary's thigh without me telling it to.

"And you?" he was asking now. "What kinds of plans and dreams do you have? You're in music, right?"

Hillary was quiet for a long beat, and then she blew out a breath. "Honestly? I don't know what I'm doing. I move around a lot. But yeah, music is really important to me."

"Do you get tired of moving?"

Honest question. Why hadn't I thought to ask her that?

"In the past, not really. It was almost like . . . like I needed to keep going or something might catch me. Does that make any sense?"

"Sounds like fear."

I watched the side of Hillary's face as she had this honest conversation with my teammate, and realized I hadn't really spent the time to learn what she wanted, where she was headed. And Samuels was managing deep conversation over a plate of Bolognese.

My thumb rubbed a line along the side of her thigh as Hillary answered. "Maybe. Yeah, probably."

"So what's next?"

She shrugged and glanced at me, giving me a flicker of a smile. "I don't really know. I'm only here a month. So, just a few more weeks."

I felt like she'd elbowed me in the gut, and a surging need flooded me suddenly. I didn't want her to leave. The idea that I hadn't even really gotten to know her, and that she was already contemplating her next adventure—without me—it made me feel sick.

"Hey," I said, rising and reaching for her hand. "Steal you for a minute?"

She looked back and forth between me and the puppy. "Uh yeah, of course. Excuse me?"

"Yeah. Nice talking to you, Hillary." Samuels smiled as I pulled her away.

"What's up?" she asked as I practically picked her up and carried her to the back of the house. We passed the den where Luca was focused on the video games he was playing, and Mamma and Uncle Julius sat on the couch, apparently deep in conversation.

I all but shoved Hillary into my room and shut the double doors behind her, locking them. My heart was hammering, my head spun, and all I knew was that I didn't want her with Samuels. I wanted her with me. Now. Maybe tomorrow. Maybe for a lot of tomorrows.

"I just . . . " I stepped close to her, pressing her back against the door. I felt like a jerk, but I didn't want to stop. I wanted her. "I just wanted to get you alone for a minute."

Her arms slid around my neck lightly, resting on my shoulders as her fingers toyed with the hair at the back of my neck. She relaxed against the door, a playful smile lighting her face as my hands pressed the wood on either side of her head. "Oh yeah?"

"Yeah." I stepped closer, putting myself between her legs, our bodies centimeters away from being pressed together from top to bottom. My hands fell to her shoulders.

"Did it make you jealous? Me talking to John?"

Her tone was teasing, but her words struck pretty damned close to the truth. "Maybe." I crowded her more, letting myself inhale the sweet summertime of her scent, finding that undertone of something exotic. I didn't like her calling him John, either.

"So you needed to stake your claim?" she whispered, her hand wrapping the back of my neck.

We were so close now that the only answer I could give her was the one I offered. I pressed my mouth to hers and felt her yield beneath me, a little moan escaping into my mouth that drove me nuts. I took her in my arms, giving myself better leverage, and felt my need ramp up when she molded herself to me. Her tongue met mine, and I spun her so that her back was to the huge four-poster bed in the center of my room.

We were tongues and hands and heat, pulling clothing away from our bodies and dropping it in a trail to the bed. When we got there, I pulled back and scooped her up in my arms. My hip gave a silent protest, but I ignored it and deposited her in the center of the bed—my Goldilocks in nothing but a bra and a pair of worn jeans.

"You're so fucking pretty," I told her, giving myself a minute to just appreciate her. Hillary's chest was heaving, and she reached for me, her pull a magnetic draw I couldn't ignore.

"Come here, Goalie."

I pushed down my slacks and joined her atop the thick duvet.

Her hands traced the muscles of my torso and she rolled us so I was on my back, Hillary sitting atop my aching erection and toying with me gently. She dropped kisses over my pecs, her hands tracing soft lines across my stomach, around my waist. She scooted lower, putting herself at mouth level with my straining dick, and I groaned. Just the sight of her there could send me off.

When her eyes shot up to meet my gaze, that bright light that always surrounded her pulsing with heat, I thought I would lose it. But then she slipped her fingers beneath the waist of my boxer briefs and pushed them down, freeing my erection and then taking it in her hand. Sensation coursed through me as she gripped me and then gave my head a cursory lick with her soft tongue.

I let my eyes shut as she worked, her mouth making circles around the tip as her hand pumped me and I struggled for control. But when she sucked me deep, my eyes popped open. That was a sight I'd have imprinted on my mind for the rest of my life. Goldilocks with her soft blond hair and bright golden aura, sucking my dick while everyone I knew was just outside the door.

As hard as it was, I didn't think it was fair to let her do all the work, so I made myself pull her back up to my mouth to kiss her. "That was . . ."

"Well, you didn't let me finish. You don't even know what it could've been," she whispered.

"I wanted a turn," I told her, rolling her to her back and planting kisses in a line down her stomach, and peeled her jeans from her body. Her panties were lacy and soft, a faded blue color that felt perfect for Hillary. She was just like those pretty undergarments—soft and special, comfortable, but beautiful. Every time I saw her, I wanted to wrap myself up in her and never leave.

So for now, I set myself to making her feel as good as I possibly could. I pushed the scrap of fabric aside and inhaled her scent—so fucking sexy.

"You're soaked," I told her, sliding my finger through her slick folds.

She moaned in response, and when I followed the finger with my tongue, she gasped. She wasn't quiet, and my mother was just a room away, but I didn't care.

I sucked in her clit, gently at first, as my fingers teased her. When she writhed beneath my attention, I slid two fingers inside her and picked up the rhythm.

"Oh god," she whispered. "Goalie . . . "

I loved it when she called me Goalie, and it pushed me on. I listened to every breath she took, every noise she made, and tuned myself to the way her walls fluttered against my fingers. She was close. And when she locked her feet behind my neck and her hands pulled ferociously at my hair, she came—gloriously and at length. And kind of loudly.

I pushed myself back up her body to swallow the last of her moans with my mouth and then reached to pull the duvet around us.

"Shit. Was I loud?" she giggled, pushing her face into my neck as I pulled her close.

"A little bit," I told her. I loved every second of it.

She pulled away to look at me, her eyes round and wide. "You don't think your mom heard? She already hates me."

"She doesn't hate you. Her previous requirements for appropriate girlfriends for me were very loose. You definitely fit them."

"She acts like she hates me."

I thought about that. I didn't like Hillary feeling unwelcome, but I knew what my mother's agenda was. Still, I hated how rude she'd been. "I'll talk to her. You're just in her way right now. She thinks if we weren't together that I'd hop on a plane back to Italy, I guess."

"Would you?"

"No. My life is here." Even as I said this, I knew it wasn't that easy.

Hillary's body was warm and soft, and one of her hands had slid along the side of my hip and was cupping my balls. "Yeah?" she purred as that hand moved upward, teasing me.

"Yeah," I managed to answer, my brain begging to short circuit as her hand started working my shaft. "For now, at least. Till Samuels . . . " I let it go. I did not really want puppy in my bed with Hillary and me.

Hillary didn't say anything else either, slipping back down my body and taking me into her mouth as her hand continued to work my shaft.

I was a goner. It didn't take long before I was warning her off. But she didn't move, and I felt a bone-deep satisfaction as the tension and stress of the past day shot out of me accompanied by groans from both of us that made the whole thing that much hotter. This time, I was the one struggling to stay quiet.

"Fuck, you're hot, Goldilocks."

She pushed herself up my chest and let her weight rest on me, warm and perfect. "So are you, Goalie. But do you think anyone is missing us out there?"

The sounds of the party hadn't softened, and they created a kind of bubble that made me feel safe in here with Hillary. Like we had a separate little piece of the world all to ourselves. But I supposed it was rude to abandon one's own party.

I sighed and wrapped her in my arms. "I don't want to care."

"But you're the host."

"I am."

"And you like to do the right thing and follow the rules. You like things just so."

"Just so, huh?"

She winked at me, and I felt a little twist of satisfaction inside my chest that she understood me so well, and yet she was still here, in my arms.

"We should get dressed," she said.

"We should."

"Maybe you can come over later?"

I shouldn't. I had an early practice the next day. "Okay."

She grinned at me, and everything about her glowed. I had an errant thought that all I needed in the world was to find a way to keep her close, that keeping her near would make my whole world lighter and brighter too.

But she was like a firefly floating over a summer field—just passing by on the way to somewhere else. And if I put her in a jar, she would flicker and fade, and eventually disappear.

Besides, forever wasn't part of our deal.

CHAPTER 20
HILLARY

PRINCESS PEACH WILL KICK YOUR
PATOOTIE

That was twice now. Twice I'd fallen into bed with the goalie, and twice I'd come away feeling like I was just making everything harder. It was bad enough being around him in general, with him being so conscientious and sweet, attentive to how I'm doing, how I feel. But now? Knowing he's equally attentive in the bedroom . . . it was mentally devastating.

We wandered back out to the party, Stephano's mother immediately stepping to his side to whisper in his ear (once he bent down, of course). I cringed. Was she scolding him for having loud sex during a party?

John Samuels had been in the den with Luca when we'd walked by, and after picking a water bottle from the tub on the kitchen counter, I went back to join them.

"I think I'm ready to defeat you in Super Smash Bros," I told Luca, who responded with a cackle.

"Unlikely," he said.

"You like video games?" John asked, grinning at me and scooting over on the couch to make room for me.

"I don't not like them." I'd played a few times before, but not for years. Video games had been a med school thing, a way to blow off steam that didn't require too much time away from studying and didn't leave me inebriated or exhausted. I wasn't good at them, but that didn't mean I didn't talk shit. I'd learned from the best. Marcus had won every single time.

"She likes not being around Mamma," Luca guessed.

"That's not really true," I said, but my insincerity was difficult to hide. I didn't want to be around Lucia right then, with her perceptive gaze and disapprovingly pursed lips. It wasn't up to me whether she got her way or not, but I understood why she thought it was.

"Princess Peach," I said, when Luca handed me a controller and pointed at the character selection screen.

"She knows the characters," John stage whispered. "We're in trouble."

"You're definitely in trouble," I said. And then I proceeded to mash every single button on my controller as fast as possible. In the past, this hadn't been a super effective strategy, but today I got lucky.

"Holy shit, you weren't kidding," John laughed.

"How are you winning?" Luca asked, turning to me with wide eyes.

"I have many hidden talents," I laughed, every bit as shocked as they were.

We kept playing and my lead began to fade, and John asked me questions as we played. It should have been concerning—after all, the more I talked, the more likely someone would figure out that while the goalie and I had something going on now, we were lying about a past together.

"You and Mizzoni been together long?"

"No, not at all."

"So it's not serious?"

"I . . . " I thought about that as I did a flying, twisting leap right off the side of the platform on the screen. "I don't know."

"Sorry, not trying to be pushy."

"It's fine," I said quickly, conscious that Luca was probably a direct conduit to Stephano's mom. "We're just figuring things out."

"So what's the plan after you're done housesitting?"

I was beginning to regret telling John so much about my situation. I was pretty sure Luca and Lucia had believed I owned the house next door.

"Ah, I don't know, really. I might go to Los Angeles, do a little recording, performing."

"Or maybe you come to Italy when Stephano comes home," Luca suggested.

I stifled the laugh that threatened to shoot out of me at the ridiculousness of the suggestion. Goalie and I barely talked about tomorrow, and he certainly wasn't going to want our fake relationship to span international trade lines. "Maybe," I said, but it was unconvincing.

John's character Link unleashed a torrent of kicks and punches on Princess Peach then, and I lost track of both the game and the conversation. I'd never really understood Smash Bros in the first place. What was even the objective? It was like chaos on the screen, constant motion and no clear goals or outcomes beyond crazy movement.

A lot like my life, actually.

"Where do you live if you don't live next door?" Luca asked, putting down his controller and turning to look at me.

"I mean . . . I had a place in LA a while ago." I tried not to picture the apartment Marcus and I had shared on Robertson. Every time I conjured the image, I saw him there, lounging on the couch with his easy smile, making me eggs in the kitchen, locking the front door as we both headed out to school. "I gave it up."

"You don't actually have a home?" Luca said, seeming not to understand this. "Furniture? Photos? Where do you keep your things?"

This was getting a little personal now, and I wasn't sure how much of what I said would get back to Lucia. Or Stephano, for that matter.

"I have a storage unit, and some of my stuff is at my parents' house. Another round?" I lifted my controller, hoping to distract Luca, who'd become a little too interested in my life.

"There you are." Lucia stepped into the room behind us. She was looking right at me. Guilt bubbled inside me, though I'd been doing nothing wrong. "Come. There is much to do."

Despite her commanding tone, I was relieved to drop the controller to the table and stand, leaving the interrogation behind. "Thanks for the game," I told the guys. And then I followed Lucia from the room so she could suggest in a not-so-subtle way that I wasn't being a very good hostess.

"People are beginning to depart." We walked by the front door just as Sly helped Clara and Katie on with their coats.

"Hey Hillary, it was nice to meet you officially. Look after our goalie, will ya?"

I smiled at Sly's easy attitude, and at the way he hoisted Katie easily to his hip as she laughed.

"It was so nice meeting you all," I told them.

"Very nice to meet you," Lucia echoed.

Clara gave me a hug, and then they disappeared out the door, followed rapidly by the rest of the team. Within a half hour, the house was quiet again, and I began gathering scattered plates and glasses.

"You don't have to do that," Stephano told me, taking a stack of plates from my hands.

"I'm happy to help," I told him. I could feel Lucia's eyes on us as we tidied up, and she was always nearby as I scrubbed platters and boxed leftovers in the kitchen. When the place was neat and shiny again, I was ready to get back to Teresa's, away from the eagle eyes of Lucia Mizzoni.

"Thank you for all the work you did here," I told her. "The food was incredible."

"Of course," she said, sniffing a bit. "I love to cook for my boys."

I wasn't sure if she meant the hockey team or just Stephano and Luca, but either way, it was pretty clear she didn't mean me.

Stephano met me at the door. "Thanks for coming over," he said, his voice a low rumble in my ear that sent my tummy twisting.

It was dark out now, and the snow scattered in our yards twinkled beneath the streetlights.

"Thanks for, uh . . . having me," I told him, hoping he'd catch my double entendre.

"Literally, any time," he murmured, pulling me close.

"Come over?" I whispered, pressing my face into his neck, breathing in the scent of him.

"Give me a half hour," he said.

"I'll leave the door unlocked."

"Don't do that." He gave me a stern look, pulling back to make sure I saw he was serious.

The twisty thing inside me heated at his concern. "Okay," I said. "Text me when you're on your way?"

"Or maybe I'll just climb the fence and appear in your backyard."

I smiled up at him, feeling a connection I was going to miss when it was time to end all this.

"Stephano. A word?" Lucia appeared at our side and I gave Stephano a quick kiss on the cheek.

"I won't keep you. Thanks again."

"Luca, walk her home," Lucia said, catching her younger son as he strolled by.

He let out a heavy sigh, but did as directed, all three of them ignoring my protests.

"Thanks," I told him when we'd reached my door.

"You're welcome," he said. "And for the record, I like you. I think you and my brother are good together." He said this like he was defending me somehow, and I knew he was the only visiting Mizzoni to feel this way.

"Thanks," I said, giving him a little kiss on the cheek before disappearing inside Teresa's warm house.

I went straight to the couch and snuggled into the corner again, checking my phone for messages.

My stomach soured when I went through three voicemails from the loan people. If I didn't send a payment soon, they were sending the account to collections. I dropped the phone and clenched my eyes shut. The universe was not helping me here.

I scanned through my banking app, trying to move money that did not exist into one place so I could make a payment. But the minimum payment at this point was a much bigger number than the one in my account. This was bad. I felt like I might throw up and did my best to force my mind to something else. I'd worry tomorrow.

The phone dropped to my lap and I snuggled down, letting my mind roll down the path it found inside me. What was I doing? Why had I let myself become entangled this way, to the point where Stephano's mom disliking me actually hurt my feelings? Why did I worry her feelings might disrupt things between us—when things between us were supposed to be temporary, anyway?

For the first time in a long time, I found myself longing for permanence. It wasn't that I'd changed my mind about anything, not really. It was more that I realized that sometimes it was nice to have something to hang onto when things were rough.

CHAPTER 21
STEPHANO

STAY GOLD, HILLARY

I sat down with Mamma and a cup of tea.

"Your friends are . . . exuberant." She gestured toward the pool area where Craft and Wylder might have gotten a bit tipsy and dared one another to swim. Since the pool was closed for the winter and tarped down, they settled for the hot tub. Aaron Craft had leaped in fully clothed, while Adam Wylder had stripped down completely naked. In front of the windows. While my mother sat just inside. At least that had kept everyone from wondering where Hillary and I were.

"They're athletes, not princes," I said, maybe a little too bitterly.

"Your uncle says they care about you."

I lifted a shoulder. Of course they did. "Some of us have been playing together a decade. We travel together, we're away from home and family a lot. So . . . yeah."

Mamma nodded, staring down into her tea. Then she looked up at me, and I watched the determination come back into her eyes. "Julius does not think we should rebuild the winery."

That was a surprise. I would have expected Uncle Julius to be behind the plan. "Why not?"

"He is a sentimental old fool."

That didn't really answer the question.

"The investor called this morning."

Mamma seemed determined to go on without requiring an answer from me, so I sat still, waiting.

"He has another opportunity and wants our answer. In the next week."

I blew out a harsh breath—not quite a laugh. "That's ridiculous. I'm in the middle of the season. I can think about this after playoffs. He knows I'm a hockey player, obviously. Tell him we'll need to wait."

My mother dropped my gaze, staring at the glass tabletop, her shoulders crumpling slightly. When she looked up at me again, it was with shining dark eyes. My stomach twisted at the familiarity —Mamma's eyes had been sad like that for a long time after my father died.

"This is what I want," she whispered. "My sons at home where they belong. Their father's memory honored. Our family heritage restored. This is the way things should be, _piccolo_."

The fight left me at the use of Mamma's familiar term of endearment and at the evaporation of the tough, stern exterior she'd worn since arriving here. I hated seeing her this way, defeated and sad. I had to do something.

"Send me the investor's information. I will speak with him."

"Will you come home?" Her voice was quiet. A plea.

I stared at my mother, feeling the weight of the decision on my shoulders as the lateness of the hour and the stark quiet of my house settled around me. "I don't know. I have a career here. Friends. A home."

"A woman." Her mouth shut into a sharp line and she stood, head bowed as she rose. "I will see you in the morning."

"I'm going to practice early," I said. "I'll see you when I return. Around noon."

She nodded and disappeared into the back of the house. I carried our mugs to the sink and then pulled on a coat. I didn't want to think about our family, my heritage. I wanted to not think. With Hillary.

I texted her that I was on my way. A moment later, I was knocking softly on her door, which swung open almost immediately.

Hillary had swapped her jeans for leggings and the Wombats sweatshirt she'd worn home the first time I'd met her, and everything about her looked soft and welcoming. I stepped inside, shut the door, and pulled her into my arms.

"Hi Goalie," she whispered, her arms going around me.

Holding her felt like a cure for all the distraction and confusion inside me. She was warm and soft, and as I inhaled her fresh scent, I allowed myself to forget everything Mamma had said, to become completely present. Here. With my Goldilocks.

"Hi," I said, finally releasing her but keeping her hand in mine.

"You want anything to drink? Hungry?" Hillary asked, looking up at me from beneath thick dark lashes.

"Just you," I said, earning a wicked little smile.

Hillary pulled me into the living room, but I didn't settle onto the couch, giving her hand a little tug toward the hallway instead.

"In a hurry?"

"I need to touch you," I whispered.

Hillary's eyes darkened, and she turned, leading me down the hallway to a bedroom painted in a dark shade of teal. It was beautiful, but it wasn't the master. "You didn't take the master?"

She smiled. "It feels wrong. I never do."

There it was, that way she had of being in the world—comfortable, but unassuming. She was adaptable, fitting herself into whatever situation she was in, molding to the world around her. I wondered if my own rigidity was part of my problem. I was so structured that when changes came around, I couldn't adapt, couldn't bend. But how could I possibly bend to make both my mother and myself happy?

I didn't want to think about any of it.

Hillary led me to the bed, covered in a satiny deep gray duvet, and then crawled over the covers. I followed eagerly, climbing over her on my hands and knees, looking down at the way her shining golden hair fanned around her beneath me, that aura glowing all around her.

Since we'd been together just hours earlier, my need for her surprised me a little, but it felt like if I didn't get my arms around her, if I didn't feel every inch of her against me as soon as possible, I'd explode. I had never heard of anyone spontaneously combusting from an overwhelming need for someone else. But I didn't want to be the first.

And mostly, I just wanted to stop thinking and worrying about what was right or wrong, about what Mamma wanted or what the Wombats needed. I wasn't a selfish person. But at that moment, I didn't want to consider anyone else.

Me.

And Hillary.

And when my mouth met hers again, everything else slid away. I kissed her slowly, ready to take my time now that we had it, now that there was no one waiting for us, looking for us. But she had other ideas.

Hillary's hands were frantic, pulling at my clothing and sliding themselves over my flesh. She moaned and writhed beneath me, fighting the slow pace I was trying to set, and finally I let her push me over onto my back and smiled up at the little look of triumph on her flushed face.

"You're going too slow," she said, grinning at me as she whipped the sweatshirt off over her head. She didn't have a bra beneath it, and the sight of her sitting atop me, glowing, her lovely breasts asking to be touched—well, it made me decide maybe slow could wait. I reached for her, taking those perfect globes into my palms and then rubbing my thumbs across the pretty pink nipples as Hillary's head fell back.

Her hands moved to my waist, unfastening my pants and sliding down my body to remove them. Her hair trailed across my torso as she worked, and I sucked in a breath—It tickled.

"It's crazy how much I want you," she said, pressing herself against me as she moved back up my body. She'd removed her own leggings and now we were flesh to flesh, and I took a moment to close my eyes and just feel her pressed along me, warm and soft and perfect.

And then she was moving again, kissing me as her hips ground into my erection, pressing her soft wet center against me. It was electrifying, and need and want mixed with something like happiness, flooding my nervous system with a series of signals that made me wish this could go on forever.

"I'm on birth control," she said, pausing in her movements for a second to look me in the eye.

I stared up at her, so beautiful and bright, knowing what she was suggesting. "I haven't been with anyone in a long time," I told her. "And never without a condom."

"Oh. Is this . . ."

I answered by pressing my hips up slightly, lining myself up perfectly with her soft wet entrance. She braced her hands on my chest and pressed back, lifting those glorious breasts in front of me again as she arched her back to take me in. She moved slowly, taking a little at a time and then moving back off until I thought I might scream. I wanted to feel her, all of her, as much of her as I could possibly experience at once—and the sensation of being inside her bare, with nothing to dampen the experience—It was heady.

Finally she slid up and then all the way down, taking the length of me inside her, and I groaned with pleasure. I could feel her heat, along with the most tantalizing little flutters and pulses. It was almost impossible not to thrust up into her, but I made myself stay still. She stared into my eyes, a tiny smile pulling up the corners of her lips.

"Shit, Goalie . . ."

"You're fucking perfect, Goldilocks."

Those words unlocked something in her. She sat up, her hands braced on my chest, and began pumping me for real, her beautiful curves undulating before me as she took me deep and then slid off, driving down deep again in the next second. It was like ratcheting up higher and higher in a roller coaster, approaching the apex of the tracks, knowing you'd be flinging down the other side at any second.

When she arched her back, taking her own breasts into her hands, I nearly lost it.

"Oh god," she said, her chin jutting toward the ceiling as she sat over me, riding me with her golden skin glistening and her hair all around her. "Oh, my god." She dropped one hand to my chest, and I moved one of mine from her hip to add just a bit of pressure to her clit. Her eyes flew open and then her mouth made a round O just before she let out a series of moans that were the most erotic thing I'd ever heard.

She came apart around me, and I struggled to wait, to contain my own release so I could enjoy hers. And just as her moans quieted, I let go, every ounce of tension and stress unspooling with the waves of pleasure that hammered through me.

When she was slumped over my chest, both of our breaths ragged, and my arms banded across her back, I felt happier and more relaxed than I could recall feeling. Ever.

And that was why words I didn't plan slipped from my lips.

"Stay," I heard myself murmur. "I wish you could just stay with me."

"I'm not going anywhere," she said, a chuckle in her voice.

"You're only here a few more weeks."

"You're the one thinking of making an international move," she said, lifting her head to look into my eyes.

I sighed. Just like that, all the stress and worry were back.

Practice was early the next morning, and when I woke to my jingling alarm, it didn't feel like I'd had nearly enough sleep. Because I hadn't. I'd stumbled back from Hillary's at nearly three in the morning and rolled out of bed just a few hours later. Thankfully, Mamma was still in bed when I left, so there were no complicated conversations to add to the already packed concerns in my head.

"Thanks for having us last night," Samuels said from where he sat with a yogurt and a cup of coffee in front of him.

"Yeah Mizzoni. Let us know if your mom needs us to come eat any more lasagna," Rock chimed in.

"I don't think there's any more lasagna left in the world after your efforts last night," I told him, sitting with my own coffee and eggs.

"You look like shit," Rock told me.

"That's not very nice," I said.

"Yeah, but you look like the kind of shit that was maybe up late with a very pretty blonde distraction," Rock added. "So maybe it was worth it. I mean, your aura's a little off, but—"

"Shut it," I warned. My aura had been off since I was eighteen. Darker than it had been when my dad had been alive. One more thing to wonder and worry about. Also, Rock didn't know that. He was just giving me shit.

"I like Hillary a lot," Samuels said.

I turned to look at him, ready to snap something back, but his face was open and smiling. He was being honest, and there didn't seem to be an ounce of innuendo there.

"Yeah," I agreed. "Me too."

"So we'll do some of those drills today?" Samuels asked, his eager puppy eyes back.

"Sure," I said.

"See you out there." He rose and headed for the lockers, and I took a deep chug of coffee, wishing it could make up for four hours of missed shuteye.

"Pretty grumpy for a guy getting sex on the regular," Rock commented.

"I'm just tired," I told him, taking a deep breath and steeling myself for what was sure to be a rough practice. It should have irked me to have Rock so deep in my business, but I found I didn't mind. I liked talking about Hillary.

"She seems like she might be worth it," he added.

I thought about that. Hillary had shown up completely unexpected in my life. At a time when I really wasn't even thinking about dating. And even though she was another complication in what was beginning to feel like a tangled mess of unsolvable problems, I was glad she was there. In fact, I didn't like thinking about what would happen when she moved away, went on with her life. I didn't like it at all.

Practice was exhausting, and my hip screamed all the way through it, forcing me to acknowledge that soon something was going to have to give. I focused on helping Samuels, giving him some insights I'd spent the last decade picking up, and telling him what I knew about the Titans, who we were traveling to face on Thursday. Given the pain in my hip and the way everything felt like it was building into an enormous threatening wave that would undoubtedly topple over me soon, I knew he'd need to be ready. And so would I.

Like a child, I avoided Frank, who undoubtedly wanted to send me out for the MRI he'd been threatening. He'd worked on me after practice, and talked about it, and I'd slipped out before we could cement anything. But when I got home, Mamma made me think maybe some time in a steel tube would have been preferable.

"Stephano, sit. We need to talk." Mamma was speaking Italian again, now that no one else was around. I slipped back into my native tongue easily.

Mamma perched on one of the tall stools at the island, making her look even smaller than she was. But her stern face left no questions about the strength of her will or her opinions.

"Okay," I sighed, pulling a bottle of tea from the fridge and then sitting on the stool next to her, exhaustion sweeping through me. "Did you sleep well, Mamma?"

"Yes fine," she said. "I want to talk about Hillary."

Dread and anticipation warred inside me. Was Mamma finally going to give in and accept that I was with Goldilocks? Or had she figured out that we weren't actually together? At least we hadn't been when she'd arrived. "Okay. You like her?"

"Not important. She is after your money."

Mamma might as well have slapped me in the face. I sat up straighter and laughed. Of all the things Hillary might be accused of being, money-hungry was definitely not one of the ones I'd have come up with. Flighty and directionless? Maybe, but that was part of her charm. And maybe she just embraced her lack of certainty while the rest of us pretended to know what we were doing. Weren't we all just stumbling through life?

But she wouldn't take my money the couple times I'd tried to give it to her freely. She certainly wasn't scheming to steal it.

"She's not."

"Stephano, look at the facts. She has no home. Luca says she keeps her belongings in a storage locker and roams around, staying at other people's houses."

"She's a house sitter." Why the hell couldn't Luca keep his mouth shut?

"I think she knew exactly who lived next door when she agreed to house sit here."

I shook my head. It was a ludicrous idea. "I guarantee she didn't. Mamma, she didn't even know I was a hockey player when we met."

"As far as you know. She is a performer. She was acting."

This was insane. "Hillary is not after my money."

Mamma crossed her arms over her chest, her face stern. As I stared at her, trying to think of how to convince her, I noticed the lines around her eyes and mouth that hadn't been there before. There were scant streaks of gray in her dark hair, and her eyes looked slightly sunken. Mamma was getting older. I didn't like to notice it.

"I think you should not see her."

I'd had enough. "Mamma, I love you, but this is not your business. Hillary is a good person, and—"

"What color?"

"What?"

"You know what I am asking." Mamma knew I saw colors around people because I'd seen them since I was a child. When I was young, I'd use the colors I saw to describe people, asking things like, "when is the green man coming over again?" Mamma figured out what was going on, and had relied on me sometimes to vet people who came into our lives.

"Dark, Stephano?" Mamma knew that when I saw dark or nondescript colors, they'd often correlated with people whose intentions ended up being less than pure.

"Not even a little bit. It's a glimmering gold, Mamma."

"Hmph."

"It's not like the colors are definitive anyway," I told her. "You're looking a little smudgy lately, you know."

"It's because I am so worried."

I sighed. "I know." I took a sip of the tea. "I will call the investor today. We'll figure this out. But please, Mamma, leave Hillary out of it. And stop pressuring me to leave the team. The season is going well. We can talk about this when it ends."

She said nothing, but her face softened slightly.

"For now, let's just enjoy your visit."

She sighed, and after a moment, I stood. "I'll go call this guy now, and then we can talk about dinner."

I went to my office and shut the door, and then went to sit on the edge of my desk. I pulled up the contact Mamma had sent with the investor's name and number. There was no point putting this off. And if the man really did understand my position, he'd know I couldn't leave mid-season. He'd wait.

Emilio Marino.

I dialed.

There was no answer, only a generic voice mail prompt, so I left a message in Italian. "Hi. This is Stephano Mizzoni. My mother is here visiting me in Virginia, and she's told me about your interest in our wine, and in me. I'd like to discuss the details when you have time. Please give me a call back." I left him my number and hung up, and then joined my brother in the den to play video games.

That night we just hung out as a family. But every time I closed my eyes, I saw flashes of gold and felt a rush of warmth. I wanted more.

CHAPTER 22
HILLARY

FAKE IS A STATE OF MIND

For the next few days, Goalie and I worked hard at putting the "relationship" in "fake relationship." It felt like we'd moved past the pretense, and somehow had fallen into something far more real than either of us had ever intended.

Lucia went to bed early, leaving Luca to enjoy Stephano's television and video game console, which seemed to make him happy. And it left Stephano and me time to spend together. I didn't push to involve myself more in time with his family—it was clear enough that Lucia wasn't my biggest fan. I kept myself busy writing and recording. Whatever I had going on with the goalie had unleashed a storm of creativity I didn't even know I possessed.

"You know it isn't you, right?" Stephano said Tuesday night as he held me after we'd spent an hour rolling around in my bed.

"It's not? You sure about that, Goalie? I'm pretty sure if I was Italian and lived in the village you're from, she'd be just fine with me."

"That's what I mean. She's worried about the circumstances, not the person."

"I get it," I told him. But it still hurt my feelings a little bit that Stephano's mother didn't accept me.

Stephano traced a line up my arm as he held me, and I snuggled into him, timing my breath with his, feeling more in sync with him than I'd been with any other person.

"We should go out," he said quietly.

I glanced at the clock next to the bed. "It's pretty late."

He chuckled. "Not now. Tomorrow night. I want to take you on a real date." Those dark eyes found mine, and he looked hopeful, an easy smile on his usually stern features.

A little thrill shot through me. "Really? But what about your family?"

"They evidently intend to stay forever. They'll be okay."

"You know a real date would be slightly at odds with a fake relationship."

Stephano stiffened slightly beneath me, and the smile slipped away. "Does this feel fake to you?"

"Are you referring to the hard thing poking me in the hip?"

"Ignore that." A fragment of a smile lifted the corner of his mouth. "That's one hundred percent real. I meant this. All of this. You and me."

"It feels real," I said honestly.

"It does."

Warmth crept through me at the idea. We were dating for real? Was it possible Stephano felt the way I did? That maybe there was a chance for us? I pushed away all the uncertainty around our circumstances, ignoring Italy, music, and my very temporary time here.

"Go out with me," he said softly, following the words with a kiss on my temple.

"Okay," I agreed easily. "But you know what this means."

"What?"

"Karaoke." I grinned at him.

"Only for you," he said with a sigh. "But I'm taking you to dinner first."

"Deal."

Stephano had never spent the night, and even though I wondered what it would be like to wake up in his arms, an entire day ahead of us, I knew he had responsibilities I didn't share. When he left, I often spent another hour or two in bed, loving the smell of him on the sheets, the knowledge that he would be back soon, that this thing between us wasn't over yet.

And the morning after our talk about what might be real between us, I wondered what that really meant.

I had feelings for the goalie. There was no doubt there. And it seemed like that was mutual, an idea that gave me a giddy little thrill. But deciding we were real didn't change the situation ahead of us. I had two more weeks in Wilcox before Teresa returned. And Stephano hadn't said anything about his plans at the end of the season, only that he didn't want to return to Italy. But he didn't say he wasn't going to.

His mother was a strong force in his life, and I wondered exactly how much pressure she would exert to get what she wanted.

I lounged longer than I should have, and when my phone chimed on the nightstand next to me, I rolled over to pick it up.

HEL: Score any goals lately?

Me: More than I'd planned to. He asked me out, Hel.

HEL: Only you could do a relationship completely backward. You're supposed to get asked out before all the sex stuff.

Me: I'm a free spirit.

HEL: So what does this mean?

Me: It means I'm going to make him sing to me.

HEL: Not everyone loves karaoke.

Me: But I do! We're going to dinner first.
Everyone gets something they want.

HEL: Doesn't this guy have like . . . games?

Me: He's leaving town Thursday morning for an
away game.

HEL: Mom going with?

Me: I don't think so. She avoids me now.

HEL: And the brother?

Me: I think he likes me, actually. But I've been
keeping my distance.

HEL: Probably a good idea, I guess. She still
talking about getting him to come home?

Me: Yes.

HEL: So . . . how is your head with it all?

Me: Fine.

HEL: You're okay with the idea that this is just a
fling?

Me: It's totally fine.

Three dots danced across the screen for a while, and I got tired
of waiting for an answer. I put the phone down and got up,
heading for the bathroom. When I came back out to get dressed,
Hel had written "be careful."

I wanted to be. After Marcus, I'd made "carefree" my mantra
when it came to everything except my heart. That, I'd guarded

ferociously, working hard to avoid anything that might ever let me feel that kind of pain again. But now, here I was.

Did I love the goalie?

It was too early for thoughts like that, I told myself, and I forced the question away. We were having fun, and that would be enough for now.

I hadn't heard from Teresa since sending her my new tracks. I imagined she'd probably realized that I wasn't like the pros she worked with. The song she'd liked had been a fluke, and I was willing to bet that when I'd sent her the follow-ups, she'd come to her professional music producer senses and realized I was a house sitter, nothing more.

That was okay with me, I realized. The idea of moving back out west wasn't especially appealing to me, though it wasn't as if I had other plans. And that was something I needed to get to work on. I needed another job when this one ended in two weeks. I needed real money. And the goalie had distracted me just enough to make me forget the roiling pit in my stomach that I remembered whenever my phone rang or I got an email from the loan company. I was screwed either way.

I made a huge cup of coffee, even though it was already past noon, and opened my laptop on the coffee table. There were a couple sites I used to find housesitting gigs, and now I logged in and applied for a few, attaching the personal references I'd accumulated along the way. Teresa's name would make a nice addition to my growing list of happy customers, I realized, so I made a note to send her a request when this job ended.

And then I took advantage of the house I was sitting, working out in the little gym downstairs and then taking a long bubble bath in the master bathroom's jetted tub. When I was done, it was nearing four o'clock, and I checked my phone to see what time Stephano planned for dinner.

Punctual and reliable as ever, there was a text waiting for me.

Goalie: Pick you up at six-thirty.

I loved that about him. I never had to wonder or wait—he always let me know when I'd see him again, what to expect. Even when we'd been officially fake, he made sure there was no uncertainty about anything. Kind of the opposite of everything else in my life.

I'd chosen this life. I'd decided to let the universe decide what was next for me. So why did it feel so scary suddenly?

At exactly six-thirty, there was a knock at the door, and I opened it to find Stephano standing on the doorstep looking ridiculously handsome in a dark blue suit with a wool coat on, and a bouquet of deep red roses in his hands.

"For me?"

"No, no," he said, his face completely serious. "These are for the hostess at the restaurant. An old girlfriend."

"Jerk," I said, reaching for my roses.

His face broke into a smile as he handed them to me, and then his eyes darkened as he looked me up and down. The short red dress I'd chosen, paired with black tights and knee-high boots seemed to be doing its job. "You look incredible."

"So do you," I told him. "I'll just put these inside." I turned to set the vase just inside the door and then pulled my coat from the hook.

"Let me." Stephano helped me into it, and then we were making our way down the path to the driveway, where his truck sat idling, the tailpipe puffing a white cloud of steam into the frigid night air.

He helped me into the car, closed the door, and went around to the driver's side.

"I chose seafood," he said. "Will that work?"

"That's perfect," I told him.

Soon, we were sitting at a corner table in front of a glass window overlooking the river that flowed through Wilcox, the evergreens on either side of it reaching toward the dark winter sky. It was cozy, and since the table was set off from the others nearby, it felt a bit like our own little retreat away from the world.

I ordered a glass of pinot noir, and the heady rush of the good wine only helped to make the night feel that much more perfect. Of course, the handsome dark-haired man at my side helped too.

"Tell me about growing up in Italy," I suggested, sipping my wine.

Stephano's eyes clouded for a millisecond, and then he dropped my gaze and cleared his throat. "It was good," he said. "When I was small, we lived next to the winery where my grand-parents' house was. I spent most of my time running through vineyards and exploring the winery."

"Both your parents worked there?"

He nodded. "It was the family business. Dad and his father did it all—tending the grapes, making the wine. Mamma and my nonna ran everything else."

"Was there a tasting room? Did you get, like, bachelorette parties?" I'd been winetasting once in med school, and my mind went immediately to the party limo we'd rented and the very drunk med students rolling around inside it.

He chuckled, a low rumble that stirred my blood. "Not really. It was a small operation, and the tasting room was just a long table in a side room next to the winery. But people did stop by, and Nonna cooked and let them taste the wine."

"Amarone," I said.

"You remember." He smiled, and I had the sense he was proud of me.

"I read about it. Someday, I'll have to taste some."

He smiled, but there was a tightness to his features that hadn't been there before. "Things changed a lot when my father died."

"I can imagine."

"I was seventeen. Luca had just been born the year prior."

I wanted him to tell me the story, but I didn't want to drag him through a painful past, either. I gave him an option to switch tracks. "Was there an ice rink there? How did you find hockey? Your uncle?"

"Eventually. Uncle Julius grew up with my father, but he moved away when he turned seventeen. He'd always been restless, I guess. He wasn't interested in the winery, or helping my grandparents."

"Why not?"

Stephano shook his head. "I don't know. He's a little bit of a mystery. They adopted him when he was ten. I'm not sure how they even knew of him, or where he came from. No one talked about it. But he didn't want to stay, and so he went to Milan. Picked up hockey."

"How did he do that?" I wondered out loud. "As a kid with no connections in a strange city?"

Stephano shook his head. "He doesn't talk about it. But he was good. And when my father died, he got an offer to play for a team here, in Washington state. He thought the money would help his parents."

So much for lightening the conversation. Uncle Julius's story was just as sad as Stephano's father's.

"So if you went back to Italy, you could play there?"

He lifted a shoulder, his face somber. "I think my days on the ice are coming to an end either way."

"Why do you say that?" I thought of the game I'd watched Saturday, the way he'd been everywhere at once. He was incredible.

"It's physically demanding," he said, but there was hesitation in his words, something there that he wasn't saying.

"That's why you train," I pointed out.

"Injuries still happen." Stephano said this in a low voice, dropping his eyes to the plate in front of him.

I took a bite of my own food, my mind turning over his words. "Are you injured?"

He looked up at me and then shook his head. "Not officially."

"What does that mean?"

The waiter stopped by just then to check in on us. "Everything good?" It was clear he recognized Stephano, but he was very respectful and reserved, careful not to fawn.

"Everything is perfect," Stephano told him. "I wondered though, do you happen to have an Amarone in your wine cellar?"

The waiter frowned, tilting his head. "I can certainly check with the sommelier." He looked at my single glass of pinot noir. "If we do, though, I don't know that we offer it by the glass." He sounded very apologetic about this.

"I wouldn't expect that you did," Stephano said. "Will you send the sommelier over?"

"Of course."

A few minutes later, Stephano was in discussion about wine with the tall, thin woman who'd appeared at our table with the wine list, and a few minutes after that, she was back with a dark bottle sporting a label that was intricately lettered in Italian. The whole thing made me feel pampered and taken care of, impressed that Stephano would go to this length to share something important to him.

Two new glasses had been delivered in her absence, and now she opened the bottle and presented Stephano with a taste. Watching him was fun—he'd clearly done this many times before. He took the glass and watched the wine as it swirled the bottom of the globe before he put his nose into the top and then tasted it.

"It's perfect," he said.

The sommelier poured a glass for me and then moved to pour

for Stephano, but he covered his glass. "No thank you," he said. I was a little disappointed to be drinking alone, but I understood why.

A moment later, she was gone, and I held the glass, looking down into the deep, ruby red wine. "It's so dark," I said.

"It darkens as it ages. Imagine what the wine my brother found must look like."

I nodded and took a tentative sip.

The wine was velvety smooth and tasted somehow as dark as it appeared. It was full of raisins and plums, cherry and something deeper than fruit, something earthy and old. "Wow."

"That's not my family's, obviously, but now you understand a bit more about Amarone. To some, it is almost revered, legend."

"It's more than wine to your family," I suggested, knowing it was true. Lucia wasn't just trying to make wine again. She was trying to reclaim her family's heritage.

"It is legacy. Blood."

I stared down into the deep red wine. Blood.

Ew.

"Now I can't drink it."

Stephano's serious face faltered and then he broke into a grin. "Because I said blood?"

I nodded, and he laughed. "That's okay. We have an appointment to get to, anyway."

"An appointment?"

"I want to hear you sing," he said. "Ever since the first time I met you, I can't get your voice out of my head."

"When I sang 'I Will Survive'?"

"While dancing around a stranger's kitchen with a whisk in your hand." He laughed, "I think I fell in love with you right then." His mouth shut abruptly, as if realizing what he'd said.

I wanted to pause, to let those words sink in, but it was clear he hadn't planned them, so I let him off the hook, tucking them away inside me to examine later. I stared at the bottle of wine on the table. "You bought a whole bottle."

"It's okay. We'll take it home. Later Mamma can tell me how much better our wine is."

I suspected that would make Lucia happy.

We drove to the little karaoke bar situated along the main thoroughfare in downtown Wilcox, and Stephano helped me from the car.

"What are you going to sing, Goalie?"

He shook his head, tucking me against his side as we approached the door. "Nope. Merely a spectator."

"We'll see."

The place was quiet, since it was mid-week, but there were still a few people willing to take the stage to belt out their favorite tunes. I sipped a martini and listened for a bit, snuggled with Stephano into a booth facing the stage. But after three off-key performances, he turned to look at me.

"Well?"

"You want it, Goalie?"

That low chuckle rumbled through him. "That's later. Right now, I want to hear you sing."

I took a sip of my drink and winked at him. "Your wish . . . " I slipped out of the booth and approached the DJ stand, a tiny jumble of nerves in my belly. When I found the song I wanted, he handed me the microphone, and I stepped onto the stage to a few scattered hoots and claps.

My song started low and slow, and I kept my eyes closed for the first few words and let the nerves dissipate into the notes, but as I sang about the dock and the bay, I found Stephano's eyes and really let it go. I could feel my body working as I belted out the lyrics, though I lost myself for the rest of the song in the momentum generated by the music, the crowd's sudden rapt attention, and most of all, Stephano's gaze. When the song ended, people stood to clap, and something inside me acknowledged the feeling, like "yes. This." I loved it.

I got back to the table, and Stephano watched me sit and sip my drink. His face, as usual, was inscrutable, but those eyes were deep and dark and full of something that looked like admiration. "You're fucking incredible."

I pretended to preen. "I know."

"No, I mean it. Your voice . . . " he shook his head and leaned in to kiss me, soft and long and deep.

"You liked that, huh?" I asked, breaking away. Adrenaline was shooting through me, partially from singing, partially from his praise.

"I more than like it," he said. "You could have a career if you wanted one."

"I don't think it's that easy to break into music," I told him, my mind circling the fact that a prominent music producer had my songs at that very minute. "But there's actually one thing I haven't told you . . ." I explained about the song, about Teresa and told him what she'd said.

He watched me, his face serious but smooth, something like pride gleaming in his deep coffee eyes.

"So now I'm just waiting to see what she thinks. And it's been super quiet, so they're probably total crap." But, God . . . I didn't want them to be.

He frowned. "I'm sure they're not. She's busy."

"Yeah."

"You'll get what you set your mind to getting. You have a way about you, a way of being in the world . . . your universe gods are looking out for you."

"You think I'm nuts. With the universe stuff." Plus, the universe hadn't been especially forthcoming in the last week or two.

He shook his head lightly. "I can see it."

Someone had begun to sing a duet on stage, a man and woman doing their best with Lady Gaga's "Shallows." Something about the tone of the song and the darkness of the bar made it feel cozy and safe to talk about dreams and the universe with my goalie.

"You can see what? The universe?"

"Maybe."

I smiled at him—so serious about the topic—and the line of his mouth told me there was something else he wasn't telling me.

"I see colors," he said finally. "I always have. It's bizarre. Just a little smudge around most people, a hint at what they might be like."

"You see auras?" This did not fit in any way with the stern and serious man I'd come to know. And yet, it drew me to him even more.

He nodded. "And you're gold. Shimmering gold. I've never seen anything quite like it."

I didn't know what to say to that as a pleased shiver went through me, so I just smiled and absorbed his words.

"You're like everything good and bright," he went on. "Maybe you really are touched by the universe."

I laughed. "What color are you?"

He grimaced and his eyes dropped, then flitted to the stage.

"Goalie?"

"I'd rather not say."

"Now I have to know. Come on."

He made a face at me, his eyes squinting as his mouth pursed. "No."

"It's that or you sing 'Call Me Maybe.'"

"I don't sing. That's your department."

"Come on . . . I told you about my song. And I sang for you just now!"

"If I tell you, can we go home? I have some more plans for you."

He really didn't need to convince me after that. I was already imagining the feel of his strong, rough hands on me. "Tell me."

"Pink. My aura is little-girl, bubble-gum pink."

I squealed with delight, and then Goalie grabbed my hand and led me out the door.

CHAPTER 23
STEPHANO

NO ONE SCREWS OVER MAMA MIZZONI

We were on the tarmac in Santa Fe when my phone rang with an international number—the investor.

"Mizzoni."

"Stephano Mizzoni, hello. My name is Emilio Marino. I'm returning your call." Emilio spoke in Italian, so I followed suit.

The investor. "Thanks, yeah. Hello."

"You asked about the details of the offer. Do you have a moment now?"

"I do."

"Perfect." Emilio explained what he'd offered my mother. It wasn't only money to rebuild. He wanted an equity stake in the business in exchange for handling the rebuild. "In addition to 51 percent, I want the assurance that you will promote the brand."

"Which I have to be present to do."

"Preferably."

I didn't like the deal. If Mamma wanted to rebuild, she should at least own the product when it was done. "A 49 percent stake does not compel me to uproot my entire life here and end my career."

"I see." He sounded thoughtful.

Cade Simpson was at my side, and though he'd been gleefully

snoring throughout the entire flight, now he was openly staring at me, his enormous beard practically poking me in the nose. Shit. Did Simpson speak Italian?

"If you can revise the arrangement, I might consider it." At least this would buy me more time, but it didn't hurt to be clear. "And I have a hockey season to finish. You could certainly start the build, but I cannot participate until I'm done. My contract is up this season, so I'd be clear to leave."

"Or perhaps I take the deal elsewhere."

"Perhaps you do," I agreed, knowing I'd have a lot of explaining to do if I bullied the guy away from the deal that Mamma seemed so desperate to take. And if this offer dissolved, the issue of the money I was trying to save for them became more pressing. But maybe what I had would be enough.

He was quiet for a moment, and I pulled the phone from my ear, wondering if the connection had dropped. But he was still there, and finally he said, "Stephano, I am not trying to take advantage of you. I was friends with your father when we were young. I grew up living next to your grandparents' winery. I want to see it restored."

"As do I."

"Then let's work something out."

"My mother gets the majority share." I wasn't going to budge on that.

"And you'll come to help?"

"Once I've seen some paperwork, we'll talk."

"I'll send it next week after I've spoken with my lawyer."

"All right."

We ended the call, and I did my best to ignore Cade's beard and his questioning gaze as the door of the plane popped open and everyone began to gather their bags.

"Dude." Now he was looming at my side as we stood, bending down and nearly inserting his beard into my personal space.

"What?" I snapped. Sometimes the closeness of my teammates was just too much . . . closeness.

"I took Italian in college. And I can't pretend I didn't hear that. You said 'end my career.' Something going on, Mizzoni?"

"It was just a bargaining chip," I lied, glancing around to be sure no one else had heard. "There's a guy trying to swindle my mom."

I knew it didn't begin to explain the situation, and Cade frowned at me. But then he said. "No one screws over Mama Mizzoni."

"Right." I was relieved Cade was willing to let it go.

We headed down the aisle and out into the relative warmth of a Santa Fe February to face the Turquoise Titans.

We went straight to the arena, settling ourselves into the dressing room and starting the routine of preparing for the game. It was comforting, and almost eased the constant screaming of my hip, allowing me to tell myself that everything was fine, that it was just a strain, my age beginning to affect me.

I took it easy in warmups and took my time gearing up for the game. Samuels, at my side, looked eager as ever, and it was hard to hold a grudge when I'd seen how good he really was. Coach Merit was right. The guy was a good get for the Wombats. We were lucky to have him.

Still didn't mean I had to be excited about the idea of stepping aside, but the idea was less awful now that I was thinking of walking away, anyway. My team would be in a good position if I did.

I moved into the rink, eyeballing the opposing goalie. He was good, but I was better. Or at least I used to be.

All of that flew from my mind as soon as the puck dropped.

I settled into the crease, the chill of the ice seeping through my pads, and the metallic taste of adrenaline in my mouth. For the first period, I held them off, dodging and flying from one side of the goal to the other and avoiding getting caught in the trap. I was tired, and I didn't like it.

I could tough my way through this game, I decided. And then I'd let Frank send me for that MRI. I'd make some decisions. But not yet.

As the second period started, Fitz, the Titan's winger, flew down the right flank, his skates carving into the ice, spraying a mist of frost. Elks and Simpson were on him, but Fitz clearly wasn't letting it go easily.

I shuffled across the crease, ignoring a scream of pain from my hip as I tried to anticipate the next move. Fitz executed a quick deke, shaking off Elks, and my heart tried to climb into my throat. "Stay square," I told myself, my glove hand twitching in anticipation.

In an instant, Fitz sent a crisp pass to the center barreling down the middle at me. The puck slid effortlessly across the ice, like a black comet across a white winter sky. My legs shot me across the crease, every muscle screaming.

Time slowed as I stretched out my leg, the blade of my skate biting into the ice. The centerman wound up, and I could feel the blood rushing through my veins as I braced for impact.

One second later, the puck was a blur, a black streak flying off a blistering slap shot. I stretched my glove hand up, my body coiling, trying to make myself as big as possible. I could feel every eye on me, every breath held as the puck neared the goal.

For a split second, I felt invincible, like I could stop anything. I felt the way I had early in my career, when it was all so easy. When everyone told me I was a natural. The puck screamed closer, and I could almost feel it in my glove. But as something broke free in my hip with a sickening tear, the puck clipped the edge of my glove and ricocheted into the top corner of the net.

The arena erupted in noise as the red goal light blared behind me, and I crouched low, trying to hide the pain ripping through me. I tried to take a deep breath, to feel the cold air fill my lungs, but my breath was coming in tiny gasps. I imagined myself standing, tapping the posts with my stick, and starting again, but I couldn't make my body do it. I sank to the ice as I realized it was over.

For me at least, this game was over.

I pulled off my helmet, and the whistle came almost immediately.

The next few minutes felt like they happened to someone else. I watched distantly as the doc came out and helped me back to the bench. Samuels gave me a quick pat to the shoulder, and then he was over the wall and flying toward the goal. My goal.

The rest of our time in Santa Fe was a blur. The docs examined me in the back as my team played on without me. As Samuels did my job. As they won. Without me.

The pain was one thing. It was visceral and fiery, and it hurt like fucking hell, don't get me wrong. But it was a whole different kind of pain, knowing the Wombats really didn't need me. They could win without me. I wasn't essential. The place I'd belonged for a decade, the place I'd built my life, my identity. They didn't need me anymore.

And nothing had ever hurt quite like that knowledge.

Despite the pain and the certainty that something in my hip was very wrong, I didn't want to extend my stay in New Mexico any longer than was necessary. I wanted to go home. So the trainers and my teammates helped me onto the plane and I sat with men who I'd come to think of as my family, knowing I wasn't on the inside anymore.

The guys checked in with me and made jokes about the location of my pain, but I felt it. The beginning of the separation. There was the team—the guys on their way to playing for the cup this season. And then there was me. The searing pain inside me told me I wouldn't be with them out there.

"Dick sprain?" Rock suggested, plopping into the seat at my side. "Overuse injuries are no joke, man."

"It's not a dick sprain, asshole."

"Ball tear?"

"Funny."

"I like Hillary, you know. She seems like a good match for you."

I was angry, and I was confused. And the words just came out. "She's not even my girlfriend. We're just pretending for my mom." Shit. The second the words were out a deep pit opened in my gut.

Rock's eyebrows shot up. "Seriously?"

"Seriously."

"Looked pretty real to me." Rock shook his head like he was having a hard time believing this news.

"How would you know what real looks like? You're famous for changing girlfriends more often than you change your pants."

"Not anymore." Rock pulled himself taller and pressed his lips into a stern line. "I'm a one-woman man now. Drea and I are married."

He was so offended I almost felt bad. "Yeah. I know."

"Look, Mizzoni. This dick sprain of yours will heal. And whatever's going on with your neighbor? You'll figure it out. All I know is the way she looks at you . . . you can't fake that." He clearly sensed there was more going on in my head, but he hadn't quite hit on the thing that had me most worried.

Now there was no reason I couldn't go home and do my duty to my family. Except one very beautiful, very compelling golden distraction. Who I was pretty sure I was in love with.

INTERLUDE

JULIUS RAMON

Seeing my nephew go down on the ice was heart-wrenching, especially knowing it was happening thousands of miles away. That I could do nothing.

If it had happened in Wilcox, I would have been every bit as powerless. I'd managed to appoint myself some kind of silent watcher over him, over this team. Powerless, except to revolve in circles adjacent to theirs.

As difficult as it might be to know that his hockey career may be at a close, I believe that could be the thing that saves Stephano.

We are alike, him and me. Driving ourselves in service of things we cannot control, paying penance for things that we had no part in creating.

But my nephew still has a shot at redemption. And if there's any small thing I can do to steer him in that direction, I'll do it.

Even if I am just the Zamboni driver now.

CHAPTER 24
HILLARY

OUCH.

I watched the game at the sports bar on Main Street in Wilcox with Clara Connors—Sly's fiancée. She'd reached out after the party at Stephano's and invited me, since we were both local. Not a lot of the guys were seriously dating anyone, she said, and some of them had wives and girlfriends out of town, like Rock Stevens.

"It'll just be us, if that's okay with you. And my friend Andie."

"That's fine with me. I need to get out of the house," I'd told her. And it wasn't like I had lots of friends in town, unless you counted Stephano's brother.

"Think Stephano's family wants to join?"

"Will you mind if I don't ask? His mom is not my biggest fan." I felt a bit embarrassed admitting this.

Clara had been fine with that. She and her friend Andie had arrived before me, and I met them at a high-top table near the big screen, chatting and watching the start of the Wombats and Titans game with the other local fans.

"Sorry to cut straight to the chase, but Clara says you're dating Stephano Mizzoni." Andie's dark gaze was bright, interested. "I've had the biggest crush on him forever. He's why I love watching hockey."

"Really? He'd be so flattered," I said. "Yeah, we're just casual. It's new."

"He's so . . . intense," she said, sounding dreamy.

I laughed. "That's accurate."

"Why doesn't Stephano's mother like you?" Clara asked, her blue eyes wide and wondering.

I lifted a shoulder. "Stephano says it's nothing personal. She wants him to go home."

"To Italy?"

"Yeah. Something about starting back up the family business and needing him there." I wasn't sure how much it was right to share. This was Stephano's family business. But I needed to talk to someone.

"Is he going?" Andie asked.

"I don't think so," I said, realizing I really didn't know what his plans were. "He hasn't made any definitive statements, at least. It's hard, because it's all related to his family's history, and there's some investor making an offer, I guess."

I didn't have to worry about telling them more because everyone in the bar was yelling suddenly, erupting in cheers as the Wombats scored on the Titans. I cheered along with them, my eyes on the guy at the end of the rink, hovering inside that net like his life depended on it. He didn't celebrate like some of the other guys who skated around and threw their arms around each other or chest bumped as they flew around the ice. He threw up a single arm in victory and then seemed to get back to the business of guarding his goal.

So serious. So stern. I thought of him hovering over me, that same intensity focused one hundred percent on me, and suppressed a shiver.

I barely had time to settle back into my seat when the action ramped up again, only this time, it was all heading in the other direction. At Stephano.

He braced and flew across the net, watching the action draw closer to him, and then when the shot came, he looked ready. He sprang up out of his crouch, one gloved hand shooting into the air. But then he crumpled, drawing himself into a heap at the bottom of the net as the puck sailed over his head and the red lights flashed.

"Oh no!" Andie squeaked, her voice high.

"What happened?" Clara asked as everyone in the bar let out disappointed groans.

"I don't know. He just . . . fell." A sick feeling stirred inside me as I stared at the screen. The cameras had slid away to the celebrating Titans, but now were back on Stephano, who remained down. He pulled his helmet off, and I got a split-second glance at his face, twisted in pain. Then he was swarmed by teammates and doctors, and a few minutes later he was taken, limping, off the ice, and the game went on.

All the elation had slipped away, and the glass of wine in front of me might as well have been poison. I wanted to leap up and rush out, but where would I go? Stephano was in New Mexico, and I was in Virginia. I couldn't exactly rush to his side.

What would happen now? How would I know if he was okay?

"Are you okay?" Clara asked me, looking across the table with concerned eyes.

"I mean . . . yeah," I said. Why shouldn't I be okay? "I'm just worried, I guess."

"He'll be fine," Andie said. "Toughest guy on that team."

"He'll be all right," Clara said. Her head turned suddenly as Sly Remington filled the screen and then shot past, sending the puck flying toward the opposing goal. When the other team's defense intercepted it, she turned back to me. "Do you want to try calling him?"

Was that my place? I didn't know what to do. I wasn't officially his girlfriend or anything . . . but we were dating, weren't we? Would he want to hear from me?

"Yeah, I guess." I slipped off my stool and headed for the relative quiet of the hallway by the bathrooms. When I had my phone in my hand, I chickened out, typing out a text instead of calling. I didn't know if he'd even have his phone on him. And wouldn't he be with doctors?

> Me: Hi. Watching the game, and now I'm super worried. Will you call me when you can? Hope you're okay.

My fingers hovered over the keys. It felt like I should add something else, but I couldn't think what it would be. Take care? Hang in there? If we were serious, it might be "love you." But that wasn't where we were. I gave up and hit send, waiting a few seconds for a response, and then shoving my phone into my purse and returning to the table.

"Any luck?" Andie asked.

I shook my head.

"He'll be fine. The team doctors are great," Clara said.

"What if it's something serious?" I asked. Oh god, his mother was probably watching at his house. What must she be feeling? Worry raged within me, making it impossible to sit still.

Clara blew out a breath and picked up an onion ring. "If it's super serious, they'll find a hospital to treat him there, but they usually try to do all the medical stuff here. He'll probably be home tonight. They get in super late. Maybe they'll take him to the med center from the airfield."

I nodded. That all made sense. "I wonder if maybe I should go talk to his mom."

"You think she's watching?" Clara asked.

"Of course she is," Andie said. "If that hottie was your son, wouldn't you be?"

Clara shot Andie a narrow-eyed look, suggesting she might pipe down, then turned to me. "I'm sure she'd be happy to see you."

"Well, that's probably overstating things, but maybe I should go, anyway. She must be freaking out. Do you mind?"

"Of course not," she assured me. "Hope to see you again soon.

Text me, okay? Let me know how he is." She stood to give me a hug.

"Thanks." I hugged her back and then headed to Stephano's house, where I was pretty sure his mother would not be pleased to see me. Still, it felt like the right thing to do. And part of me wanted to be there, at his house, to feel closer to him somehow. Maybe it would ease some of the aching worry inside me.

CHAPTER 25
STEPHANO

INVENTIVE OFFERS NO ONE LIKES

Hillary had sent me a text, and even though the dark mood that had stayed with me the duration of the flight tried to keep me from responding, I didn't want her to worry.

Me: I'm fine. On the way back. Talk to you soon.

My mother, on the other hand, was a tougher thing to figure out. She didn't text, but my brother did, and there was no question he was her mouthpiece.

Luca: Mom is worried. You okay?

Me: I'm fine.

Luca: You didn't play the rest of the game.

Me: I'm aware.

Luca: So you aren't fine.

Me: I'll BE fine.

Luca: Mamma says they have good doctors in Veneto.

Fuck.

I didn't want to think about that. About the deal, about my family, about the fact that if I wasn't playing, there were very few reasons not to go home. I'd come here for hockey. If hockey was over, what was keeping me here besides an entanglement that was supposed to be fake.

The texts with my brother were making me wish I hadn't refused the painkillers the doc had offered me before we got on the plane. The naproxen wasn't cutting it, and there wasn't a single position that didn't remind me that there was a screaming tear of something inside my hip. It felt like a hot poker was pressed into my groin the entire flight.

Worse, there was a wheelchair waiting for me at the bottom of the stairs when we got home.

"Want us to carry you down?" Rock and Cade peered out the window where I sat, all of us watching the medical team approach the plane in the glaring lights on the tarmac.

"Want me to twist off your nipples and shove them up your asshole?"

"Ew," Cade said, exchanging a wide-eyed look with Rock. "I'll pass."

Rock looked like he was considering. "Very inventive, Mizzoni, but I'm gonna take a raincheck on that."

Despite the refused offer, they sandwiched me on the way down the steps, like they thought I might topple forward or back. As much as I hated it, I also appreciated their loyalty. By the time I survived the trip down the stairs, I was grateful for the stupid wheelchair.

I sat in the chair and held my duffle on my lap, feeling like an invalid when the nurse holding the handles asked how I was doing.

I didn't feel like answering. I didn't feel like talking to anyone, seeing anyone. Except . . . a part of me that I was trying hard to ignore would have been happy to see Goldilocks standing down there waiting for me. Even if we were married, she wouldn't have been able to meet the plane that way, but it didn't stop my imagination from putting her there, a worried look on her face.

Shit. Why did I want Hillary worrying about me? Why did it feel nice in some fucked up way to imagine her like that, as the one person I'd want around when I wasn't strong?

I didn't have much time to consider it deeply, because they loaded me into a fucking ambulance, and then I was at the medical center in Roanoke. They threw me into the MRI machine almost immediately, despite it being the middle of the night, and by the time the sun was coming up beyond the UV-coated windows of my hospital room, they'd scheduled surgery. It was all a blur, and I barely acknowledged the doctor breaking the news to me.

There were a few hours to wait, and though I couldn't sleep well, I tried. I was starving, but they didn't want me to eat since I was headed into surgery in the afternoon.

I picked up my phone, knowing I owed my family a report. Mamma would be worried. I would call her, I told myself. But my fingers made other choices first, and a moment later, Hillary picked up.

"Goalie! I've been so worried."

"Hey." I instantly felt better.

"How are you?" she asked tentatively, as if she was maybe not supposed to ask this question, or like she knew the answer wasn't going to be good.

"I've been better."

She laughed lightly, and the sound filtered through me, untying some of the knots in my chest. "I guess so." A pause. "You're in Roanoke?"

"Yeah, how did you know that?"

"The team doctor called your mom."

"I gave him her number. I figured she'd be worried. She called you?" That was a bit of a surprise. Mamma had been working pretty hard to keep Hillary out of things. I wouldn't expect her to purposely include her.

"Luca texted me."

Aha. Luca. I never thought my seventeen-year-old brother would become the rational one among us, but he seemed to be the person unfazed by his feelings about the land, the wine. If he even had any. He'd been young when Dad died.

"So . . . surgery?"

"Yeah, torn labrum."

"And are they gonna keep you there for a while?"

"Actually, no. It's outpatient technically. They admitted me last night because it was so late, and I guess because . . . "

"Because you're a hockey star and you get special treatment." She laughed.

"Maybe, yeah."

"Do you have a ride home?"

"I'll get a car," I said. I had no doubt the team doc was around here somewhere to help get things lined up.

"I'll come get you."

"No, Hillary, don't do that." It felt like too much. Like if she did that, I'd have to acknowledge the truth I already knew. That this was real. That I loved her. That maybe she loved me too. And that I had one more reason why I couldn't do what my family wanted.

"Don't be ridiculous. I'm coming."

Why did it feel so good to have her argue with me?

"Okay. If you're sure."

"That's what girlfriends do," she said.

Goldilocks was my girlfriend. "Thanks."

"Are you going to call your mom, or do you want me to go update her?"

I couldn't let her do that. Mamma would want to hear from me. "I'll call her. I've got surgery at one. I'll give them your number, okay? They'll keep you updated if I tell them you're the one picking me up."

"Okay," she said.

"Thanks."

"Of course. And Stephano?" Her voice lowered, became soft.

"Yeah?"

"It's gonna be okay."

I wasn't even sure what she meant. The situation between us? My family? The team? It didn't matter. Just hearing her say those words made me feel better somehow.

"Yeah. Thanks."

I closed my eyes for a long moment after we hung up, picturing my glowing Goldilocks, her easy smile, her happy outlook on everything. I was becoming attached, even though I definitely hadn't meant to. Shit, I wasn't *becoming* attached. I was attached.

One more complication. But one I didn't want to untangle myself from. One that felt worthwhile.

I sighed and dialed my mother's number.

"Stephano." The worry and fear in her voice twisted my heart.

"Mamma. I'm okay."

"The doctor called and said you were going to have surgery."

"It's not a big deal. A tear they have to fix. I'll be home after."

"We will come get you."

"No, Hillary's coming. It's okay. I don't want you to have to drive." Mamma was a notoriously tentative driver. I couldn't even imagine her on the highway in my truck.

"Hillary," Mamma repeated in a soft voice. "That's good."

"It is," I said, relieved that she hadn't fought this time. "She's a good person. I care about her."

"I know." The word was laced with resentment, but I didn't have the energy to dive into that topic now.

"I spoke to the investor. He's going to call me back Monday with new terms." I knew Mamma was worried about this, so figured I should address it even if the timing wasn't ideal.

"New terms?"

I explained to my mother that there was no point giving up the majority share if she was going to do this deal, making her see that if the man was serious, he wouldn't walk away.

"And if he agrees?" The question wasn't explicit, but I knew what she was asking.

"Let's see what he proposes. Then we'll figure it out."

"This injury, Stephano. It might mean you are done with hockey, anyway."

I squeezed my eyes shut. Leave it to my mother to say the one thing everyone else was thinking, but wouldn't dare say out loud.

"We'll see."

"I'm making food for when you are home."

"Thanks, Mamma." Food. Mamma's love language. "I'll see you soon."

We hung up and I slid the phone to the table at my side, exhausted. Everything about my future hung in the balance, and when they came to prep me for surgery, I felt like a man standing on one side of a dark imposing door, having no idea what was beyond. But I was about to find out.

"Just breathe," the anesthetist said as I looked up at her, the mask in place over my mouth and nose.

I let my eyes slip shut, and slept, everything dark until I awoke back in the hospital room, tight dressings wrapped around me and a nurse smiling at my side.

"Hey there," she said softly. "How are you doing?"

I felt like I'd had a long nap, but woken up somehow a different person, in a different body. "Yeah, I'm . . ." My voice was raspy and rough.

The nurse gave me a cup with a straw sticking out of it. "There's someone here to see you and take you home when you're ready. Is it okay to send her in?"

Goldilocks. "Yeah." Relief and happiness replaced everything else inside me.

A minute later, my room glowed gold as Hillary stepped in, smiling and holding a bouquet of daisies. "Hey, Goalie," she said, glancing nervously between me and the nurse.

"The doctor will be in to brief you in a while, and then we'll get you discharged."

"Thanks," I told the nurse, and a moment later, she was gone.

Hillary stood uncomfortably a foot or so from the bedside, holding the vase in front of her.

"Hi," I said, trying for a smile.

"Should I . . ." she gestured with the flowers as if trying to figure out what to do with them. "Maybe here?" She found a low table near the side of the bed.

"Thanks. That was sweet of you."

"I didn't know what else to do," she said. "I didn't stay in med school long enough to learn about post-surgical foliage protocols."

"Yeah, I hear that's one of the toughest parts of that whole med school thing."

She nodded earnestly, and we both grinned.

"Thanks for coming," I said, meeting her eyes and feeling my whole body tingle.

"Of course." She stepped close and took my hand. "Are you in pain?"

I shook my head.

We both looked down at the dressings wrapping my hips. The sheet was pulled up over them, but I knew they wrapped the top of my right leg too, in some crazy half-pants kind of thing.

"Too bad," she murmured.

"What, that I'm not in pain?"

She nodded. "I could see if kissing it away helped."

A shiver went through me at her words and an immediate mental image arose. "You are a very naughty girl."

She laughed and pulled up a chair. For a few moments, we sat in silence. Hillary held my hand between hers and I let my eyes drift shut. I wasn't in any pain and I vaguely recalled a mention of a nerve block being described to me before I went under. For the moment, I felt nothing in my hip. My heart was a different story.

I must've drifted off because the next thing I knew was awaking to the doctor coming in with a tablet in hand and laughing jovially with Hillary. She squeezed my shoulder, coming to stand next to me, and the doctor smiled down at me.

"Ready to hit the road?"

"Sure," I said, blinking away the groggy confusion.

"That nerve block should hold you another hour or so, get you home at least. But let's stay ahead of the pain, okay? Take the Percocet for the first couple days, even if you think you might not need it. And ice every couple hours." He looked at Hillary. "You can help with that?"

"Sure," she said, glancing at me as if asking permission before smiling up at the doctor.

"The circulatory devices need to stay on at all times for the first forty-eight hours," he went on, handing Hillary a box with pictures on it that matched the wraps on my legs. I hadn't really even noticed them before, but as the drugs began to clear my system, I became aware of the noise and pressure of the inflating wraps on my lower legs. "Don't need a blood clot," the doctor said. "But you should be up and moving around in twenty-four hours."

He looked at Hillary. "He has PT scheduled for tomorrow?"

"Uh . . ." She looked at me.

"Can you coordinate with the team doc?" I asked him.

"Sure. No doubt they'll have you moving quick. No skating, though."

"For how long?" I asked, knowing we had to talk about this even if I'd rather live in denial.

"We'll see how things go. There was a lot more scar tissue in there than I expected. You've torn this before."

It wasn't a question, and so I didn't bother with an answer. I'd been injured for a while. I just hadn't known how badly.

Before long, I was in a wheelchair yet again, and Hillary pulled her silver mini SUV to the curb and then came around to help me in. Once we were on the road, headed back toward home, everything hit me at once.

Despite Hillary's brightness, despite the not-awful prognosis, I felt as if darkness was swamping me, seeping in around any loose edges and unguarded gaps in my awareness. I was too tired to fight it.

I pulled my phone out and checked email. The investor had said he'd send something next week, but his name was sitting there in my inbox, just as I'd suspected it might be. I opened the message and quickly read through it.

Mr. Mizzoni:

Find new terms attached. The Mizzoni estate retains 55% if you promote in person for the first three years of the brand's establishment. I've attached a tentative schedule of events where we'll premiere the new label.

All the vineyards except the two closest to the structures are viable with some attention, and we should be able to begin production year one or two, and can source locally until then.

We are eager to get started. Please let us know your thoughts and the earliest date you might be available in person to finalize details.

I look forward to your response.

Emilio Marino

I closed the email and let the idea sink in.

I was going to have to go home. To Italy. The deal was perfect for my family, for my mother. And I couldn't give her the security this deal could, even though I'd saved for years. Now the money I'd set aside would just be a nice addition to the security the winery would provide.

Either way, I'd be heading home soon. I no longer had a choice.

The thought didn't inspire any nostalgia or warmth. In fact, when I thought of walking away from the brightness and warmth sitting right next to me, all I felt was cold.

CHAPTER 26

HILLARY

THIS IS NOT THAT

Mrs. Mizzoni must've been watching out the window, because she was out the door and at the passenger side of my car before I'd even managed to properly park in Stephano's driveway.

"Oh *Mimmo*," she cooed when he opened the door. Then she let out a long, melodious chain of words in Italian that sounded exceptionally motherly and concerned.

My goalie let his mother fawn over him, asking her to back up as he struggled to his feet with the crutches on the icy driveway.

"Careful," I said, unable to help myself.

Stephano narrowed his eyes at me as he came around the front of the car—pro hockey players didn't appreciate being told to be careful, I guessed—but then his face cleared. "Thanks for driving me."

"Should I come in? Help you get settled?"

"I think I'll have more help than I need." He angled his head at his mother, who was still murmuring to herself in Italian and wringing her small hands.

"Okay," I said, wrapping my arms around myself as I stood there in the cold, feeling suddenly useless, unneeded. "Well, I hope you feel better soon . . ." It was more than awkward watching Stephano's mother take over and shepherd him up the two steps and into the house, fretting all the way.

As she stepped across the threshold, she turned to me. "Thank you for bringing him home."

I nodded, and as the door shut, I felt left out in the cold, both literally and emotionally. What happened now?

The drive back to the house next door was obviously brief, and once it was done, I had little to do to distract my mind from wanting to run next door to care for my goalie.

Dammit. How had this happened? He wasn't supposed to be my goalie, and I wasn't really supposed to care. We weren't fake. That had been clearly established. But I didn't know what we were.

And what did that leave me with now? Another week in a house that wasn't mine and no real plans for the future, while even the thought of packing up my bag and leaving Wilcox had my chest aching.

This.

This was exactly why I tried to avoid attachments. It was why I moved around so much. It was why I ran.

Because if I kept running, there was very little chance anything like the pain from my past would ever catch me.

I sank onto the couch, curling up in my favorite spot, which I thought still smelled vaguely of Stephano if I closed my eyes and breathed deeply. But now I closed my eyes and saw the scene on the ice replay, over and over, felt the fear inside me mushroom and vine throughout my body, taking over. And as that old companion shadowed the room, and my mind, the image flipped.

I was back in my apartment at med school, picking up the phone, which was ringing with Julie's name. We were med school roommates, at least until Marcus and I had gotten engaged and moved in together.

"Hey you," I trilled into the phone. "Bring me a cheeseburger if you guys are stopping, okay?"

"Hill." Julie's voice was thin, broken.

Without intending to, I shot to my feet. "Julie, what's wrong?"

Julie sobbed at the other end of the phone and adrenaline had me racing for my keys, though I had no idea where I needed to go. "Tell me where you are. What's happened?"

"We were in an accident," the words were almost unintelligible.

"What happened?"

"It was so fast," she said, her voice breaking but the words clearer. "Head on."

"Oh god." Dread pooled in my stomach.

"Hill, Marcus and Sue didn't . . . they aren't . . . they died."

My legs went out from under me, but I kept the phone pressed hard to my ear, as if there was a chance I'd just heard wrong. Something inside me forced out one word. "No."

I stood and made myself go out the back door, the bracing cold snapping me out of the memory. That was then. I'd survived it, and moved ahead. And I wasn't going back.

This was not that.

Stephano was fine.

I took a deep breath and went back inside, telling myself that for the rest of the day, I'd let him settle and would work on my own things.

I found my laptop, set up at the kitchen island with a big cup of coffee, and began going through email. There was nothing surprising there, but it still took over an hour to weed through everything I'd ignored for the last couple weeks. Just as I was finishing deleting the loads of spam, my phone chimed.

My heart spun in a little circle, hoping it would be Stephano, but it wasn't.

It was Teresa Palmer.

> Teresa: Call me when you have a moment.

Good. More distraction. Even though I knew it could be bad news, I dialed.

"Hey, that was quick," Teresa said.

"Too eager?" I laughed.

"No, it's great. Listen, sorry for the delay in getting back to you."

"Oh, no. It's fine." My insides were tightening in anticipation, preparing for the disappointment.

"I really liked the second version of that track you sent. I played it for a friend of mine, and he agreed it's really good."

"Oh." I wasn't sure how to respond. Surprise and a flare of giddy excitement roiled around in my gut. "Great."

"Yeah, so I wondered if I could send you a contract."

"A contract?"

"The friend I played the song for is a music supervisor."

I shook my head. "I have no idea what that is."

She laughed. "Right? There's a million jobs in production. It's a lot. So this guy, Luke, is in charge of selecting and licensing the music that will be on the soundtrack for movies and television shows."

"Oh, wow." I honestly had never thought about how that happened.

"He's working on a new show and they're really interested in licensing the song."

"For a television show?"

"It's called Chaos. They want to use your song for the theme."

I let that sink in. Shock made my thoughts slow as I tried to understand what this meant.

"You're quiet."

"I know, sorry. I'm just . . . surprised."

"So if the series does well, your song could take on a life of its own. It would be the music people associate with the series, the actors, the story . . . it would be in commercials and promos. This is a pretty big deal," she said.

"Wow." I found myself staring out the back windows, but didn't recall getting up from the counter. "Wow," I said again, the information finally beginning to coalesce into some logic.

"Can I email you the details?"

"Yeah," I said. This wasn't bad news. The universe was delivering. This meant money. Potentially a career. Maybe an end to my debt?

"I'm not an agent, so I worked with another friend of mine to put this together," she said. "I want you to retain as many rights as possible so that if this thing does get big, you'll be able to strike future deals for more money. And if you want, I can have my friend give you a call. You might want to think about getting an agent."

"Right." I had no idea what kinds of rights she meant, or what in the world I'd need an agent for after this, but was willing to defer to her expertise. "Thanks." Teresa promised to send the initial contract and the agent's information by the end of the day.

"Have you been working on anything else?" she asked just before we finished up.

"A lot, actually."

"Great! Can't wait to hear it. Send me whatever you want."

"Okay." This all seemed like a dream. Could one of the biggest music producers in LA really be casually suggesting I just send her my music?

"How's the house?"

I looked around. "Pretty much like you left it, I think," I laughed.

"Have you met my grumpy neighbor?"

She could only mean Stephano. I chuckled. "Yeah, I have."

"He's mostly friendly."

"We've, uh . . . actually kind of become friends."

"Have you?" she asked, her tone clearly indicating that she knew I meant something beyond friends. I hoped she didn't think less of me or consider me less than professional now. "Nice. Okay, well, I might end up out here another week or two, but you don't have to stay if you've got plans."

"I don't really." And nothing would be better than a couple more weeks with the goalie. Especially now that it looked like I might have an actual future.

"Well, I'd love it if you can stay. I'll Venmo two more weeks' pay."

"Wow. Okay. Yeah." Two more weeks before I had big decisions to make, and now I might have actual choices in the matter. I'd take it. "Thanks for everything, Teresa."

"No problem. The universe works in mysterious ways. I'm glad we met."

"It does." I hung up when she said goodbye and looked out at the clear blue sky over her backyard, offering a bit of silent thanks to the universe.

CHAPTER 27
STEPHANO

TALKING AND WALKING. TOO
MUCH.

Mamma played caring nurse for about two hours, making sure I took the pills they'd given me for swelling and pain as she set me up on the couch and then set an array of food at my side on the coffee table.

"I made all your favorites."

I didn't have the heart to tell her I was nauseous, so I did my best to eat a bit. She sat across from me and watched me expectantly. Luca wandered through to get another soda from the fridge before returning to the den to hang out with his best friend, the X-Box.

"You okay?" he asked me.

"I will be."

I wished my mother would be satisfied so easily, but instead, she seemed to be contemplating how to approach the discussion she clearly wanted to have.

I was just dozing off when she finally found the question she wanted to ask.

"Stephano. What does this mean?"

I blinked my eyes open again and let out a groan without meaning to. "It means I'm supposed to lie here until tomorrow and then go see the physical therapist."

"No, what does it mean for us?"

"You're asking if I'm coming home." I didn't want to talk about this—or anything—right now.

"Yes."

I sighed and struggled to find a comfortable position where my hip didn't scream. The nerve block had worn off. "I don't know."

"Why would you stay here now?"

"Mamma, can we talk about this later?"

She clucked and leaned back in her chair. "Of course. You rest."

But rest did not seem to be in the cards for me. My phone chimed at my side as soon as I laid my head down again. A text from Shotz.

> Shotz: Call me when you can talk.

I groaned again and dialed. "I can talk. I just can't walk."

"That bad?"

"I mean, I don't know. They fixed it, I guess. Labrum tear. The doctor said I'm supposed to start weight bearing and moving in twenty-four hours."

"And skating?"

"I guess Samuels is getting his wish." Though I hated the thought of it, I was glad the Wombats still had a shot at a great season without me. And part of me still hoped I'd be back after a few games, but I doubted that was true.

"What are you thinking, Mizzoni? About everything."

I sighed. I'd known this call was coming. If I was honest, I'd known it since October when even pre-season didn't feel like it had before. My body was betraying me, forcing decisions my brain wasn't ready to make. "I guess it's over."

"The season, or the game?"

"Everything." Desolation sucked the emotion from my voice.

"You want some time? We don't have to decide anything today. I just wanted to get a pulse. Your contract is up this season, but that doesn't mean you can't come back strong next season. I can talk to Merit."

"I don't need time. It's over. My family wants me back in Italy, anyway."

"Oh shit. Okay. Well, your contract gets paid out, even if you don't play. But if you're that sure, we can talk about a lump sum settlement instead."

"Whatever's good for the Wombats."

"I'll talk to the owner and Coach Merit. Get back to you in a day or two, okay?"

"Yeah." I knew I should care. I should focus. But I just couldn't. Everything I'd known, everything I'd built. Hell, everything I'd lived for was burning down. And the worst part? I'd known it was coming. I'd told myself it would all be okay, let myself get wrapped up in the comfort and warmth of the girl next door and the false promises between us . . . and it was all crashing down. I shoved the phone back onto the table and let the darkness overtake me, falling into a pain-addled sleep.

When I woke, the sun had set outside, and the house smelled like garlic. The pain in my hip was sharper, more focused, but my mind was clearer.

I struggled a bit and got myself to a sitting position.

Mamma appeared at my side immediately. "How are you?"

"Better, I think." I reached for the crutches and got myself to standing.

"Where are you going?"

"Just to the bathroom, Mamma."

She clucked and fussed as I moved slowly to the bathroom and then did the same as I moved from there to the kitchen to sit down again.

"What can I get for you, *piccolino*?"

I smiled at the fond expression. I was too big for it, but I liked it anyway. "Just some water please, Mamma."

She put a tall glass of water in front of me and sat at my side, looking expectant and worried.

"I'll call the investor tomorrow to let him know I'm coming back home. We can review and sign paperwork in person. I'll call a realtor to handle things here."

Mamma took a sharp breath in. "You're sure?"

I looked into her familiar face, the face that had always been the one to share my triumphs and my tragedies. She'd cared for me my whole life, and it was time I returned the favor. "Yes. I'm sure." I pushed away the few doubts I had left, most of which came in the form of a beautiful blonde with a bright aura and a honey-soaked voice. "It's the right choice."

"Hillary?" Mamma said her name softly, carefully.

"I'll tell her tomorrow." I did my best not to picture her face, but was glad I hadn't repeated the words that had been on the tip of my tongue the last few times we'd been together. Love would only make this worse.

Mamma worried her little hands in her lap. "She will be upset. She cares for you."

I squeezed my eyes shut, working to force away the feelings I had for her.

"You care for her too."

"Yes, but it doesn't matter now."

"There are nice girls in Italy," she said, and I felt a surge of resentment at how easily she brushed away the feelings I'd just admitted to having.

But it wasn't worth the argument. I'd made my decision. I'd do my duty to my family. Maybe someday I could come back, though I didn't know what a washed-up hockey goalie could possibly find to do after walking away from it all.

It was over.

Once I got settled into bed, I pulled my laptop open and sent Emilio a quick email, letting him know we'd handle things in person and forwarding our arrival plans. Then I emailed the realtor who'd sold me the house a decade earlier to ask about selling the place furnished or even renting it out.

And then I shut the laptop and held my phone in my hand. I needed to talk to Hillary. But I wasn't sure what I wanted to say. I sent her a cowardly text.

Me: Thanks for bringing me home.

Goldilocks: Of course! How are you?

Me: I'm okay. Better. Crutches are lame.

Goldilocks: I'm sure. Can I visit tomorrow?

Me: I'll come to you after PT, okay?

Goldilocks: Okay. What time?

Me: See you around two?

Goldilocks: Can't wait.

I put the phone down, but then it chimed again.

Goldilocks: I miss you.

I missed her too, but telling her would only make everything harder. I put the phone on the nightstand and switched off the light.

CHAPTER 28
HILLARY

OKAY, SO AN NFT IS LIKE...
NEVER MIND

If the universe were a person, I'd ask it to sit down with me over a glass of wine and explain itself. Why did it always seem like good came with bad, opportunity coupled with difficulties? Why would it send me this opportunity at the same time Stephano was struggling so much?

But asking the universe to make sense was like trying to explain NFTs to . . . well, anyone. Pointless.

Still, I was excited about the news I had to share with Stephano, and I thought there was a chance it might even lift his spirits a bit. I wasn't sure what his injury meant for his career, but I knew it couldn't be good. And even if it wasn't terrible, this was Stephano we were talking about. He wasn't exactly a glass half-full kinda guy. So as the time for him to visit neared, I braced myself for the grumpiest of grumpy goalies.

I might have also spent a little extra time curling my hair and touching up my mascara, putting on one of the soft sweaters I knew he liked on me. I couldn't help it, I loved seeing him pleased, knowing I was responsible for his rare smiles.

When the doorbell rang, I rushed to help him in. It was odd, seeing Stephano standing there on crutches. The physical change was obvious, but there was something else about him as I ushered him inside, something in his face. There were lines around his eyes, a duller cast to his skin. He looked defeated.

"Hi," I said, wanting to throw myself at him and also a little afraid to touch him. I didn't want to hurt him.

"How are you? Are you okay?"

"I'm okay. Therapist said everything is right where it should be. Of course, that was after forcing me to move around in the most painful ways possible."

"Oh no," I laughed, ushering him in toward the couch. "Here, sit."

He did, slowly and with a grimace, and then he leaned his crutches next to him and let out a sigh. His expression didn't loosen when he was off his feet—he still looked like the world was crashing in on him.

I sank down next to him, laying a hand on his strong thigh. "I've been worried about you. This can't be easy."

He didn't answer right away, and he didn't look at me. A tiny cell of worry sprang to life inside me and began to multiply. "No, nothing about this is easy."

"I want to talk about it," I said, earning me a look I'd rate a seven on the Mizzoni Scowling Scale. "But first, I have some news. Maybe it'll cheer you up a bit."

"I'm cheery." This was delivered with a look that easily pinged nine on the scale.

"Right. Sorry, I get your happy face mixed up with your mad face sometimes."

He blew out a breath, staring down at his hands in his lap, then looked up at me, his expression tamped down toward a three. "I'm sorry. Things are just . . . hard."

"It's okay," I said, my heart warming when he took my hand between his. "But I'm dying to tell you my news."

"Tell me." His face opened a bit as he looked at me.

"Well, you know I play around with music."

"I know you have a beautiful voice," he agreed, making me smile.

"I didn't tell you that there's a recording studio downstairs, and I've been messing around down there sometimes."

An eyebrow raised.

"Don't judge. I have permission."

"That's good."

"Anyway, before I had permission, I accidentally sent a couple songs to Teresa, the producer who lives here."

The eyebrow again.

"And," I went on before he could say anything, "she liked one of them. An original song I wrote. She asked me to work on it a little and send her a couple more versions."

He nodded, his eyes lighting just a bit as he certainly anticipated the good news part of the story. I couldn't wait to tell him the rest.

"She played one version for a guy she knows who was looking for music for a show he's working on, and he wants my song for the theme song!" I was bouncing, the excitement leaping out of me.

"Goldilocks, that's awesome, congratulations."

"There's a contract and money, and everything! Like a real musician."

I could feel the smile stretching my face. Life felt like it was finally lining up right. Stephano was here, holding my hand, filling my heart. And my music was about to turn into a real career, something I could be proud of, something I could use to pay my debts, maybe even the one I owed my parents.

"Thanks," I said, leaning into him.

Stephano shifted, pulling my hand until I was close enough for him to wrap his other arm around me. I looked up into those deep, dark eyes and felt my love for him surge within me. I hadn't meant to, but I knew I'd fallen for him. And there was something inside those espresso pools that told me he felt the same.

I lifted my chin, and he took the lead, claiming my mouth with his. His hand dropped mine, going around the back of my neck and sinking into my hair, positioning me so his mouth had better access. And then he was devouring me, kissing me like I imagined men about to deploy for war zones might kiss their wives.

One of us moaned—it might have been me—and I shifted my weight to straddle him.

The moan that escaped him then wasn't one of ecstasy, however, it was pain.

"Oh god, sorry!" I slid off quickly. "Are you okay?"

"Got carried away."

"Me too. I'm so sorry. Did I hurt you?"

His eyes were still deep, hooded, and fixed on mine. "No, but . . ." Those dark eyes squeezed shut and a chill went through me. "It's probably better if we don't . . . "

He pulled his hands from my body, and foreboding washed through me. But it didn't make any sense. Everything was fine. Better than fine. Once his hip was healed . . .

"I need to tell you something." His voice was flat, and without even speaking the words, it told me pretty much everything I needed to know. He was leaving. The details didn't really matter.

We were done.

I scooted back, widening the gap between us.

"I have to go home, Hillary."

"To Italy."

"Yeah."

I'd known. Somewhere down deep inside, I'd known from the moment I met his mother.

"For good?"

"I don't know. Probably. The contract specifies a three-year term to start."

I dropped his gaze, stared down at the leather of the couch visible between us, and tried to will myself not to feel disappointed. Not to feel anything. "I see." I steeled myself and looked up. "And this . . . whatever this is? With us?"

He gave me a half-smile that wasn't a smile at all as he lifted a shoulder. "I mean . . . I guess we were never meant to be real in the first place, right?"

It would have hurt less if he'd slapped me. "Right." I managed to put a little pep into my voice.

"It could have been," he said suddenly. "I wish it were."

It didn't matter. Whatever we had been lay between us in shattered fragments. I almost laughed—I'd been so close to telling him how I felt. I stood. "But it's not real. When are you leaving?"

"Day after tomorrow."

"So soon? You just had surgery."

"They'll give me blood thinners for the flight. It's not ideal, but I need to get back."

"Great!" Now I sounded manic, but cheer was the only defense I had against the overwhelming sadness that was threatening to swamp me. I wasn't going to cry in front of the goalie. I wasn't going to show him that I'd let myself get carried away, believing in a fairy tale that clearly wasn't coming true.

"Hillary . . ."

I couldn't hear whatever he was going to say. I was too close to losing it. "Well, safe travels! Tell your mother goodbye for me. And Luca!"

"Goldilocks—"

I leaned across him to hand him his crutches. "It's been . . . fun . . . pretending with you."

He rose, with some clear difficulty, and paused. I could feel his stare on the side of my face as I forced myself to look out the window, to avoid falling even deeper into the dark pools I'd thought I might lose myself in forever. "Okay."

I moved to the door, pulling it open and letting a blast of frigid air wash into the room. It was bracing and helped me keep my emotions in check as I shivered.

At the door, Stephano turned to face me one more time. "For what it's worth, if circumstances were different . . ."

"No worries," I chirped. I could not hear how things might have been. I already knew.

"I'll miss you."

"Okay!" I practically pushed him out the door, leaving him to manage the front stairs and the icy walkway on his own. Because I didn't have time to help him. The second the door shut, the tears came like a tornado.

I tried to hold them in, to keep them under control, but they were sudden and ugly and painful, and I leaned against the door and cried, eventually slumping into a heap in front of the door. The cold tile seeped through my leggings, chilling me and making the sobs that wracked my body compete with shivers. Somewhere, in the back of my mind, I knew I was crying for more than just the loss of a potential connection with Stephano. I was grieving someone I'd never allowed myself to grieve. I was saying goodbye to love as a whole, paying penance to the pain I'd run from for so long.

And as I let myself hurt, curled in a ball in front of a stranger's front door, I realized how wrong my life had been since med school. You couldn't run from pain and grief. You couldn't escape the things in life that were ugly. You had to stand and let them assail you. And sometimes, I understood, you might not be strong enough to withstand the assault. Sometimes, what didn't kill you didn't make you stronger.

It just made you a sad, darker version of the person you were before.

CHAPTER 29
STEPHANO

LUCA HAS A SECRET

I nearly fell down the front steps as Hillary slammed the door behind me. It would have felt right to collapse at her door in a heap. It was what my heart was suggesting I should do. Give up. Call it. Admit there was no point.

But it was cold, and my hip was screaming after the slog over to Hillary's. And I faced the return trip like a man on his last ounce of determination because that's exactly what I was. When I got back through the door at my house, it was going to be the Mamma Mizzoni show.

And I didn't have the energy to struggle against it.

We'd go home. I'd promote the winery. I'd make sure Mamma got the recognition and honor she wanted for my father, that she had something to do with her days that kept her busy and content. And I'd . . .

I didn't even know.

But it didn't matter.

"Stephano!" My mother was waiting by the door when I came in.

"Mamma." I shuffled past her, something inside me well and truly broken.

"Your brother called with news."

For a moment, I was confused. My brother, as I'd come to know him, lived in my den with an X-Box controller permanently attached to his hands, muttering into the mic attached to his headphones.

"He is engaged."

"Cristiano is going to get married?" In my head, my middle brother was still twelve or so, lanky with floppy hair and skinned knees.

"Yes." Mamma didn't sound pleased, which was confusing.

"An Italian girl, right?" I shuffled to the lounger and stretched out. "So you should be thrilled."

She made a little noise and sat on the couch. "It's not what I wanted, is all. It's just . . . I pictured all of us home. Family dinners. Getting to know the women in your lives slowly, over food and wine. But both of you . . ." she shook her head.

"Mamma, this is good news. Cris is happy, right?" At least someone got to be happy.

"But we barely know this girl."

"You've met her?"

"Yes. Two times. Briefly."

I sighed. Mamma's version of courtship was based on her own. Slow growing romances where parents played a pivotal role not only in the dates, but in the introductions themselves. The fact that Cris had somehow met a woman without Mamma's help seemed to be part of the issue.

"Mamma, times are different. You know most people meet on dating apps now, right?"

She clucked and tsked, demonstrating her view of matching technology.

"It'll be okay," I told her, but the heaviness in my chest made me wonder if anything really would be. Ever again.

Over the next two days, details were settled. I signed forms and sent checks, deposited my payout from the Wombats, and did my best to avoid any and all goodbye-related events. I ate, drank, handled logistics, and slept.

The night before we were to head back to Italy, I shuffled past the den after midnight. I thought my brother had gone to sleep, but he was still sitting up, the television glowing with life in front of him, controller in his hand.

I was about to snap at him to turn it off, when I heard him speaking quietly into the headset.

"I miss you too," he said in Italian.

I was pretty sure he wasn't talking to me. I paused, listening in the dark. Creepy, but I didn't care. I was the big brother. Hell, I was practically this kid's father.

"Tell your mama I'll be back soon, and we'll introduce you both to my mama."

What? Who was he talking to?

"I know," he whispered. "Me too."

This sounded romantic. Was Luca in love with a video game?

"Who are you talking to?" I asked, my voice too loud in the darkness.

Luca spun around, whipping the headset off, his mouth dropping into a guilty expression. But as I shuffled into the room, his mouth shut and a sheepish smile took over his face. "Vittoria."

"Vittoria," I repeated.

He nodded.

"When you're in here playing video games all hours of the night, you're talking to Vittoria?"

He shrugged a non-committal agreement. "She is my girlfriend."

Shock dropped my jaw, though after a second, I realized there was no reason for surprise. The kid was tall, strong, good-looking, and seventeen years old. "In Italy."

"Of course. She lives down the street. The Foscaris. You remember?"

I nodded. Of course I remembered. The Foscaris were as established a family in Fumane as the Mizzonis. "Mamma doesn't know?"

"Not yet," Luca said. "I'll have them over when we get back."

My heart lifted just a bit. "She'll like that." I thought of Mamma's face when Luca told her he was dating a local girl, that they'd share the meals she'd missed with Cris and me. "That's good."

Luca grinned, and I saw that goofy light in his eyes, glimmering even in the darkness to match the faint green glow that had always surrounded him. He was in love. And I was glad for him.

"Go to bed," I told him.

"Okay, dad," he said, emphasizing the sarcastic tone on the word dad.

"Love you," I told my brother.

"Love you too, Stephano."

CHAPTER 30
HILLARY

NOTHING SURPRISES PEOPLE LIKE A SURPRISE

I didn't know if there'd be moving trucks arriving or if Stephano's house would be put up for sale right away, but I didn't want to see any of it. I didn't want to witness more of the truth that was breaking my heart over and over again.

So I did what I always do.

I left.

I forced myself not to think too much through the flight to LAX or the ride to Helly's house. And when she opened the door, I did my very best to be my bright and sunny self.

"Surprise!" I sang, loving her shocked expression.

"Hill? Did I know you were coming?" she asked. "No, of course I didn't. Because you do everything the exact opposite way a normal person does things."

"You're not happy I'm here?" I struggled to maintain my happy face, everything inside me pulling apart and threatening to break.

She glanced at my bag, and back up at my face, a little exasperated sigh leaving her as she reached out to hug me. "Of course I am. It looks like you're staying a while?"

"Is that okay?"

"Yes, always," she said, pulling me inside. "Just would have been nice to have a little notice. The guest room is like a wedding planning hurricane."

"I don't mind." I didn't. I would have slept on her floor. I just wanted to be home. Or close to home. Near someone who loved me.

"You okay?" She squinted into my face like she could diagnose a problem if she looked hard enough. "What's wrong? What happened in Virginia? With the goalie?"

"Nothing," I lied. "Just wanted to visit."

"Right." I knew she didn't believe me. But that was the thing about sisters. They'd let you lie for a while if they thought you needed to.

"I'm going to dinner at Mom and Dad's tonight," she said, her voice carrying a note of warning. "Which means you are too."

"Perfect," I said. I meant it. I missed my family. And this time I'd have real answers about my life, my debt. Even if the answers didn't make me happy without the thought of Stephano to share my happiness.

Helena got me set up in the guest room, shoving aside piles of magazines and boxes holding shoes and other wedding-related items. Her wedding was still six months away, but she was much more of a planner than I'd ever been. Even when I'd been a planner.

"I think I might just take a nap until dinner," I told her, needing a few moments alone.

"Sure, sis. I'll wake you at five thirty."

"Thanks."

I laid on Helly's guest bed and tried to force myself to sleep.

Maybe if I slept, I'd get a few minutes of peace, away from the endless looping cycle of questions running constantly through my mind.

Had I imagined the connection I felt between the goalie and me?

Had I gotten carried away and embellished us into something we were not?

Had any of the sweet things he'd said to me been real? Was the conversation about it being real even real?

I was angry with myself. Angry for getting too involved when I'd known from the very start that we had an expiration date. Either I was leaving town when Teresa came back to claim her house, or the goalie was going back to Italy. One way or the other, I'd had no business imagining there was any kind of future for us.

And wasn't that exactly how I liked things?

No strings, no chance of getting hurt . . .

Only . . .

I *was* hurt.

"Hill? You awake? We should head to Mom and Dad's in about fifteen minutes." Helly's voice came through the door.

"I'm awake," I said, my false brightness sounding like a stretch, even to me.

Helly pushed the door open a crack and peered in. She'd put on makeup since I'd arrived, and looked very put together and pretty. The complete opposite of how I currently felt.

"Are you really okay?" My sister moved to the bed and sat, dropping a hand on my shin and squeezing me gently.

"Probably not, not really," I admitted. I wanted to say more, but I could feel the tears threatening again. I wanted to tell her that I thought maybe I hadn't been okay in a really long time, but I didn't risk it.

"Little sis," she whispered, and moved in to curl up next to me, pressing herself in close like we had when we were kids. She draped an arm around me and snuggled me. I breathed her in, that familiar scent of my sister making some of the panicky worry calm inside me just a little.

I hugged her back, feeling lighter, like maybe the world wasn't going to crash down on me just yet.

"Sis?" Helly said softly.

"Yeah?"

"I'll tell Mom and Dad we're going to be a little late. You need a shower."

I punched her gently in the arm. "That's mean."

"But true."

"At least you're honest."

"Always."

"Okay, I'll be quick." I slid off the bed and pulled some clean clothes from the bag I'd brought, heading into the bathroom. But just as I stepped in, I leaned back out. "Don't tell them I'm here. We'll surprise them!"

"But then they'll think I'm the reason we're late," she moaned. Helly did not like to be late. But she especially didn't want to be thought of as being late.

"Don't worry, once they know I'm here, they'll know it was me."

"You're right. Okay."

I closed the door and took a quick shower, sampling a few of my sister's fancy bath products. I did feel better when I was done, and there was no doubt I smelled better. The man next to me on the plane had enjoyed two bacon cheeseburgers on the flight, and I would have put money on each one having extra onions. I'd absorbed some of his lunch.

When I'd dressed and twisted my hair into a knot, we headed out to Helly's car, a cute two-door sports car she'd saved for after she began working as a nurse practitioner. Very responsible. Very stable. That was my sister.

"They're gonna be so excited to see you," she told me as she drove the speed limit the four miles to the house where my parents moved after we'd both gone to college in Los Angeles. They'd downsized, but since we both went south, they told us they would too. To keep the family close. Even though I'd been doing the complete opposite for years now.

Helly pulled up in front of the little bungalow in Pasadena, a beautifully restored yellow arts and crafts house with immaculate landscaping—my mother's pride and joy.

We headed up the walkway and the front door opened just as we topped the steps.

"Oh my gosh, am I dreaming? Is it really Hillary?" Mom stepped delicately down the steps as a huge smile spread across her face.

"It's really me. Hi Mom." I hugged her, Mom's tall frame wrapping me as it always had. I sank into Mom's embrace, the familiar comfort of her closeness enveloping me.

"What a wonderful surprise. Your dad will be thrilled." Mom took my hand, and we walked back up the front steps together. "Hi Helena," she said as we went in. "I'm happy to see you too, just got a little overwhelmed with the surprise."

"It's okay, Mom." Helly headed in before us, and led the way to the living room where Dad was bent over a jigsaw puzzle in the corner.

"Harvey, look who's here." Mom said, her voice holding a little teasing note.

"Helly," Dad said, without looking up. "Always good to see you, honey."

"Hi Dad," I said. It took a second, but Dad's head turned slowly and then he was up and out of his chair to pick me up in a big bear hug.

"Hilly! You're home! What a great surprise!" He put me down and grinned at me, and then reached for my sister, giving her a hug too. It was nice, being back at home, and for a moment, I forgot how miserable I was.

"I had no idea your sister could keep a secret," Mom said.

"I can't. She just showed up today or you would have known for sure," Helly said.

"But you didn't let it slip that she was coming," Dad said, trying hard to congratulate my sister.

She wasn't having it. "She didn't warn me, just showed up on my doorstep."

That got their attention, and suddenly the celebratory mood fizzled, and both of my parents gazed at me with worried expressions, their joy at seeing me replaced with the usual concern. Mom snapped out of it first. "Well, let's get some drinks, and we can sit out on the porch and hear everything that's going on."

We arranged ourselves on the big front porch, Mom and Helly in the swing, and Dad and I in matching rockers facing them, a little table between us and gin and tonics in all our hands.

"So," Dad said. "What brings you back to LA?"

I wanted to break down and cry and tell them that my heart was broken and unfixable, that I was home because I had nowhere else to go. But I'd been enough trouble to my family and caused them enough disappointment. So I went a different direction.

"Well, I have a really awesome opportunity, and it's here in LA!"

"In medicine?" Dad asked, ever hopeful.

"No," I answered, trying not to feel guilty at his misplaced excitement. "In music. I've been house sitting for this really famous producer, and she heard one of my songs and got me a contract for it to be the theme song for a new show on that big streaming service. It's called Chaos."

"Ironic," Dad said under his breath.

I ignored him as Mom gushed, "That sounds incredible, honey."

"It's a big deal," I explained. "The song will be licensed for use in commercials and previews, and they'll use it for all kinds of promotion . . ." I trailed off.

"So you get, like, royalties?" my sister asked.

I'd seen the contract, but hadn't really gotten into the details. I knew there was a significant advance, and that was all I'd really paid attention to. "Maybe. It's all in the works."

"Well, honey," Dad said, and I could hear that strain in his voice that crept up when he was trying to be supportive but failing to find the ability to do so. "That sounds promising."

"Thanks," I said, the excitement I'd coaxed for this big revelation dissipating.

"So you'll be going back to Virginia? Or are you moving home?" Mom asked. "Helly says you're dating a hockey player?"

I shot a glare at my sister, who mouthed "sorry." She really was the worst at keeping secrets.

"No, no," I waved this away, trying to make it sound casual. "We weren't serious. Not at all." I guzzled my drink, trying to make myself stop talking and hopefully dissuading anyone from asking me anything else, seeing that I was occupied.

Helly and Mom talked about the wedding planning a bit, and Dad seemed to be thinking about something else, lost in his own world. Before long, Mom suggested we go in for dinner. I was relieved for the distraction.

Mom had made Italian food.

It wasn't that this was unusual in itself—my mother was a great cook, and growing up, we'd had everything from Thai to Italian to French dishes on a regular basis. But tonight, the scent of garlic and the sight of the dishes on the table were a surprising gut punch.

"I tried something new tonight," she said, as we sat. "It's called *fondi di carfiofo*. Fried artichoke bottoms."

What were the odds?

"Hillary, you don't have to try it." Mom was holding the dish over the table, standing next to my father and staring at me with concern.

"I thought you liked artichoke, peanut," Dad said, his eyes full of worry.

It actually took me a moment to understand why the whole table was now staring at me—the tears had come so easily, so involuntarily, as if sadness was my new default. Tears were no more complicated than a smile.

"Oh, god. Sorry." I wiped at my face, struggling to pull everything together.

"Hill . . ." My sister said softly.

My mother dropped into her chair, the dish plopped onto the table in front of her, forgotten.

"It's just artichokes. You don't have to eat them," Dad tried again.

My mother swatted his arm. "It's obviously not about the artichokes."

"I mean, it kind of is," I moaned, dropping my head into my hands and just giving into the sobbing that had become my most natural state of being.

"Tell us, honey. What's this about?" Mom's voice was gentle, and as I made myself look up at them, I realized I should talk to them. These were my people. If anyone could make me feel better, I hoped it might be my family.

I told them. I started with the hot tub and ended with Stephano's injury and decision to go back to Italy.

"Oh honey," Mom said, sympathy lacing her words.

"I can't believe any man would choose some Italian winery over you," Dad said, his indignation making me smile a tiny bit.

"He didn't, he chose his family," I said. I thought about it a bit as my family comforted me. "And it makes sense, really. What was I to him? Some girl who lived temporarily in the house next door. No home, no career, nothing to show for myself, really."

"Hill," my sister said, her voice carrying a note of warning, like she didn't want me to piss myself off or something.

"What?" I challenged. "I've given up on everything I've ever started. I've spent most of my adult life making sure I wasn't weighed down. And I've ended up sabotaging every opportunity I've ever had."

"Honey—" Mom said, but I was on a roll.

"And in the process? I've disappointed you over and over

because I'm so terrified that if I actually try, I'll just end up disappointing you, anyway." The words flew out of me, surprising all of us. But as soon as they were out, I realized how true they were, and that this was the exact truth I'd been running from for so long.

"Disappointing us?" Dad asked, looking confused.

We all stared at each other for a moment, my family exchanging muddled looks even though I'd just explained everything to them.

"Yeah. You," I clarified. "I'm your daughter, the flighty failure."

My dad shook his head. Slowly at first, and then with more dedication. "No. That's not true, and I'm not going to let you put this on us."

He was angry? This was all worse than I thought it would be. This was why I tried not to come home.

"You don't get to blame us for your unhappiness," he said.

Ouch.

"Harv," my mother warned.

"No, honey. It's time we had this talk." Dad straightened his silverware on the table. Straight silverware was evidently critical when one was approaching the topic of one's daughter being a complete disaster. "Hillary, listen to me. You have never failed at anything. You have stopped trying at various pursuits along the way, but I have no doubt that continued perseverance in any of those fields would have led to profound success."

I stared at him, looking for the words to refute his belief in me.

"I think you quit before any of us ever have the opportunity to see if you'd succeed at things. And I don't know exactly why you do this, but every time you start something new, all your mother and I hope for is that it will finally be the thing that makes you happy."

Tears continued rolling down my cheeks, and I'd given up wiping them away. The navy T-shirt I wore was beginning to feel stuck to the top of my chest, soaked through with tears.

"That's the real question, Hillary," Mom said. "Are you happy, honey?"

I looked around at them all, and then down at my soaked shirt. "Do I look happy?"

"Oh, Hill, is it the goalie?" Helly asked.

"It's everything. I'm just so tired of disappointing you all every time you see me."

Mom was out of her chair and kneeling at my side. "Honey, I don't think we've ever been disappointed with you. Worried, yes. Concerned, definitely. But you are not a disappointment."

"I dropped out of med school." There. I'd said the thing. I sucked in a deep breath and raised my eyes to meet my father's, expecting to see the anger there that comes from spending tens of thousands of dollars on an education that wasn't appreciated or used.

"Med school wasn't a good fit for you," Dad said simply.

"But all that money," I breathed.

"It was an expensive way to find out it wasn't a good fit," Dad shrugged. "But the last thing I'd want is for you to spend your life doing something you hate because you feel like you have to."

I exhaled a heavy breath, feeling almost like someone had knocked the wind out of me. But also, it was a relief, like I'd been holding that breath for years.

"But that's the problem," I said as Mom rubbed my back. "I don't know what I do want to do."

"Let's hear this song," Helly suggested.

Surprise snapped my head to look at her. "Right now?"

"Oh, yes," Mom popped up. "Can we hear it?"

"But, dinner?" I said, looking at the rapidly cooling dishes on the table.

"Can wait. Play us the song," Dad said.

What if I played it for them, what if they hated it? What if the hope and encouragement on their faces slipped away when they realized this was one more thing that wouldn't work out?

I swallowed hard, and then I pulled my phone from my pocket

and searched for the track Teresa had liked. "It won't sound great on the phone," I warned them.

"Connect to the speakers," Helly suggested.

"Oh, right." I did, and a moment later the first chords filled the space around us. I sat in a kind of suspended emotion as I watched my family listen to me sing, listen to the arrangement I'd worked so hard to put together just right. Even I thought it sounded good, better than I'd remembered.

As the song faded, my voice disappearing into the darkening evening air in the house, my parents both beamed. My mother's eyes filled with tears. "Honey, that's amazing. Your voice is lovely."

"That was really good, no wonder they want to buy it," Dad said.

My sister just watched me, her eyes satisfied, and her chin raised. She winked.

"Yeah?" I asked, unused to the feelings washing through me. My family was proud of me. I didn't even have to wonder, I could see it in their eyes. All these years, I'd been running and avoiding, when maybe if I'd just involved them more, asked them for support, they would have been right there, on my side.

"Can we eat these artichokes now?" Dad asked, reaching for the dish.

Relief washed through me.

"I've had this once," I told my mother. "It's delicious. Did you know it's Venetian? This is the part of Italy that Stephano's family is from." Tears threatened, but I held them in.

Mom smiled at me, and we all busied ourselves eating. As we each enjoyed our first few bites, my dad put his fork down again and looked at me.

"Hill, Helly, I just want to make one thing very clear to you girls. Your jobs in this world are not to pay us back or to make us proud. You do that every day in so many ways, I can't even count. Your jobs are to go out into the world and live. To find the things that make you happy." He swallowed hard as we both sniffled.

"And if that happiness enables you to pay rent, well, that's good too," he added.

I went to bed that night feeling just a tiny bit lighter, freer.

But my heart still ached for the man who hadn't chosen me, the man who'd be on a flight to Italy the next day. The man I'd probably never see again.

CHAPTER 31
STEPHANO

KEEP THE ROYALTY ON THE LOW DOWN

The ride to the airport was surreal. I remembered the first time I'd arrived in Virginia, this ride reversed almost exactly. Even my driver was the same.

"I will miss you, Stephano," my uncle said from behind the wheel of my truck. We'd loaded Mom and Luca into the back seats and Uncle Julius had promised to take good care of the car for me. I'd wanted to sell it, but he was strangely against the idea. I figured maybe he needed a car and just didn't want to say it. He could have it. He was family, and I wouldn't need it anymore.

"I'll miss you too."

"The team won't be the same."

"That ship has sailed," I told him, thinking of the money I'd taken to essentially cut ties with the Wombats. In the end, it had been anti-climactic. No goodbye party, no cake, no sendoff of any kind. I'd shaken hands with Coach Merit and the owner, and Sly, who was taking on some managerial responsibilities, and left the arena for the last time. I hadn't talked to a single Wombat in the last few days. I wondered what they'd think of me leaving town. I'd gotten a few texts wishing me well after my injury, but I didn't think any of them knew I was gone yet.

The rest of the ride to Dulles was silent, each of us in our own worlds. At the curb, Uncle Julius had hugged us all goodbye, promising to visit soon, and then we were checking in.

At the gate, I found myself struggling to keep from speaking. Everything felt wrong. Leaving the team without saying good-bye . . . Leaving Virginia on the heels of an injury, like a hurt animal limping to safety . . . Leaving Hillary without a fight.

But every time words popped into my head, I reminded myself that my mother had cared for me for years on her own, raised me without my father, sacrificed so much. Couldn't I sacri-fice for her?

"Mamma," I said, almost not intending to.

She turned, and the stern expression on her face faded a bit as our eyes met. Could she see the pain in my heart?

"I don't want to go."

"I know, Mimmo."

I waited, but she didn't tell me it was okay, that I didn't have to come. She didn't let me off the hook. But everything about this felt wrong. She had to know that.

"I feel like there has to be another way. Something we haven't thought of."

Her face softened, and she sighed, sinking into her seat. For a long moment she was silent, but then she spoke. "I am struggling. It is my job, as your mother, to do anything I can to make you happy. And I know that what I want more than anything in the world is something that is making you unhappy. But how can I explain my love for your father in a way you will understand? How can I tell you that this last thing we can do for him, this one action, is the only way I can hope to keep him near?" A tear hovered on the edge of my mother's eyelid, and her lip quivered. I'd seen my mother cry exactly one time before, and my heart squeezed with sympathy. It took a lot.

"But how can I ask you to do something that is making you so unhappy?"

I shook my head, torn between duty and love for my family,

and the pull I felt to Hillary. Why did it have to be impossible to have both?

"Do you ever think that there is a chance the universe will deliver the right thing if we let it?"

Mamma's eyebrows shot up in surprise. "You are speaking of fate? You believe in that?"

"Mamma, I see auras. I believe in Bigfoot. Of course, I believe in fate."

She chuckled then, and lifted a hand to my face, tracing the line of my cheek with a fondness in her eyes I hadn't seen since I was a boy. "My sweet Stephano . . ."

Mamma dropped her hand and her gaze and was silent. I waited for her to finish, and finally she looked back up at me. "You must do what you feel in your heart. And if it is not the thing I hope for, maybe your universe—your fate—will provide for me too."

It wasn't acquiescence, not really. And it didn't clarify things completely. But it was close. I needed to think. I rose, telling Mamma and Luca I was going to get a bottle of water at the little shop.

"Need a push?" my brother asked, indicating the wheelchair they'd brought me down the concourse in.

"Absolutely not," I told him. I could walk. A little bit, at least. "I'll take it slow."

And I did, taking my time moving to the little shop down the walkway from our gate, my heart feeling like it was weighing me down every bit as much as my healing hip. I lingered outside the little shop, my eyes scanning the headlines on the newspapers and tabloids they had displayed there without really taking any of it in. I was making up my mind, moving closer and closer to a hard decision and blocking out everything around me. Until something caught my eye. Someone, actually.

"Cris?" I uttered his name, as if my brother could answer me from the photograph. He was there, on the front of an issue of

Them Magazine, his arm around a beautiful dark-haired girl above a headline: *Italian Royalty Princess Alessia Engaged.*

Princess Alessia?

My brother was engaged to the Italian heir?

It was true we didn't have a sitting king at this point, but Italy still had a royal family, and they were well known and respected. And the king had one daughter. Princess Alessia.

She was beautiful and famous, constantly the subject of our tabloid speculation. She was an artist, a model . . .

And evidently, she was engaged to my brother Cristiano.

I pulled the magazine free and paid for it, hurrying back to where my mother sat—as much as that was possible with my hip and crutches. I handed her the magazine and waited.

Mamma took one look at the photo and sniffed, rolling her eyes and handing it back angrily.

"You knew?" I ask her.

"I knew who she was. I did not know he was going to propose until he told me."

"You might have mentioned this," I said, looking to Luca for support. Luca shrugged. "You knew too?"

"Cris said we were keeping it on the low down."

"The down low."

"Yes."

My brother was going to be a prince? Were you a prince if you married a princess? Or more like a consort or something?

"It is just one more example of everyone finding ways to leave your home behind. He will go, live a fancy life, travel the world with his princess." Mamma pressed a hand to her heart as if she'd been betrayed.

"Did he say that?" I asked.

"It is obvious. He has been away so much."

"Because they were trying to keep this secret," I suggested.

Mamma waved a hand at me, clearly not interested in talking through my brother's intentions.

"He is gone." She sniffed again.

I exchanged a look with my younger brother and slid my phone from my pocket, dialing the number for Cris, who I hadn't spoken with in way too long.

"Stephano," he said when he answered.

"Prince Cris."

"You heard."

"I read. You're front-page news in the airport."

"So much for keeping things quiet," he said.

"Tell me what's going on. Mamma won't say a word except to complain that now you'll never come home."

My brother laughed lightly. "She has no idea. Alessia wants to settle in Veneto. She isn't quite the princess you imagine, not like they make her out to be."

"You're coming home to live?" Surprise trickled through me and I felt my heart begin to lighten, a little at a time as I realized something.

"That is the plan," Cris said. "I haven't told Mamma yet. But I don't like being away from the family so much, and Alessia wants to give our own family a more traditional life than she had growing up."

"Family, huh?"

"Hopefully." I could hear the happiness in my brother's voice.

"Congratulations, Cris. I'm happy for you." The words were true, but the ache of what I'd just given up was more painful than before.

"Why are you in an airport? Traveling for games?"

I'd forgotten he didn't know. I gave him a brief recap of the situation, Mamma's visit and the investor's plans.

"So you'll give up hockey? Just like that?"

"I can't play now, anyway."

"For a while."

"I ended my contract. And Mamma needs me."

"You are very famous," Cris said. "And I see why the investor thinks having you around will help. But you're not *that* famous."

"Ouch," I said.

"Just hear me out."

When I hung up with my brother, a new plan had taken shape. And by the time I was seated on the plane in business class, watching the familiar DC skyline recede from view, I was more nervous than I could remember being, maybe ever.

CHAPTER 32
HILLARY

I HAVE NO MO

The day after dinner, I texted Teresa to let her know I was in Los Angeles and see if she wanted to meet up. She'd forgiven me easily for leaving her house unattended when I told her I was here, and I'd reversed the money she'd sent. She arranged a meeting with the guy who wanted to use my song, and at two o'clock, I was sitting in the lobby of Teresa's studios and trying to calm my breathing.

My face was still puffy from the night before, when I'd cried more than I'd thought it was possible to cry, especially after my parents told me how they felt about everything. We even talked about Marcus, which only led to me crying harder. The good news was that I was pretty sure I was completely out of tears.

Stephano was gone. The past was behind me. I was sitting here, the sun shining in through the tall windows of this lobby, and I was forging a new path.

Maybe I'd even rent an apartment. Put down some roots. The idea was comforting.

"Hillary?" A petite woman with a bob of curly dark hair strode into the lobby, confidence in every step she took. Her face was friendly, but her attitude screamed business.

I squared my shoulders and stood. "Yes, hi. Teresa." I stuck out a hand, but then thought better of it, smoothing my skirt instead and dropping her eyes.

When I looked back up, Teresa's hand was out, and she was grinning. "Gonna leave me hanging?" she asked.

I felt like an idiot, but reached out and shook her hand. "Sorry, I, uh . . . shaking hands isn't part of my usual MO."

"No?" she chuckled, waving us toward a bank of elevators. "What is?"

"What is what?"

"What's your regular MO, Hillary?"

"Ah . . . yeah, I have no idea. Listen, I'm super nervous. Normally I'm not so . . ." I thought about what I was about to claim. "No, I am. I mean, I'm always . . . shit."

"You're definitely not shit, and there's nothing to be nervous about," she said, her laugh alleviating some of the tension I felt. "This is a formality really, since you expressed interest and Luke is all in. We'll just give the song a listen again, Luke will tell you why he loves it, and then we'll look at some numbers."

"Okay." I tried to calm the excitement floundering inside me as the elevator took us up thirty floors.

We exited into a functional office space that held a small reception desk, though there was no one seated at it. There were a couple leather chairs scattered around, but we passed directly through the space and headed down a hallway.

"Luke's in my office," Teresa told me over her shoulder as she kept a furious pace down the hallway.

We stopped at a glass door and Teresa waved me in to where a bald man with glasses sat, staring at his phone in his hand. He put the phone on the edge of the coffee table and stood when he saw us.

"Hi there," he said with a broad smile. "You must be the talented house sitter with the golden voice. I'm Luke Shanks."

"Hi Luke. I'm Hillary Watters."

"Luke freelances," Teresa told me as she moved around the space, picking up some folders and then coming to stand around the low coffee table where Luke and I faced one another. "He's one of the most sought-after music supervisors in the business, so directors and producers take turns trying to snag him for their projects."

"This one's for a premium streaming service," Luke said. "Did Teresa tell you about the show?"

"Not a lot," I said, sitting as Teresa waved us into chairs. "Just that it's called Chaos."

"Right," Luke smiled and nodded. "It's poised to be the next *Game of Thrones* if we do it right. Huge production, star-studded cast."

"Dragons?" I asked before I could think better of the question.

"No dragons," Luke laughed.

"I love dragons," I said. Dammit, what was wrong with me? Things just kept ejecting themselves from my mouth.

Luke and Teresa both laughed. "Well, that's good," she said.

"It's more of a generational drama. Here's the casting list," Luke said, sliding a piece of paper across the table for me to look at. I recognized several names on the list. "And the production schedule, all somewhat tentative," he said, moving another piece of paper into my little pile. Filming had already begun.

"There's going to be a pretty big ramp up ahead of the premiere, which will be about a year out," Luke said. He put another piece of paper on my pile, this one detailing a list of promotional plans from commercials to movie trailers to print promos. "And this is all based on a book," he went on, "so the author will be heavily involved too. For the record, we played the song for her and she loved it."

"That's amazing," I said, a light bubbly feeling fizzling through my body. This all felt unreal. Of course, I was a nobody, and the numbers Teresa had mentioned over the phone were nothing until they were written and signed. I braced myself.

"So here's the proposal," Teresa said, putting another stack of papers in front of me. "A lot of legalese here that you'll want your lawyer to look through, but it's all pretty standard. The important parts are here. My company will publish your song and license it to Luke for use in a variety of mediums. We'll own the rights for the specified period, and our royalty split would be fifty-fifty."

I nodded, having no idea what was typical or correct. I was going to need a lawyer.

"I'm also offering an advance here," Teresa pointed to a number that was slightly mind-boggling, "because I have a few other projects coming up that I think your voice and vibe would be really good for. But that would require us working together to make some more music. Would you be up for that?"

"Um, I mean . . . Yeah, totally." Here it was. The career.

Teresa laughed as she looked up at my face. "You look shocked."

"I just . . . I've never done any of this before," I admitted.

"I know," she said kindly. "And I'll walk you through it. Did you call the agent I suggested?"

I shook my head, feeling stupid. I'd been too swamped with heartache.

"It's okay. If we get serious moving forward, I know a few more I can introduce you to and you can see what feels right. They generally negotiate these kinds of contracts. Of course, they take a cut too, so this deal is a little bit special."

I nodded. I'd never thought I'd have an agent or need one. But I remembered Stephano talking about his agent, someone he called "Shotz." It made me feel oddly close to him, thinking we'd share something like that.

"Can I show you something?" Luke asked, standing and moving to pick up a remote on the edge of Teresa's desk, aiming it at the flatscreen on the wall.

"Of course," I said, excited.

Luke aimed the remote and the flat screen sprang to life, the screen filled with the image of a beautiful woman and the word "Chaos" in a medieval font scrawled across the screen. When he hit play, the picture sprang to life, and I sat slack jawed as my voice sang out over the moving images, providing the soundtrack for what I was seeing.

When the promo ended, I couldn't find words. It was the most surreal moment of my life.

"What do you think?" Luke asked.

"It's perfect," I said. "I just . . . I can't really believe it."

"It is perfect," Luke said, putting down the remote and coming back to sit. "I knew it the first time Teresa played it for me."

I shook my head, everything feeling just a little unbelievable.

"So have your lawyer look over the contract," Teresa was saying, tucking everything into a folder for me. "The cast list isn't released yet, so I can't let you take that, but everything else in here is solid. When the contract's done, we'll get started re-recording together, and then we'll start working on other things if you're up for it."

"Yeah. Okay," I said. I was up for it.

On the drive back to Helly's house, my mind skipped and danced through reruns of the meeting. As unreal as it all felt, there was also something about everything Teresa and Luke had said that just felt right. The ability to work from anywhere. The freelancer status. I would keep my flexibility and freedom, but I still had a real job. It was perfect.

I practically sprinted back into my sister's house, giddy with my news.

"Did you crash my car?" Helly asked from where she was bent over peering into her refrigerator.

"No, but thanks for the confidence. And even if I did, I could just buy you another one with my big ass advance."

She stood up and squinted at me. "Tell me everything."

I did, and my sister's happiness for me just compounded mine. Everything felt so right suddenly, except for the one very deep hole in my heart that still ached. I hoped that with time, even that ache could heal.

Helly and I planned to go out to dinner to celebrate, and her fiancé Anson was going to meet us out, but just as we were about to walk out the door, Mom called. Helly's face went through a variety of expressions as she listened to whatever Mom was saying, and I realized that we shared that trait. I couldn't keep anything I felt off my face, either.

When Helly hung up, she turned to me with an expression I was surprised I couldn't read. Either some kind of excitement or a sudden and uncomfortable nausea. "Change of plans. We're going to Mom's house."

"We had dinner with them yesterday," I pointed out. "Though I'm excited to tell them my news."

"Yes, good. That. We should go there to do that."

"You okay?"

"Good. Yes. Why?"

"I can't tell if you're acting weirder than normal or not."

"I need to tell Anson about the change of plans. Do you want to maybe change clothes?" She was peering with disapproval at my ripped jeans and baggy T-shirt.

"Not really."

"Go change."

"So going to our parents requires something more casual than what I have on?" My sister was confusing.

"No, definitely nicer. Dress up. Maybe a little sexy."

"To eat dinner at Mom and Dad's?" Now she'd lost it.

"I'll dress up too."

"Why?"

"Mom said to," she lied.

"You're a terrible liar."

"Runs in the family. Could you please just play along?"

I sighed. "Okay, fine." I headed back to my room and changed into a sundress that had bright yellow daisies scattered on a white background and pulled out the wedge sandals I loved. Something was up, but I was too eager to share my news to worry about what it might be. You didn't dress up for a bad surprise, I figured.

"Better," Helly said. She was wearing a sundress too, and

looked somewhat less frazzled than she had a moment before. "Let's go."

My family was strange. But I loved them. "Okay."

Mom was waiting inside the door as we came up the walk, and she looked every bit as out of sorts as my sister had been.

"What is going on?" I asked them both.

Mom made a noise that was half-squeal, half-scream as she hugged me and pulled me inside.

"We're going to eat on the patio out back."

"Okay," I said, beginning to feel very suspicious. Just inside the door, my dad was waiting awkwardly, his hands shoved in his pockets and a half-smile on his kind face. Anson was sitting on the couch in the living room. He, at least, looked normal.

"Hey Anson," I called. "Dad," I said, hugging him.

"Hi honey."

"What's up, Hill?" Anson gave me a hug. "Big night, eh?" He grinned and gave me a thumbs up. He'd been doing inappropriate thumbs-up signs since I'd met him. They seemed to pop up whenever he said anything, and I wondered if there was something that could be done about it. I wasn't even sure he knew it was happening.

"Is it a big night?" I asked, confused as my dad shot Anson a stern look.

"Let's go out," Mom suggested, and when I headed for the kitchen, she took my shoulders in her surprisingly strong hands and steered me the other way. "We'll go out through the bedroom."

"Because . . . ?" I was so confused. Something was definitely up, and I wondered if the heavy scents of garlic and olive oil were still hanging around from the previous night's dinner, or if we were having Italian again. Helly and Anson followed us out.

"You sit here, Mom said, pushing me into a chair with my back to the kitchen door. Have wine." She poured me a huge glass of red wine and then went back inside, leaving Helly and Anson to fend for themselves.

"What is going on?" I asked them, but neither one would answer. My sister wouldn't even make eye contact with me. She sprang up as soon as she'd sat down, and headed for the kitchen door. "Be right back, I just want to, uh, check on something."

I could hear voices rising inside the kitchen, Mom and Dad, Helly's bright laughter, and then another voice. Deep, rumbling. Familiar. Who else would be here, though? Oh god, I hoped they weren't setting me up.

"Anson, what the hell is going on?" I pinned my sister's fiancé with a stare. But even Anson stayed tight-lipped.

As I sipped my enormous glass of wine, I realized this had potentially been the strangest day of my life so far. But when I glanced back toward the kitchen door to see my goalie standing on the other side of the glass wearing one of my mother's aprons, it blew every other strange day completely out of the water.

CHAPTER 33
STEPHANO

THERE ARE ISLANDS. AND THIS
STREAM, SEE?

Dammit. I'd glanced outside, unable to stop myself from trying to get a glimpse of Goldilocks, and she saw me.

I'd spent most of the day with Hillary's parents. The first part was hard, because I had to explain exactly who I was and how we were involved and then admit that I'd been about to give her up, which her father did not seem very impressed about.

Hillary's mother was easier to win over, especially when I told her that I hoped to support her daughter in whatever she pursued and that I thought one day we might even have a family of our own.

Family, I was beginning to realize, was more important to me than anything.

It was something my brother had said on the phone, about the kind of childhood he wanted to give his kids, about his fiancée's wishes to settle near our home. I'd had it good. And I had an incredible family. I wanted to honor that by living in the same tradition, putting family at the forefront of all the decisions I made from now on.

But there were things that needed handling first.

"Oh no. She saw me," I said.

Hillary's mother gasped dramatically and pulled me away

from the door. "Okay, we'll have to change the plan." She looked around as if a clipboard bearing the heading "NEW PLAN" might be laying on a counter nearby.

"I'll handle this," Harvey said, stepping to the door.

"Dad?" Hillary's voice came in as he pushed open the glass. "Who's in there? Is that—"

"Just me, honey. And your mom and sister. And the caterer."

"Caterer?" Hillary's voice told me she neither believed this nor thought much of her father's ability to cover the truth. "That was Stephano."

"Who?" her father tried.

"Maybe we should just fast forward the plan a little bit?" I suggested.

Stella and Helena both nodded while I removed the frilly pink apron I'd had on all afternoon and handed it to Helena, who looked vaguely confused by this entire endeavor.

I did have a plan. Or I'd kind of thought of one.

I'd managed to track down Teresa Palmer, and convinced her to admit that Hillary was in Los Angeles and no longer at her house in Wilcox. That was what had led to me buying a ticket to LAX. From there, I'd had to play investigator, which had involved a lot of phone calls and Googling. The online phone books I'd found were useless—Hillary had a pretty common last name, and I didn't know her folks' names. Her mother had proven to be the key, since she volunteered at a huge foundation in Pasadena that was evidently investing heavily in PR. Her photo was in multiple articles, and she looked so much like Hillary, I had no doubt about who she was. I tracked down the foundation's number and used my former position on the Wombats to get Stella's phone number. Getting her to cooperate after she'd accused me of breaking her daughter's heart had been a tiny bit harder.

Once we'd worked through all that and Stella had agreed to help me, I'd had to figure out how I was going to win Goldilocks back.

And that had resulted in several phone calls to teammates that

I kind of regretted. I'd gotten suggestions ranging from stacking fake wombat poop into a tower while singing to staging a homecoming parade, or performing Broadway hits. None of those options had seemed like a good fit, though Rock had called me back several times now with suggestions for Broadway tunes he assured me would win back any woman's heart.

I didn't think singing "For Good" from *Wicked* was going to do the trick, no matter how vehemently Rock argued for green face paint and full costume. But I knew the answer—for my Goldilocks at least—probably did involve music.

I turned to Hillary's family. "I'm going out there. Do you think you could give us a few minutes?"

"Oh, of course, honey," Stella said, patting me on the chest. I'd spent the afternoon in her kitchen, and she'd become increasingly motherly as time went on. I liked her. A lot. And Hillary's dad had warmed up too, once he'd given me a stern talking to about hurting his daughter.

Now I just needed to work on Goldilocks. I hoped it wouldn't be too hard.

I pulled open the kitchen door and stepped out to find her sitting on the couch, an enormous glass of red wine between her palms and her eyes narrowed at me. I was doing better walking now, but steps were still difficult so I had to hobble a bit. A sharp bolt of longing hit me as soon as I saw her. She was so beautiful. Anson stood and disappeared through the other door.

"I knew it was you." She took another enormous gulp of wine and then set the glass on the low table in front of her.

"Surprise?" I said, wishing we'd been able to stick to the original plan. The one where I warmed her up before we had this conversation.

"Aren't you in Italy? Promoting a winery for your mom?" There was no tone of accusation. Just fatigue. Like she was disappointed in me. I hated that I'd hurt her.

"I didn't go."

"Yet."

"I'm not going," I clarified, moving closer.

"What about your family? Isn't your mom disappointed?"

I gestured to the seat at the other end of the couch, a silent question. "She was, yes."

Hillary's nose wrinkled as she thought about that, her expressive eyebrows lowering as she nodded that I could sit.

"The thing is," I said, gathering myself to say what was really in my heart, on my mind, in a way I'd never done before. "The thing is, you're right, Mamma is all about family."

Hillary didn't respond, so I went on.

"And she's not wrong. Family is important, and I let mine go for far too long. I think I believed I was taking care of them, doing what they needed by sending them money, making sure they didn't have to worry, saving up so I could give them a big nest egg for the future. But what I forgot was that family is about more than not wanting for material things. It's about being together, about making memories, spending time."

"And yet, you're here."

"Because families change. They grow."

She frowned at me again. "Goalie, it's been a crazy day. And while I want to be excited that you're here, I just . . . I'm afraid to hope. I can't . . . " she shook her head, sending her hair dancing around her shoulders.

"Families expand. Sometimes we make room in our families for new people. Like when we fall in love and realize we can't live without certain people."

The frown had faded, but she still didn't look like my words were sinking in. "What are you saying?"

"I'm talking about me. And the girl who I found in my hot tub. You. I'm in love with you, Goldilocks. And I don't want to live without you." I swallowed hard, surprised how easily those words had come out. "I want to see if there's any chance my family might grow to include you. And to find out if there's any room in your family for me."

I could hear murmuring behind me and glanced over my

shoulder to see Hillary's entire family pressed up against the door. I turned back and scooted closer to Hillary, whose eyes were shining now. "I love you, Goldilocks. Do you think there's any chance you might be willing to try again? For real this time?"

She sniffed loudly and made a little gulping sound I didn't know how to interpret. But then she said actual words that gave me hope. "I had to leave Virginia," she said. "I couldn't be there knowing you would be gone. I couldn't stay in that house if you weren't going to be next door."

I reached a hand out, and she gave me hers, which I wrapped inside my palm. It felt like coming home, and I knew if she'd trust me with her heart I'd hold it every bit as carefully.

"I didn't mean to fall for you," she went on. "And it was so clear there was no way it was going to work anyway. With you going back to Italy, and . . ." She frowned at me. "I still don't understand you being here. You're not going to Italy?"

I shook my head. "No. But maybe we can go together soon. For a visit. But my life is here. With you, if you're willing."

A tear rolled down Hillary's cheek, and I wiped it away with my thumb, letting my hand linger along the side of her beautiful face. "I'm scared," she said. "Love has never gone well for me."

"Will you give it a chance?" I asked.

Hillary's mouth opened to answer, but the words didn't make it past the extremely loud music that blared to life at the same instant. Helena must've gotten an itchy trigger finger.

Stella, taking that as her cue, appeared with the microphone just then, and Harvey lowered the patio lights and then placed a second microphone on the table in front of Hillary.

"No," she laughed as she recognized the song. "You're not . . . " But she didn't get the words out, because I was already singing the first lines of "Islands in the Stream," belting out words that Kenny Rogers had certainly handled more masterfully. I didn't know if Goldilocks would pick up that microphone when Dolly's part came up. But if she did, I would know that everything would be all right.

And as I took a breath, ready to sing about how she did something to me that I couldn't explain, Hillary grabbed the mic and rose. And in the next moment, her honey-whiskey voice joined mine, and we were singing together. Joy filled me, and I thought I might actually levitate.

Hillary's family was outside with us now, swaying to the beat of the exceptionally loud speakers as Hillary and I sang to one another. She'd begun tentatively, but by the time we were hitting the chorus a second time, she was belting it out, grinning and looking me in the eye. When the song ended, she flung herself into my arms, and in that moment, I knew we'd be okay.

"That was the right song, right?" I asked her. "The one you said we'd sing together on our first date."

"Yes," she laughed, looking up into my face as I hugged her tightly. "It was perfect. I've always said that Dolly can fix anything."

"So, do we have a chance?" I asked her, loving the feel of her in my arms again.

"I think we do," she said. And then she pressed herself up to wrap her arms around my neck and kiss me. The patio and Hillary's family faded away, even when her father began singing "Love Shack," which had evidently been cued up next. All I was really aware of was my Goldilocks in my arms, saying we could try again.

"Harv!" An unfamiliar voice came from somewhere beyond the patio. "Harvey!"

Hillary and I broke apart, and we all turned to see a man hanging over the fence, his face not completely happy.

"Oh, hey Mike!" Harvey shouted this into the microphone over the music.

"Listen, either gimme some Neil Diamond or turn that down a few notches, would ya?" Mike yelled.

"Oh!" Stella ran inside and a second later the volume had decreased.

"That's better," Mike said, his face relaxing a bit. "I still wouldn't argue with a little 'Forever in Blue Jeans,'" he said. "But maybe the lady that was singing a second ago could do it."

"That's Hillary, my daughter. She's a professional musician," Harvey said proudly, beaming at Goldilocks. "Her music's going to be in a huge television show. She'll be famous soon."

"Dad," Hillary laughed, but it was clear his pride was exactly what she needed. We hadn't gotten to talk about the contract she'd been offered yet, but it sounded there had been progress. Pride swelled inside me.

Hillary agreed to sing some Neil Diamond, and Mike and his wife Stephanie ended up coming over. Eventually, we were serving dinner on the patio while the karaoke party continued, and everyone got a turn or two. Hillary even convinced me to sing Taylor Swift.

"Hillary said you were grumpy," Helena said, dropping into the seat next to me after I wrapped up my rendition of "Shake it Off."

"Uh, thanks?" I wasn't sure how to take this news. "I mean, I try not to be . . ."

"She called you her grumpy goalie when you guys were out in Virginia."

"Yeah, maybe I was a little grumpy," I admitted.

"But you don't seem grumpy now," Helena said, bumping my shoulder. Her aura shimmered around her, so much like her sister's. This whole family was golden—I'd never seen anything like it.

"Thanks. I think maybe I just needed some Goldilocks in my life," I told her. She laughed when I explained the nickname, skipping the part about Hillary's aura, and then her fiancé came to sit next to her and she repeated the story for him.

"It did seem like Hillary was trying on lots of different things," he said. "I'm glad she found you."

"Me too," I told him, everything inside me feeling warmer as I watched my Goldilocks singing to her parents.

Eventually, things settled down and Goldilocks and I found

ourselves alone out on the patio. The happiness inside me felt so huge I was surprised I could hold it all.

"I can't believe you're here. And that you played along with that crazy karaoke party and my nutty family!"

"Your family is great. They've been so welcoming and warm," I told her, guilt dampening my happiness as I recalled my own mother's icy reception to Hillary and her tired acceptance when I'd said goodbye at the airport. "You know, my mother will love you too, once she quits focusing on her own fear of losing her family."

"Yeah, about that," Hillary said. "How'd you get out of going back to be the face of the winery?"

"I realized I was running away," I told her honestly. "And that while my mother wanted me home in some kind of tribute to the great love of her life, I was losing my chance at my own. I couldn't do it."

"But what about the contract and the winery?"

I laughed. "That was luck. The investor wanted me for my fame, but I'm not actually that well-known in Italy. There are Italian hockey players who are much better known than I am. But it turns out my family is connected to someone much more famous in Italy than I could ever be."

"Who?"

"Princess Alessia. She and my brother Cristiano are engaged."

"Oh my gosh, a real princess?"

"In name only, but the royal family is still important to Italians, and she's agreed to promote the family winery."

"That's amazing. Your mom must be thrilled."

"She's thrilled that my brother is going to settle near home and wants to have lots of babies."

Hillary laughed at that. "What about you?"

"I'll settle wherever you want to. Or just follow you from housesitting gig to housesitting gig."

"I think I might stay out here a while," she said. "See how this music thing goes."

"Based on the offer your sister said you got today, I think it's going to go great."

"Do you like LA?" She sounded wary.

"I like any place I get to be with you."

"Stephano," she said, her face growing serious. "Won't you be bored? What will you do?"

I shrugged. "I don't know for sure. Coaching, maybe?"

"Because you loved working with John so much," she laughed.

"He was trying to take my job," I pointed out.

She leaned closer, and I caught a whiff of the fresh scent that followed her around, the one that was uniquely hers. "You'd be a great coach, I bet. College?"

"I was thinking kids. Little kids. Start 'em young."

"You're kidding."

"I want to be ready to teach our kids to play. I'll practice on other people's first."

"Our kids," Hillary repeated. And before I could ask if I'd gone too far, she was in my lap, kissing me like her life depended on it.

CHAPTER 34
HILLARY

KATIE THE COP

The next few months were the fullest and happiest of my life.

Stephano and I flew back to Virginia to pack up some of his things and offer his friends and teammates a proper good-bye. I got a reprise of my grumpy goalie when he hosted his own farewell party at his house and people kept forgetting to use coasters on his tables. He solved the problem by designating Clara's daughter Katie as the coaster patrol, and she spent the rest of the evening enforcing his rule firmly. It's possible Katie has a bright future in law enforcement.

The movers brought Stephano's things to California, and we rented an apartment near my parents' place. The best part of it all was that we were true partners—I paid for half of everything thanks to my sudden financial stability.

It felt good. For the first time in years I was standing on solid ground, building something that wasn't engineered to fall apart.

But Stephano missed hockey.

It was clear every time we watched a Wombats game on television, and every time he came home from the gym. He missed the workouts, the team, and the feeling of belonging. And there wasn't much I could do to help him with that. He'd looked around for youth teams that needed coaches, but even with his credentials hadn't been able to find anything that fit nearby.

So despite the way everything felt like it was fitting together in my life, I worried about him.

Until a day in June when he came home grinning and chuckling but refused to tell me what was going on.

"It's a surprise," he said. "Get dressed."

"I'm not standing here naked," I pointed out. "I am actually dressed." I looked down at my leggings and ripped T-shirt. Maybe I wasn't well dressed, but I was clothed.

"Naked," he repeated, raising an eyebrow. "Good idea. Get naked and then I'll help you get dressed."

I laughed, but he wasn't joking. Stephano stalked toward me across the open space of our living room, and came to a stop in front of me, his hands immediately finding the hem of my T-shirt.

"I thought we were going somewhere?"

"Naked first," he said in a low rumble. He kissed me then, his hands moving to my waist and pulling me against him. His mouth was soft and sweet, but the way he held me against the increasing stiffness at my hip was firm, demanding.

I kissed him back, sliding my hands up the muscle I found everywhere I touched, loving the feel of him.

"Are we going to be late?" I asked, pulling my mouth from his as he whipped my shirt over my head sending my hair flying.

"I'm in charge, so I decide when we're late," he said, and then he scooped me up and carried me to the bedroom where he deposited me gently on the bed and then worked his fingers into my waistband.

"Okay," I agreed, tension coiling in me as he slid my clothing from my body and then devoured me with hungry eyes before following suit with his mouth. When I was gasping and writhing, my hands fisting into the duvet as I whimpered and moaned, he stopped.

"Goalie," I whispered, needing him to finish, needing more.

He moved up my body, the sliding of our skin ramping up my

need even more. And then, while staring into my eyes and effectively pinning me to the bed, he notched himself and began sliding into me, a centimeter at a time.

"You're teasing me," I complained as he took his time.

"I'm enjoying you," he responded.

I was so ready for him by the time he finally gave me what I wanted, I exploded within seconds, every part of me pulsing and shivering. And he didn't take long to follow, going stiff and then relaxing over me with a satisfied sound.

His face nestled into the crook of my neck, and he placed tiny kisses there and then whispered, "I love you, Goldilocks."

"I love you too, Goalie."

"Now get dressed." He was up again, heading into the bathroom and returning with a warm washcloth.

"Thanks," I said, sitting up. "What should I wear?"

"What do new landowners wear in Los Angeles?" he asked.

"I have no idea," I told him, laughing. "Did you buy land?"

"I bought a city block."

"What?"

"Just get dressed. I'll show you."

I followed directions, putting on a dress and climbing into the truck Stephano had shipped out from Virginia, enjoying this playful side of the goalie. I'd seen it before, but his recent disappointment had begun to dampen his spirits.

We drove west, and Stephano pulled off the freeway just outside Montrose and then navigated the town like he'd done it many times before.

"You've been keeping a secret," I accused.

"A little one. I didn't want to say anything until I knew it would work out."

Stephano pulled up outside an arena that looked like it had seen better days. It was huge, though, and it took up an entire city block between the structure and the parking lot.

"Is this the block you bought?"

He grinned at me. "Yep."

"Are you going to refurbish it or something?"

The grin didn't fade. "Yep."

We got out of the car and Stephano led me inside the old arena. "This used to be a minor league hockey rink," he told me. "They built it in the seventies, but the league folded and they just left it here."

"It's huge, you'd think they'd use it for concerts or something."

"They will," he said, smiling at me. "They'll also use it to host the California Goalies Camp soon."

My heart swelled. That was perfect. "You've been very sneaky," I told him as we stood in the center of the old arena.

"I had a lot of pieces to put in place before I was sure it would happen," he said, happiness practically emanating from his handsome face. "But I think I can get the place renovated this year, which will give me time to promote the camp and finish making housing arrangements and hiring coaches. I'll open the camp next summer."

"Wow." I looked around, imagining it bright and new, kids in crazy pads skating around after their idol, Stephano Mizzoni. "It's perfect."

I hugged him, loving the way Stephano's arms went around me, pulling me close without any of the hesitation I'd once felt. Since moving to LA, he'd become so warm and loving. I was the luckiest girl in the world.

I let it all sink in as we stood there holding one another. I could never have imagined a future like this, with a man like this—the universe had definitely overdelivered, and I had no complaints at all.

FINALE

JULIUS RAMON

When Stephano called me to tell me the news, joy flooded me like a river overflowing its banks. I'd hoped for it. I'd believed in it . . . but sometimes I was certain I was just an old man with romantic dreams now.

That was why I didn't let him sell the truck.

Maybe I shared a little of Hillary's belief in the universe. Maybe I'd become a bit superstitious. But I paid to have the truck parked in a covered garage while Stephano straightened things out, as if I could help drive the eventual outcome by keeping some small attachment vital. Even if it was just a truck.

And now? Now that my biggest connection to the Wilcox Wombats and my main reason for staying there was gone?

It changed nothing.

I had nothing to run back to, nowhere to go.

The Wombats were my home and my family, even if I was relegated to the sidelines in every imaginable way.

I'd stay. And if I could, I'd ensure none of them made the same mistakes I had.

EPILOGUE

STEPHANO - 8 MONTHS LATER

"**I**s there more of that fondutti stuff?" Cade Simpson asked, leaning forward from his spot on the couch on Hillary's parents' patio and looking up and down the table in front of him, which held various dishes and trays of appetizers.

"*Fondi*," Stella said, replacing the empty tray in front of the red-haired Viking. "They are fried artichoke bottoms. Here you go."

"Thank you, Mrs. Watters. Your house is amazing, and you are a talented cook," Cade said, his eyes twinkling though his beard hid his grin.

Houstein took a couple of the fondi on the plate. "Artichoke butts are delicious."

Stella blushed and giggled, and Deck Gillespie joined in the flattery. "Really, ma'am. Thank you so much for having us all. It's been a real pleasure getting to know Hillary's family."

Most of the Wombats were scattered in chairs and stools around the Watters's big outdoor patio, where Mr. Watters had pulled a huge movie screen into the opposite side of the yard. I'd helped him set up the projector earlier that day.

"What time does it start?" John Samuels asked, his mouth half full.

"About fifteen minutes," Hillary answered, her whole body practically vibrating with excitement.

"I'm nervous for you," Teresa said, stepping close to Hillary to give her a hug. "Which is ridiculous. It's not like you're performing live, right?"

"Right," Hillary agreed. "But I'm nervous too." She was adorable nervous, by the way.

"Wanna know what I do when I'm nervous before a game?" Rock Stevens asked the group loudly.

"What?" Samuels replied.

"Nothing!" Rock laughed. "I don't get nervous." He chuckled as Corny slapped Samuels on the back.

"Kinda walked into that one," Corny said.

Samuels smiled the sheepish grin I'd come to appreciate. The guy was humble and a little naive, but he was a hell of a goalie. We'd started texting a bit, and he always called me after games, looking for input on his play. It was good practice for my work with the kids, and I respected the hell out of Samuels as a player.

"Let's get this going," Harvey said, clapping his hands together and moving to the projector. "Stella, can you get the lights?"

The Wombats settled down, and Hillary grabbed my hand and pulled me to join Helena and Anson on a blanket spread on the lawn in front of the movie screen.

The screen blared to life, and I pulled Hillary against my chest, so she was sitting between my legs, leaning against me. It was one of the happiest things in the world, feeling my girl so close to me, supporting her.

"Harvey?" Mike's voice came from over the fence. "Sorry we're a little late." He pushed through the gate between the houses, hauling two patio chairs and Stephanie, his wife, behind him.

"No problem," Harvey called back. "Grab some artichoke butts and take a seat. We're just getting rolling."

Hillary tilted her chin up to catch my eyes, and warmth flooded my body. This, I recognized, was happiness. My team was here, my girl was in my arms. I was surrounded. By family. By the family we'd made so far. The only thing missing was my own family, but with Cristiano's wedding coming in a couple months, we'd remedy that soon too.

"This is it!" Rock boomed as a low bass note reverberated across the yard and an enormous dragon took flight on the screen. Evidently Hillary's idea about dragons had made its way to the author, who suggested dragons on the family crest for the family in the show and as a symbol.

And then the intro sequence to the most hyped new series in the country was rolling over the screen, while Hillary's incredible voice wound its way through the epic images and striking melody.

The sequence ended with the word "Chaos" in Gothic font stamped onto the screen, and Hillary's voice fading gradually in the background. When it was over, the yard erupted into a whole other form of chaos. The Wombats cheered and whistled, and several came over to pull Hillary from my arms and hug her.

Stella and Harvey had taken seats next to us and tears were standing in Stella's eyes as Harvey cried, "That's my girl! We're so proud of you, Hill!"

And Hillary herself was beyond words, which wasn't something I'd seen happen too often. Tears rolled down her cheeks, and the gold that surrounded her burned brighter than ever.

"Again!" Someone in back cried as Hillary hugged her sister, and Harvey went over to stop and rewind the intro. We watched it three times before everyone settled down enough to actually watch the show. There were more hugs and congratulations when it ended, Hillary's voice flowing through the yard again, reminding us that the only truth was in chaos.

"It's funny," she said, looking up at me as everyone began cleaning up dishes and moving around again. "I used to think it was true—that chaos was all we could count on, that life was arbitrary."

"You don't believe that now?" I asked her.

She shook her head. "I think we work for the happiness we

want, and that sometimes it's risky. Things can change. But when they do, we hold on or we pivot, and we work again to be happy."

I nodded. That felt true. I still missed my team, my career. But I knew who I was and where I was headed, and with Goldilocks at my side, I knew this new version of my life would be even more beautiful than the first.

The Wombats trickled out slowly, each of them hugging Hillary and thanking her parents for hosting. They were all staying in town a couple more days to help me launch the re-opening of the arena. I'd refurbished it in record time, and with Teresa's help, had even managed to book a few concerts into the venue. In the downtime, it would operate as a pay-per-use skating rink, and I'd lined up a first group of kids for camp. They were locals—It wasn't quite what I was planning for the following year —but it was going to be incredible.

We met the next morning at the arena, and I gave them a tour.

"This place looks suspiciously like the Wilcox arena back home," Sly told me with a smile.

"I got a hold of the plans," I admitted. "And I figured there was no point reinventing the wheel."

"Just need a few Wombats logos here and there, and you'll be all set," Chris Houstein said.

"What time are the kiddos coming with their families?" Rock asked, checking his watch.

"Eleven, right?" Hillary asked, looking up at me.

"Right."

"So why are we here an hour early?" Rock asked. "I don't need that kinda time to prepare. I could've used the beauty sleep."

"Doubt it would help," Cade shot out.

"Put a sock in it Simpson, or I'll take you to a barber." Rock crossed his arms over his chest.

"Grab your skates," I suggested, waving the Wombats to the locker room where they'd dropped their stuff.

"Hillary, come with me." I helped her to the box where I'd left a pair of skates for her and mine were waiting too.

"We're skating?"

I shrugged. "Thought it would be fun."

"You know I have no idea how to skate, right?"

"Let's learn then." I helped her lace up and soon we were stepping carefully out onto the ice. We spent a few minutes going over basics as the Wombats joined us, one by one, offering tips.

I hadn't been able to fill them all in on the plan—Rock couldn't keep a secret to save his life. But Samuels, Gillespie, and Simpson knew why we were here so early. Samuels skated out now, holding a chair and placing it in the center of the ice.

Gillespie, I saw, was filling the other Wombats in as they all moved around the rink. And Simpson was helping them find their positions in line while I helped Hillary toward the chair.

"Why is there a chair here?" she asked.

"For you. Figured you might want to sit a minute."

She shook her head, her hair drifting around her shoulders and her cheeks pink from the cold. "I'm okay."

"Would you sit, please?"

She wrinkled her nose and then looked over my shoulder. "What are they doing?"

"Ignore them. They're morons."

"Goalie, is something going on?"

"Nothing at all. Sit down."

Hillary finally gave in and sat down in the chair, an amused expression on her face as she watched the Wombats shuffling and whispering to one another in a big line. I skated back to the box and grabbed the signs, returning to hand them to Gillespie, who was on one end of the line.

"Take the top one and pass them down," he told Sly Remington at his side.

Nerves were slamming around inside me, but I felt more optimistic and hopeful than I had in a long time. My hip was healed, my heart was full, and my family was around me—mostly.

"When you're ready, Mizzoni," Gillespie called.

I nodded, and skated to where Hillary sat, coming to stand beside her chair, her hand in mine.

"What are they doing?" she asked me.

But her attention shifted as Gillespie held up the first sign, penned in dark ink, across his chest. It read, "GOLDILOCKS."

Hillary giggled and I squeezed her hand, nerves making it tough to stand still.

My teammates began flipping their signs, one by one, holding them up for her to read. Unfortunately, they hadn't gotten the whole "take the top one and pass it on" thing quite right.

Hillary read out loud, "Goldilocks. I can't imagine my hot tub. And now? In it, you've taught me to live of the rest of my life. The night you jumped me, I didn't know it then."

Rock yelled out, "If she jumps you and you don't know it, there's a serious problem!"

"Put 'em down!" Gillespie yelled. "Sorry, Mizzoni, hang on."

All the signs went down and Hillary shot me a half smile. "I'm so confused."

"Morons," I muttered, hoping they'd get it right on the second try.

The Wombats were in a circle now, handing each other signs and arguing loudly.

"Right to left!" Simpson shouted.

"We're not in Japan," Elks answered him.

"Dress rehearsal," Samuels ordered. "Facing me."

All the Wombats lined up again facing away from us, and Samuels skated down the line, rearranging the signs as needed. He shot me a thumbs-up as he rounded the end of the line. "Ready now."

"Try again!" Gillespie told them.

This time, the signs were right, and Hillary read, "Goldilocks. The night you jumped in my hot tub was the beginning of the rest of my life. I just didn't know it then. Since then, you've taught me to live for the moment while planning for the future. And now? I can't imagine that future without you in it."

She sniffed loudly, turning to look up at me. "Goalie," she said, wiping a tear from her face.

"Don't cry," I said, dropping to one knee and reaching into my pocket. "Hillary, will you make me the happiest man alive?" I opened the box, revealing the simple solitaire diamond on its platinum band. "Marry me?"

Hillary ignored my suggestion not to cry, and clamped a hand over her mouth as a sob escaped. But she did not say yes.

"Goldilocks?" I prodded, the nerves making me feel sick.

She kept crying, but now her head was moving in a nod.

"She's saying yes!" Elks shouted. "Right, Hillary? That's a yes?"

"Yes!" she finally said, and I stood, sweeping her into my arms and hugging her tightly. Her arms went around me, and I saw several of the Wombats snapping photos with their phones.

When Hillary stopped sobbing and stepped back, she looked up at me, her face glowing. "I'm so happy," she said. "Yes, of course I'll marry you."

"The ring!" Rock cried as the Wombats crowded in close.

I slid the ring onto her finger and felt like it was possible my heart would actually explode.

"I love you, Goldilocks," I whispered.

"I love you too," she told me.

I kissed her then, and the Wombats cheered loudly.

And when it was time to clean up the arena and get ready for the grand opening, I caught John Samuels wiping at his eyes.

"Sentimental?" I asked him.

"Just happy for you, man. You deserve it."

"Thanks."

"Maybe a little of your luck will rub off on me." He shot me a sad smile then, and I hoped if I had any luck to give, that a little might go to him. It sure seemed like I might have some to spare, because at that moment, with the woman I loved at my side, I felt like the luckiest man in the world.

The End

Want more Wombats? There's a bonus epilogue here!

ALSO BY DELANCEY STEWART

Want more? Get early releases, sneak peeks and freebies! Join my mailing list here or scan the QR code and get a free story!

The Wilcox Wombats Series:

Checking the Center

The Wedding Winger

Grumpy Goalie

The Kasper Ridge Series:

Only a Summer

Only a Fling

Only a Crush

Only a Secret

Only a Touch

The Singletree Series:

Happily Ever His

Happily Ever Hers

Shaking the Sleigh

Second Chance Spring

Falling Into Forever

Singletree Box Set 1

Singletree Box Set 2

The Digital Dating Series (with Marika Ray):

Texting with the Enemy

While You Were Texting

Save the Last Text

How to Lose a Girl in 10 Texts

The Text Before Christmas

The MR. MATCH Series:

Prequel: Scoring a Soulmate

Book One: Scoring the Keeper's Sister

Book Two: Scoring a Fake Fiancée

Book Three: Scoring a Prince

Book Four: Scoring with the Boss

Book Five: Scoring a Holiday Match

Mr. Match: The Boxed Set

The KINGS GROVE Series:

When We Let Go

Open Your Eyes

When We Fall

Open Your Heart

Christmas in Kings Grove

The STARR RANCH WINERY Series:

Chasing a Starr

THE GIRLFRIENDS OF GOTHAM Series:

Men and Martinis

Highballs in the Hamptons

Cosmos and Commitment

The Girlfriends of Gotham Box Set

STANDALONES:

Let it Snow

Without Words

Without Promises

Mr. Big

Adagio

The PROHIBITED! Duet:

Prohibited!

The Glittering Life of Evie Mckenzie

www.ingramcontent.com/pod-product-compliance
Lightning Source LLC
Chambersburg PA
CBHW060910210726
48293CB00006B/2038